About the Author

Born in Droitwich, UK, I am a retired Manufacturing Engineer with over forty years' experience in the automotive industry. Spending the last twenty-five years of service working on overseas manufacturing projects, I have travelled extensively overseas meeting and working with a rich mix of wonderful people. Back home, I enjoy sports such as football, cricket and rugby and am currently a keen and active golfer. I have a fantastic, supportive and loving family and have been happily married for over twenty years.

Cabin

Charlie Summer

Cabin

Vanguard Press

VANGUARD PAPERBACK

© Copyright 2023
Charlie Summer

A CIP catalogue record for this title is
available from the British Library.

ISBN 978 1 80016 675 2

Vanguard Press is an imprint of
Pegasus Elliot Mackenzie Publishers Ltd.
www.pegasuspublishers.com

First Published in 2023

Vanguard Press
Sheraton House Castle Park
Cambridge England

Printed & Bound in Great Britain

Dedication

I would like to dedicate this book to my parents, Graham and Jean. I want to thank them for their continued belief in me, for always being there and for being the best parents anyone could wish for.

Acknowledgement to John Kenny for his kind assistance and continued belief and support.

Chapter One

It had been a torturous eleven years for Uncle J. Imprisoned for his part in what turned out to be a botched kidnapping, played out by an ill-educated collective of small time crooks, striving to display the impression of being a big-time organised criminal group. In a country where life is cheap in the outside world, the value placed on the life of prisoners barely registers. Prison cells were dark, dusty, overcrowded, and archaic, the only electricity supply is gleefully consumed in staff areas. The food served up at mealtimes is barely fit for a dog, and daily exercise takes place in an inhospitable yard surrounded by towering walls, giving any available sunlight scant chance of infiltrating the depressing spaces. Then there was the incessantly overwhelming heat and humidity to contend with. On top of that, prison guards treated most prisoners as if they were provided for sport. Beatings, bullying, and mental, verbal, and physical abuse were commonplace. All except for the few protected or feared captives, who had forced their way to the top of the pyramid of the prison power clique, branded 'The Family' by inmates. This elite group were either known ex-warlords, ex-high-rated officers from The Cell or physical specimens who had bashed their way to exemption.

Uncle J had managed to wriggle himself into the fringes of this select group. The minor privileges helped him avoid the regular baton beatings, but he did still take a few body blows from time to time. However, the real anguish of being an inmate was amplified for Uncle J with the incessant need for revenge that rattled around his head during every waking moment. In his mind he was not a failure, it was the inexperienced street delinquents that had put paid to a relatively foolproof plan. Uncle J still wanted his pound of flesh from the rich and privileged target, who managed to escape capture without paying the asking price. Revenge plan after plan went through Uncle J's head, playing out every scenario, every twist and turn, every eventuality, but still, the golden plan had to be conceived. Pressure was mounting to produce a workable plan as Uncle J was scheduled to attend a parole hearing in two months. His good behaviour, combined with the fact that the prison system was so overcrowded, gave Uncle J, in his opinion, a reasonable fighting chance of release. Visitor privileges were incredibly rare for Uncle J, so he had no access to his outside world-based accomplices, to bounce ideas off or provide fresh ideas for a revenge plot, which also impacted the slow progress.

It was time for supper, the inmates were being bullied into single file from their overcrowded cells to the equally inadequate dining hall. A line of drably uniformed prison guards with batons drawn lined the passageways on the lookout for signs of any aggressive or unacceptable behaviour from the line of destitute interns. The prisoners, lined up in silence to receive today's offerings, proceeded to available benches to consume their daily slop, once it had been dispensed thoughtlessly onto their metal food trays. Each prisoner outside of the reaches of The Family took great care where they decided to eat, so as not to sit in a seat reserved for a Family member, as that could be harmful to their health.

Uncle J sat down at his accustomed station staring down at his tray in disbelief. His negative thoughts were interrupted by a fellow inmate who energetically sat next to him landing on the bench with a zealous bounce.

"Hello, brother," said Umar. "How is your health and temper on this most glorious day?"

"Who gave you a happy pill?" responded a gloomy Uncle J.

"Come on, Bro," continued Umar. "How long is it now until your parole hearing? A couple of months?"

"Yeah," replied Uncle J, "and we all know how that's going to go."

"Hey, man," responded Umar, placing his arm around Uncle J's back "be positive, man, you never know, they might release you?"

11

"Get your hands off me," exclaimed Uncle J, brushing the arm away instantly. "What will be will be. Why are you pestering me with your joyous garbage?"

"Just wanted to see if there was any workable revenge plan yet?" continued Umar.

"Keep your voice down," uttered an angry Uncle J. "Walls have ears here, you never know who's listening."

"Come on, man," replied Umar. "Nobody gives a damn in this unruly place"

"Just keep it down," snapped Uncle J. "This is my business, got it!"

"OK, OK," responded Umar. "I just wondered if you had considered a slightly different angle, that's all?"

"What angle?" quizzed Uncle J.

"Kids," stated a confident Umar.

"Kids?" replied a confused Uncle J.

"Yeah, kids," confirmed Umar. "Does Mansoor have any kids? If so, I bet he would be very concerned if his kids went missing."

"You mean kidnap his kids?" asked Uncle J.

"Yeah, man," replied Umar.

"Mansoor does have two kids," snapped Uncle J "but they aren't kids anymore and they live in the U.S.A. How is that of any use to me whatsoever?"

"Just geography," quipped Umar. "With some help here and there I am sure we can come up with a strategy that works. In any case, I bet his kids feel nice and safe in the U.S.A., with no threat at all for them in their nice, safe, and stable American life. In fact, this should make you even more determined for revenge, targeting them as they have turned their backs on our homeland, preferring to make their way in life in a foreign land."

"I see," replied a ponderous Uncle J. "You might have something there. I bet The Cell would help me, after all, I was one of their finest adversaries back in the day."

"I am sure they would," added a compassionate Umar. "After all, you are still considered a legend in some parts, Uncle J."

"Tosh!" snapped Uncle J. "Legends are for story books. However, you might have something for me to build on here, let me go away and think about this angle of attack, I might be able to make it work with the right team around me this time. Handpicked warriors."

"You the man," cheered Umar. "I am sure you will make this work. I am due out of here in six months, maybe you can use a man like me on your team? After all, I may have given you the idea you were looking for."

"Maybe," responded a realistic Uncle J. "I've got to get out of this place first before I can feel any passion or excitement for this type of revenge plan, as my release is far from a given."

"Be positive, man," responded Umar. "Positive thoughts bring positive outcomes."

"I'm a realist," replied a despondent Uncle J. "Why would they let me out early? I am still a threat to society, a known felon with form, also branded a failed kidnapper."

"Come on, brother," said a reassuring Umar. "You never know, man, you never know."

Uncle J finished his substandard feast, deposited his slop tray in a bucket containing the murkiest of washing-up water imaginable and then trudged back to his awaiting overcrowded cell.

That night, Uncle J's mind dropped into overdrive. He was primarily self-punishing as he hadn't taken the children kidnap angle seriously up to now. Sure, he had considered using Mansoor's children as a possible target for revenge, but Uncle J was convinced they were established and lived a safe and protected life in San Francisco, having also attended university in the same city. Maybe The Cell could help him out with their network of contacts and connections. The main stumbling block facing Uncle J was geography. He was eight thousand miles away and there was also the Pacific Ocean to negotiate. Nevertheless, it was a start, something to build a plan around, possibly even hope of revenge at last.

The following day, Uncle J searched out Umar at breakfast time. With a newfound spring in his step, Uncle J bundled his ample frame onto the well-worn canteen bench occupied by Umar.

"So," said a slightly excited Uncle J "you think The Cell may be able to help me? Even after the failed kidnapping for which I was allegedly responsible?"

"Good morning to you as well," replied Umar adopting a very sarcastic twist. "Nice to see you again. My, I am honoured to have the venerable Uncle J's company two days running at the dining table."

"Cut the sarcasm, lad," snapped an unimpressed Uncle J. "I want some honest feedback. Do you think The Cell would be interested in helping me execute my plan of revenge? Surely there is still enough cash in that Mansoor family to muster a suitable and worthy ransom? What do you think? Does it have any mileage in it?"

"Uncle J," responded Umar. "Let's be realistic here. You don't have a plan, you have an idea, a sketchy idea at that. You want me to contact The Cell and say what? That the legendary Uncle J wants your help to implement revenge on a family? You do realise that the underworld still holds you partly responsible for a failed kidnap attempt? What meat have you added to the bones of my idea? What are the details? What are the timings? What resources are required? What? What? What?"

"Don't treat me like a fool, Umar," snapped an angry Uncle J. "I can still inflict harm on you and make life oh so difficult in here for you, so be careful what you say. I don't have a detailed plan as such, but when I get out of here, I can make that happen very quickly. All I need to know is that I have the backing of The Cell at this stage, no more than that. It was not me, after all, that was the failed kidnapping gang leader, it was Zaheer, he was the reason for failure and that is also well-known in the underworld."

"You do know that there has been a change of guard at the top of The Cell?" quizzed Umar arrogantly. "It's all change at the summit, a new breed with fresh ideas and methods."

"You know these new people well?" asked Uncle J.

"That's the reason I can help you by contacting The Cell," replied Umar. "I didn't have such strong connections with The Cell before the clear-out, but it so happens that one of my old adversaries took control, with whom I have a long-standing and strong connection."

Uncle J leaned over and grabbed Umar firmly by the throat.

"You had better not be pulling my chains now, laddie," demanded a furious Uncle J "because if you are, you will pay the full, ugly price."

Uncle J's lunge caught the eye of a watching prison guard who sprinted over to the minor incident. The guard drew his baton.

"Stop now!" shouted the guard. "Hands off, now!"

Uncle J let go of Umar and held both hands above his head.

"Nothing going on here!" shouted Uncle J. "Just a bit of friendly prisoner horseplay."

The guard double-checked that all was in order, replaced his baton in its holder and walked back to his station.

"Look," said a flustered Umar. "I am not trying to make fun of you. I have strong connections and also visitor rights. I can arrange to get word out to The Cell within the next two weeks. Just leave it with me. You just need to tell me roughly, and I mean not word for word, what you are expecting. Leave the rest to me."

Uncle J took a mouthful of breakfast slop to give him a moment's thinking time.

"When do you need my words?" asked Uncle J.

"Before the end of the month," responded Umar. "I can arrange a visit in the first week of next month, which will give you just over a week to get your request for assistance in order."

"Sounds fair to me," said a calmer Uncle J. "I had better get busy."

"We can't raise suspicion," added Umar. "We can't be seen together too often."

"What do you mean?" asked Uncle J. "Lots of inmates sit in the same places every day and with the same people."

"But we have only just started," answered Umar "and I am not sure if the prison authorities here know about my connections with The Cell. We have to be careful just in case."

"I see," replied Uncle J. "I agree, we need to keep contact to a minimum from now on, just an occasional meal together."

"Right," nodded Umar. "Now go and get busy with your words and make them count, you will only get one stab at this. I know how the new Cell works."

Over the next few days, Uncle J busied himself. He joined the prison library which completely shocked the majority of the prison guards in that area, considering that for the past eleven years, Uncle J had not even set foot in the zone of the prison containing the library building. Uncle J sold his newfound interest in books as preparation for his potential release, catching up with current affairs on the internet and reading leisure books to help adjust himself to a life of freedom as a better person. The guards seemed to have bought these ideas, considering that Uncle J had not been a difficult prisoner to maintain during his time in captivity.

Resources in the library were relatively scant. The library itself was not a grand room full of sturdy bookshelves overflowing with well-maintained books, It resembled a hospital waiting room populated with out of date magazines. There was, however, access to two computers with an internet connection, which was what Uncle J had his eyes on. Uncle J wanted to get to know San Francisco and its surrounding areas, understand where the remote Californian forests were located relative to San Francisco, somewhere he could potentially successfully hold hostages for a number of months without fear of disturbance. Uncle J completely avoided searching the names of Mansoor's children, as that may give the intended targets away from the start, assuming his internet activities would be monitored. Uncle J spent the majority of his internet time looking at maps and images of California, targeting popular beauty spots and hiking trails, as these needed to be avoided as viable hideouts, as the risk of nosey tourists and heavy hiking traffic would threaten his plans.

When back in his sweltering, noisy prison cell, Uncle J put his mind to his so-called application for assistance with The Cell. There was no Zaheer and his incompetent cohorts to mess things up this time. Uncle J could create all the plans and call all the shots. This time he anticipated success, riches, and a chance to repair the damage to his soiled name and reputation within the underworld.

It was the end of the month. Uncle J had collected his evening slop from the steaming serving barrels and was on the lookout for his newfound friend. Spotting Umar sitting at a table isolated from the crowd, Uncle J hurried over and sat down.

Uncle J put his hand in his pocket and removed a piece of paper.

"Not here!" snapped Umar. "If that's what I think it is, put it away, there may be someone watching us; inmates, or guards, they are both equally a threat."

"Where then?" begged a desperate Uncle J. "The words are ready."

"What time is your exercise time tomorrow?" asked Umar. Ten thirty until eleven fifteen a.m." replied Uncle J.

"OK," uttered Umar "I will have to give my guard an extra bribe to get my time changed. I have cigarettes, he loves my cigarettes."

"Fine," said Uncle J. "Let's call it a date."

"For goodness' sake," groaned Umar. "You have made me feel all queasy now, just the thought of a date with Uncle J, just beggars belief."

"Ha ha," replied a cheery Uncle J. "I'm a catch in here, I'll have you know, Section Four has got my picture on their wall, I am a hero."

"It's for throwing rocks at more like," responded Umar, "they need a target to aim at."

Both inmates smiled broadly and tucked into their evening offerings. Uncle J was feeling upbeat for the first time in a long time. He believed he had a creditable adversary, a worthwhile cause to follow, something to focus on and more importantly, a means to get his long-awaited revenge and riches.

The following day at ten thirty a.m. Uncle J made his way to the exercise compound searching for Umar. Once united, they made haste over to the far corner of the yard, away from the crowd and more significantly, away from the guards.

"Give me the paper now," demanded Umar.

Uncle J covertly took a piece of folded white paper from his pocket and nestled it into the palm of Umar's hand, who promptly concealed it in his prison uniform.

"Aren't you going to read it now?" demanded Uncle J.

"Too public, brother," replied a cautious Umar. "I will read it in my prison cell. I will let you know what I think at supper tonight."

"OK," replied an anxious Uncle J. "Be sure you do, time is ticking, and I want the backing of The Cell in the bag before my parole hearing."

"You'll get a reply man, don't fret," snapped Umar.

"Like I said, it had better be before my hearing, laddie," replied a concerned Uncle J. "Have you actually sorted a visit with The Cell yet?"

"I sure have, man," replied Umar. "Tuesday next week, two p.m., it's all sorted."

"Who are you meeting, if you don't mind me asking?" requested Uncle J.

"Yeah, right, Bro," replied Umar. "Like I'm really gonna reveal my contacts to you. In any case, The Cell will send a representative, it won't be anyone directly working for The Cell, they don't do their own dirty work, after all, this is just the passing of information, nothing more than that."

"Can you rely on these representatives to pass over the information?" asked a concerned Uncle J.

"You just leave that to me, brother," replied Umar. "I'll do what I do, you do what you do."

"So, what happens now?" asked Uncle J. "Do you just hand the piece of paper over to the visitor?"

"No!" snapped back Umar. "We can't just pass papers to each other, the guards will be watching, and they will confiscate anything that physically passes between the bars."

"Bars?" asked Uncle J. "There are bars in the visitor area? I've never been in there, so I don't know the form."

"Big thick bars, Bro," responded Umar. "The guards watch like hawks and listen in to conversations. I have to memorise your words and deliver them in code to the visitor."

"Word for word?" asked a surprised Uncle J.

No man," replied Umar. "I just need to get the gist of the message across. The Cell will understand what is being asked of them, don't worry, Bro."

"I'm beginning to wonder now," said a resigned Uncle J. "I thought you would pass over the paper, simple as that. I've spent endless hours getting the wording right."

"Look," responded an agitated Umar, "I've told you, leave it to me, OK. I will sort this, now stop getting all high and mighty with me and trust me."

The conversation became more and more fractious as their exercise time progressed. Umar's frustration was growing fast as the 'old school' legend appeared not to trust the communication process available. Uncle J was equally frustrated, having little confidence in his message getting through to The Cell, leaving his dreams of revenge at the starting post.

That afternoon, Umar digested Uncle J's words. The request to The Cell was reasonably predictable. Funding, false identification papers and passports, reliable resources to help with the execution of Uncle J's plans, covert transport around the city, the paper headed by the bold title 'Revenge Kidnapping'. Umar was confident he could at least get the gist of the message to be delivered, however, he couldn't guarantee success. After all, Uncle J had promised a place in the team should The Cell take up the requests and run with them, so Umar had a vested interest to make this happen.

The following morning, at breakfast time, Uncle J sought out his accomplice.

"So," barked Uncle J, "what did you think of my note then?"

"Pretty much as expected, brother," replied Umar. "I am used to these types of demands. I have issued them before, man, like a piece of cake, I'll have no problems with this one."

"OK," replied Uncle J. "So we need to make a plan to meet up on the outside so we can prepare detailed plans. I have a fairly large house in a compound, I can give you the address, so you must come to my house when you are released. When is that again?"

"In under six months now," responded Umar, "but I reckon I can work something out with my guards, they like my cigarettes and they owe me. Maybe they can put in a good word for me to grease the early-release wheels?"

Uncle J slid a small piece of paper under the table to Umar.

"This is my address," added Uncle J. "We can use my house as the headquarters for operation 'Revenge Kidnap'."

"Wow, bro!" replied Umar looking covertly at the address. "This is an expensive part of the city, you must have some serious cash, man."

"I did ok," responded Uncle J, "back in the day, when I was well paid and, quite rightly so, the muck and bullets that I have been through."

Umar offered his outstretched hand under the table; Uncle J shook the hand firmly.

"Welcome aboard, partner," smiled a happy Umar.

"Let's get one thing straight," barked Uncle J. "This is my baby, I am the leader, end of. You are in the team, but I call the shots. Got it?"

"Chill, bro," replied Umar. "I was just messing with you."

"I'm not messing," said an agitated Uncle J, "just remember that."

The pair parted having finished their breakfasts and returned to their respective prison cells. Uncle J was now challenging his thought train to determine how best to make this kidnap plan a success. It hinged on the winning over of The Cell, as Uncle J was sure he needed to be stateside in order to execute his plans. He dared not to trust anyone else, he needed to be at the coal face, holding the reins and giving the orders, punishing anything that fell short of perfection.

Uncle J's visits to the library were starting to prove fruitful. Over a short period, he had compiled a comprehensive list of the main trek trails and holiday centres around the Yosemite, Sequoia and Kings Canyon National Parks. Uncle J had separated the perceived busy areas from the perceived remote and quiet areas, to shortlist potential locations which could be used to hold his captives. Uncle J decided to use satellite views on Google Maps, inching across the landscape and searching for suitable structures which could be utilised as his kidnapping stronghold. It was laborious work, but the thought of riches and revenge kept Uncle J's fingers firmly on the keyboard. As Uncle J discovered potential sites, he recorded the exact coordinates on a notepad. He wanted to build up a portfolio of sites that met his specific needs. As a precaution, Uncle J duplicated the coordinates on a separate sheet of paper and concealed it deep in his belongings in his prison cell, just in case any of his lists were confiscated, stolen or lost. He was determined to cover all bases from the off, leaving nothing to chance; failure was not an option.

The following day four guards turned up at Uncle J's cell door, all with batons drawn. The cell door was opened.

"You," demanded the lead guard looking directly at Uncle J, "come with me, now."

"What's going on?" said a surprised Uncle J. "Where are you taking me and why?"

"Just come," growled the surly guard.

Uncle J was led away, eventually finding himself in the middle of the prison canteen, he was ordered to sit on a bench that was surrounded by baton-wielding guards.

Uncle J sat nervously for around five minutes.

"Stand up!" demanded one of the guards pulling Uncle J to his feet.

The governor of the prison entered the canteen, flanked by another six or seven muscular-looking guards. The governor was immaculately groomed which didn't look right considering the surrounding squalor. The governor strolled confidently over to Uncle J and sat down opposite him.

"So," said the governor in a confident manner, "let's cut to the chase. What's going on? Why the sudden interest in the library? Why the sudden interest in the internet? Why the sudden interest in California? What the hell are you planning, Uncle J?"

As soon as the governor had delivered his myriad of questions, a nearby guard stooped down and thrust a baton under Uncle J's chin.

"Answer me!" demanded the governor.

"It's all very simple to explain, sir," responded a flustered Uncle J. "I have always had a dream to trek in the great outdoors with the wildlife and trees. I have always had a love affair with California and promised myself that one day I will go there and fulfil my dreams. I am a changed man, sir. My days of thuggery and crime are behind me. This institution has guided me not to offend again. I don't want to spend any more time in here, it's hell. The new me is trying to plan a trekking holiday in the United States, no more than that, sir, I promise."

The governor reached into his inside jacket pocket, removed a pack of cigarettes and took one out. He offered one to Uncle J.

"Thank you, sir." said Uncle J taking a cigarette.

The governor removed a second cigarette, put it to his lips, leaned forward and lit his and Uncle J's cigarettes.

"Trekking, you say?" chortled the governor. "Uncle J trekking, that I would love to see. You treat me like a fool, you want to trek as much as I want to swim with alligators."

"It's true, sir," replied a nervous Uncle J. "I am a changed man, it is my destiny."

"Bullshit!" snapped the governor. "What is really going on? Tell me now."

The guard thrust his baton further under Uncle J's chin.

"Sir," begged Uncle J, "what can I say apart from the truth, I want to leave my life of crime behind me."

The governor looked at the guard standing directly to the right of Uncle J and nodded. The guard drew his baton and hit Uncle J firmly in the rib cage causing Uncle J to spit and splutter to the floor.

"Again," shouted the governor, "what the hell is going on?"

Uncle J looked up at the governor holding his aching rib cage.

"It's true, sir," sobbed Uncle J in pain. "I am just planning a holiday in case I get out of here."

The governor again nodded to the guard, and once more Uncle J took another baton body blow.

"Anything to say, Uncle J?" boomed the governor.

"It's true, I am planning a holiday, sir," sobbed a forlorn Uncle J.

"He's had enough," said a disgruntled governor, "perhaps he is telling the truth? Keep a close eye on him in any case and pull his library privileges, he can plan his own holiday in his own time and not mine."

The governor and his entourage then filed out leaving Uncle J in a painful heap on the canteen floor.

"Move, now," growled a guard again wielding his baton close to Uncle J.

The remaining guards helped Uncle J to his feet and took him to his prison cell to recover from his unscheduled audience with the governor.

Uncle J waited until supper the next day to try and make contact with Umar so that he could share his experience. Umar sidled up to Uncle J in the canteen.

"I heard about the governor trying to rough you up yesterday, bro," said an inquisitive Umar.

"Good news travels fast in here!" said a vexed Uncle J. "Who gave you the low down?"

"Like I said," replied Umar, "my guards like my cigarettes, they keep me informed all the time, I'm quite a fountain of knowledge when it comes to current events."

"I see," replied Uncle J, "so using your superior knowledge, do you think there are any candidates in here suitable to join our quest?"

"Nah, bro," responded Umar. "In any case, The Cell will hand-pick the team, man, that's the way they roll now, you will have little say in that."

"I bloody well will," snapped Uncle J. "It's my plan, my revenge, I am the leader and I call the shots."

"Then say goodbye to the backing of The Cell, man," stated a confident Umar.

"It's going to be like that then, is it?" replied Uncle J.

"Yeah, bro," said Umar. "Just accept the fact and get used to it."

"So, is there anything else I need to know about the new Cell?" asked Uncle J.

"They just do things differently now," responded Umar, "totally differently since the overhaul. It's for the best in my opinion. If this Cell was around in your day, your kidnap would have been a total success, man."

"How can you say that?" demanded a hurt Uncle J.

"I just know, bro," responded Umar. "It's hard to explain. The Cell does their business now in a calm and calculated way, everything is just so, they don't make mistakes and always have a contingency plan, whatever the scenario."

"Sounds too good to be true to me," uttered a bemused Uncle J. "If they are that successful, why are they criminals? Why don't they operate in a legit way?"

Umar just shrugged his shoulders.

"Oh, man," said an excited Umar. "I nearly forgot, I have news."

"You've run out of cigarettes?" chortled Uncle J.

"No, bro," added Umar. "I am up for a parole hearing, my plans have worked. I am up in front of the release committee a week after you. How good is that?"

"I don't know how you do it?" said Uncle J.

"And who said smoking is bad for you?" laughed a belligerent Umar.

"Well, the very best of luck," said Uncle J offering a handshake.

"Don't need luck, man," replied Umar shaking Uncle J's hand, "just need more cigarettes."

"You know what," said Uncle J. "I never asked, why are you in here? What did you do?"

"You won't believe me if I told you," responded Umar.

"Try me," replied Uncle J.

"I used to work for Mansoor in the Port," added Umar. "Shall I say I had a side-line selling some "excess" goods that used to come into the Port until Mansoor found out, had me relieved of my post and thrown in here for a very long time."

"Well, I never," chortled Uncle J. "It's a small world, maybe that explains why you were so keen to join the revenge team."

"In actual fact, The Cell told me I was on your team," replied Umar. "I told you; they look after the big picture and handle recruitment. I might add though, Mansoor has left a bitter taste in my mouth, so I did push my agenda with The Cell."

"Why, you sneaky little toad!" responded a surprised Uncle J. "I had better keep you on a short leash."

The pair laughed and joined together for a brotherly embrace, both hoping for better days ahead.

Chapter Two

It was the night before Uncle J's parole hearing, his head was buzzing which prevented him from even remotely considering falling asleep. His thoughts were dominated by visions of relaxing on a yacht, drifting aimlessly on a calm and sunny ocean on the Caribbean Sea, smoking a large Cuban cigar while sipping away at the finest brandy. Uncle J was desperate and driven to get out of his prison hellhole to deliver his revenge plans.

From time to time, Uncle J's blissful thoughts of a tranquil and luxurious life outside were overruled by terrifying thoughts of his imminent parole hearing and the possible outcomes. Failure was not an option, he had to gain his liberty to spare himself of further turmoil inside this inhospitable prison. His recent painful encounter with the governor was not only still causing him physical pain, but also reminded him that the governor was aware of his newfound interest in the internet and in particular, California and its offerings. Uncle J just hoped that he could sell his recent interest in trekking and living a more healthy and outdoor approach to a reformed lifestyle.

At breakfast time, Umar jostled with the crowd of ill-mannered inmates to make his way to Uncle J's side on this, his potentially historic day. Sliding up tight to Uncle J, Umar punched him gently on the upper arm.

"Hey, bro," said Umar, "you gonna smash it today at the hearing, no worries, man."

"I don't want to talk about it," responded a jittery Uncle J. "I can't face any more time in here. I am above all this inglorious bedlam. I need my freedom. I need to breathe fresh air. I despise the threat of a baton beating around every corner."

"You did the crime, now you're doing the time," quipped Umar.

"Don't start," snapped Uncle J. "I should never have got myself involved with those small time immature street criminals trying to do man's work."

"Whatever, bro," replied Umar, "it is what it is. I just want to wish you all the luck, man, with the hearing, but I don't think you will need it, if you know what I mean."

Umar rose from the breakfast bench, winked at Uncle J, and disappeared into the throng of feasting criminals.

"What the hell did he mean by that?" thought Uncle J to himself.

Uncle J picked himself up off his breakfast bench and set foot to try and catch up with Umar for a suitable explanation, but Umar's fleet of foot made him long gone.

Staring down the exit hallway, Uncle J was herded back to his cell to wait impatiently for his fate. The three hours leading up to his hearing passed by at a snail's pace. Fellow inmates in his cell knew that today was Uncle J's big day and started to pass inappropriate comments and jokes to try and rile Uncle J, but he was having none of it; he didn't want to snap and attack a fellow prisoner on the day of his hearing. So, Uncle J just switched off to the verbal circus in his cell and pretended to fall asleep facing the wall of the cell on his bottom bunk.

It was time. Four aggressive-looking guards had appeared at Uncle J's cell door.

"You!" barked the lead guard. "Come, now!"

Uncle J leapt off his bunk as the cell door slid open just enough for Uncle J to squeeze his ample frame through. Other inmates in the cell moved forward to try and hamper Uncle J's exit, but the remaining guards aggressively raised their batons, gesturing at the attempted disrupters.

It was a ten-minute walk to the hearing room for Uncle J. Escorted by a tightly grouped squad of what-looked-like henchmen rather than prison guards, marching briskly through the maze of sultry and claustrophobic corridors lined with rusty barred cell doors. Behind every cell door was a small mob baying a mixture of abuse, good luck wishes and downright nonsense as Uncle J and his posse advanced. It was a difficult walk, to say the least, and at times Uncle J struggled to keep pace with his guards, often stumbling on the uneven and ill-kept floor.

After what seemed like a lifetime, the party arrived at the parole room. Uncle J's heart was throbbing in his throat at fifty to the dozen. He was fighting back his building nerves as best he could.

The door in front of Uncle J opened slowly as the guards pushed Uncle J into a relatively small room furnished with a basic desk, a plastic chair located against the desk in front of Uncle J, with four more comfortable-looking padded chairs situated on the opposite side.

"Sit," said one of the guards, "and behave."

Uncle J nodded at the guard and sat humbly on the chair in the manner of a small schoolboy about to be set on by the headmaster.

A door in the left hand corner of the room creakily opened and four well-dressed figures emerged, one at least Uncle J recognised, as it was the prison governor.

Uncle J started to stand as a mark of respect, but this was soon compromised when one of the guards brought down his baton onto the top of Uncle J's shoulder firmly.

"You behave," said the guard.

The assembled group in front of Uncle J sat down and started to organise paperwork, folders, and plastic cups of chai in front of them. Once settled they all looked up at Uncle J.

"Right, then," stated the governor, "let's make a start, shall we? Present at this parole hearing is myself, the governor, this is Mr Ishaaq, who has been appointed as your legal support for this procedure, Mr Javed, who has been appointed as your public protection advocate for this procedure, and Mr Naeem, who has been appointed to represent the state for this procedure. Any questions?"

"No, sir," replied a humble Uncle J. "I wasn't expecting all of this."

"All of what?" snapped back the governor.

"All of these people," responded Uncle J who appeared to be slightly overwhelmed.

"It's what we do at parole hearings," continued the governor. "We do it to the book in my establishments, no comebacks if you perform your duties to the book."

"I understand, sir," replied Uncle J.

"So," continued the governor, "you have been a guest of ours for eleven years, Uncle J, and I must say that in that time you have been what could loosely be described as a model prisoner. You have stayed out of any major trouble. It was duly noted that you took no part in the major riots of four and eight years ago, choosing to remain in your cell. You also took no part in the countless minor riots and disturbances in your block over the entire period of time you have been a prisoner here, which I actually commend you for. Pity the prison is not full of Uncle J's."

The panel of four all smiled and nodded at each other.

"In addition," added the governor, "your one-on-one fight count is not even worth considering so on the positive side there is not too much negativity to discuss."

"Excellent," nodded an appreciative Uncle J.

"However," replied the governor in a steelier tone, "I am somewhat disturbed by your recent interest in the library, the internet and more specifically, California. Would you care to explain to the panel why the sudden change and interest in the library, as in eleven years you have not once set foot in that zone, let alone the building?"

"I can, sir," replied Uncle J. "As you have explained, I have been in this institute for eleven years now, cramped up, with little time or opportunity for proper exercise combined with the plethora of time available for me to think. My thoughts and dreams have been steered towards a healthier lifestyle, grasping the great outdoors where I can roam freely, trekking in the forests or taking in the fresh mountain air of California; something I have always dreamed about, but my life up to now has been distracted and perverted into a life of crime which I want to leave behind. If nothing else, sir, your prison has taught me a hard lesson that crime does not pay, and I don't want to spend any more time in your company. No offence intended, sir."

"None taken," quipped the governor. "I do understand your train of thought, Uncle J, to make a new, healthier start following a new lifestyle choice, but why just in recent weeks? Why not five years ago? Why not eight years ago?"

"Sir," responded Uncle J with real purpose, "if I had joined the library five or eight years ago and started to research a new lifestyle it would have been a torment to me, sir, not being able to live out my dreams for five or eight years. It would have made the time pass by in here painfully, so much slower, sir. It would have been a millstone weight to drag around the prison with me."

"I see," replied an intrigued governor, "so, in reality, let's say you are telling the truth."

"I am, sir, I am," butted in Uncle J.

"Silence, let me speak!" barked the governor. "Like I said, in reality, let's say you are telling the truth, how on earth do you think you will get a Green Card to even enter the United States? I hear they don't take too kindly to visitors from our neck of the woods, let alone visitors with prison records."

"I appreciate that point, sir," replied Uncle J. "I am willing to take my chances. Yes, I may fall at the first hurdle, but if I don't at least try I will never know. Plus, if I do fail to get a Green Card, we do live in a beautiful country with many mountain ranges, great plains and vast outdoor areas that I can explore up north."

"I see," replied a somewhat taken aback governor, "so California is the pipe dream, but the Northern territory is the reality then?"

"Exactly, sir," responded a relieved Uncle J. "I do really want a new life, sir. I'm sick and tired of being imprisoned, I carry far too much weight, plus I want to do some good for myself in the world rather than bring misery and pain into people's lives with crime and deceit. I am, to excuse the cliché, a changed man, I really am, sir."

"Right!" stated the governor. "I've heard enough. I will consult with the panel and let you have my decision in the next week or so."

"Are these people going to speak?" said a concerned Uncle J pointing to the remaining panel.

"Enough!" growled the governor. "I have said my piece, you have said your piece, now return to your cell, as I have told you, I will let you know the outcome of this hearing in due course."

The panel rose in unison and promptly jostled out of the room. Uncle J knew it was his turn to leave, as a baton had appeared under his chin.

"Let's go," mumbled another guard lifting Uncle J off his seat firmly using Uncle J's armpits as leverage points.

It was again time to run the gauntlet of abuse down the comedian-loaded prison corridors. The guards bundled Uncle J out of the tranquillity of the parole room into the sweaty, arid and acrid bedlam that Uncle

J wanted to leave far behind him. There was to be no respite, as once again the baying hooligans sparked into life, chanting venomous insults and abuse from behind their steel barriers at Uncle J. There was no thought of trying to identify the abuse perpetrators for Uncle J, as payback was not on Uncle J's menu just in case the parole hearing was a success, and freedom awaited. A schoolboy ruck with a jealous and uncaring felon was not going to strip Uncle J's hopes of being released away from him, so he bravely and reluctantly took everything that the baying mobs could throw at him on the chin.

Following the unpleasant and uncomfortable transfer, Uncle J found himself once again lying on his bunk, trying to predict the outcome of the parole hearing. Reliving the governor's contributions word for word, trying to make some sense of the governor's comments; always trying to interpret them in a positive manner. The hearing seemed to have gone well in Uncle J's opinion; there appeared to be no negative argument to oppose his release, but the main threat to his freedom was his knowledge of the authorities, who were known for fickle decisions based on shallow, unreasonable reasoning, just as long as they could flex their muscles of power on the prison low life at every given opportunity. This was a real and valid worry.

Later in the day, Uncle J was ushered once again to the canteen to receive the delights of evening dining. Having queued up in an orderly fashion to receive his portion, Uncle J scoured the room for a seat giving him distance from the throng so he could continue with his parole hearing assessment in peace.

"Hey, bro," said a smiling Umar as he bumped into Uncle J's rib cage with vigour, "so, come on then, how did it go, man? How was the hearing?"

"I'm really not sure," replied a lacklustre Uncle J. "I can't make up my mind. All seemed to go well but you know the governor as well as I do, he plays his cards like a steely poker player, when you think you are in with a chance, he will crush you with an ace that has been concealed up his sleeve."

"Maybe picture him in a t-shirt, then he will have no sleeves to hide his winning cards," quipped Umar.

"Very funny," replied Uncle J. "I wish it was as simple as that."

"So, man," continued Umar, "who was at the hearing? How many dudes were in there with you?"

"Well," responded Uncle J, "there were two guards positioned on both doors in the room, I sat alone on one side of the table and there was the governor, of course, my brief and some advocate dude, whatever that means?"

"You had a brief?" quizzed Umar.

"Exactly," responded Uncle J, "it was all news to me as well. I guess the prison appoints a solicitor as part of the process. I'd never seen him before in my life and he was a puppet, room meat, just present to tick a box, as he never said a word in my defence. In fact, he never said a word at all."

The pair relived the parole hearing for as long as they could until the impatient guards demanded that they return to their cells with their fellow inmates. It was going to be a tense time until judgement hour for Uncle J; he wanted this freedom so badly. He needed to get back on the revenge trail and celebrate his pound of flesh.

Three days had passed since the hearing and time was elapsing in slow motion for Uncle J. He imagined that every movement in the corridor outside his cell was indeed the posse of guards to summon him to the governor for his decision. Whenever Uncle J was out of his cell for meals or exercise, every gesture from or eye contact with a guard was interpreted as a possible calling from the governor. Uncle J absolutely made sure he steered clear of any inclination of trouble or unrest wherever he found himself. He had to keep a clean record whatever the circumstances. Uncle J feared a counter plan from the governor, maybe fabricating a situation to place Uncle J in a position of false guilt, just to take away that glorious chance of freedom, but thankfully this didn't materialise.

On the fourth day following the hearing, Uncle J's mid-morning nap on his bunk was interrupted and not rudely. Four guards had appeared at the cell door, all with batons drawn and a mean look in their eyes. Gesturing a baton at Uncle J the lead guard demanded

Uncle J come forward. The other ten or so prisoners in the cell were told to get away from the cell door in no uncertain terms. Once in the corridor, Uncle J knew that the totally unpleasant but worthwhile running of the gauntlet was upon him again. Enduring the barrage of inmate banter and abuse, Uncle J was transferred back to the parole hearing room. After a protracted and difficult transfer, Uncle J was guided through an open door into the parole hearing room and told to take a seat. The featureless, acrid and intimidating room was populated by just Uncle J and the customary two guards on each of the two visible doors. Uncle J stared at the dusty desk in front of him, thinking that it needed a good clean when the door in the corner swung open vigorously and the governor appeared.

The governor sat in one of the four seats opposite Uncle J, he reached into his jacket pocket and removed a packet of cigarettes plus a fancy zippo lighter adorned with an image of a skull. The governor took out two cigarettes and offered one to Uncle J.

"Thank you, sir," said a humble Uncle J taking the cigarette, "very kind."

The governor offered the smallest of nods of his head, leaned across and sparked his lighter into life. The governor then sat back in his chair, took a long draw of his cigarette, and leaned forward again.

"Uncle J," said a confident governor, "I have the outcome of the parole board concerning your case for release undertaken four days ago. I guess you have some level of interest in what I have to say?"

Fearing the worst, Uncle J just nodded his head and said nothing.

"I'm not sure how," added the governor, "but it appears that you have the Gods on your side, Uncle J, as they have recommended that you are released, with immediate effect."

Hearing this news, Uncle J, immediately broke down in tears of joy, his brutal ordeal appeared to be finally over.

"However," continued the governor, "there will be certain conditions imposed on you. For three months, you will be on curfew, you will not be allowed outside of your home after six p.m. each evening until eight a.m. the following morning. Plus, you will have to sign in at your local police station every day before four p.m. By my reckoning based on where you live Uncle J that will mean you have to sign in daily at Precinct twenty-seven police station. If you breach any of these conditions at any time you will be dragged straight back here, where you will serve out your sentence in full, and more. Plus, when your three months are up and your daily sign in is no longer valid, you will not be permitted to leave the country without the personal permission of the chief of police. I want to know if you actually do want to travel to California to live out your dream. Do I make myself clear?"

"Certainly, sir," replied a tearful Uncle J. "Precinct twenty-seven it is then, sir. I will follow your guidelines to the letter, sir, fear not."

"Also," added the governor, "the authorities will be keeping an eye on you. Any signs of criminal activity and they will come down hard on you, again dragging you back here to serve out your time, do I make myself clear?"

"Oh, yes, sir, perfectly," replied Uncle J. "As I said at my hearing, sir, I am a changed man looking for a fresh start away from my past life of crime and disorder."

"Let's see, shall we," replied the governor, "Now, go back to your cell and prepare yourself for release. The guards will pick you up after this evening's mealtime, make sure you don't miss the bus, Uncle J."

The governor paused momentarily and stared at Uncle J eye to eye in a very suspicious but silent manner before turning to leave the room.

"Let's hope we never meet again, Uncle J," said the governor as he arrogantly left the room.

Uncle J's evening mealtime couldn't arrive quickly enough. He had already collected together his meagre belongings which were stashed in a pillowcase-type sack ready for the off. Later, in the evening, once in the bustling canteen, Uncle J was desperate to find Umar and tell him of his news. Uncle J had remained tight-lipped about his successful parole hearing so as not to promote jealous and spiteful reactions from less-fortunate fellow inmates. Fortuitously for Uncle J, the guards seemed to have also remained unusually secretive about the parole hearing outcome, which helped Uncle J steer clear of unrest or aggravation.

Very quickly, Uncle J and Umar sited themselves in a sparsely populated area of the canteen to conduct their parting feast and chat. Umar was ecstatic with Uncle J's tremendous news. They shared a brotherly embrace as covertly as they could so as not to attract unnecessary attention.

"Right," said an excited Uncle J, "you know where I live if you do get out of here early. You still have my address?"

"Sure, bro," replied Umar, "it's as safe as houses in my secret hiding place, I won't be losing that beauty."

"OK," replied Uncle J. "I will be there all the time except for signing in at my local police station, but there is one thing that the governor said to me. He informed me that the authorities will be watching me, whatever that means, so when you do come over to my place, have a good look around just in case you are being followed or watched, and maybe come up with a good reason why you are visiting me, just in case we get a house call from the authorities."

"Funny you should say that, man," responded a jovial Umar, "it just so happens that I have just realised that my life after prison will be taken up with a newfound interest in trekking with my brand new friend. The authorities can waste a can load of film on you and me out trekking around the local hills. They will enjoy following us and probably need the exercise."

"Good plan," said a smiling Uncle J. "I like your thinking. You will go far, lad, if you stick by me."

Uncle J and Umar finished their final prison meal together, shared another small brotherly hug, and returned to their respective cells.

Within half an hour of the return to his cell, Uncle J was collected by six guards and led for a final time through the corridors of criminals who were once again chanting their unruly and invective abuse.

Uncle J was led to the handover room where he was reunited with his own clothes and belongings he had on his person when he was first admitted to the jail. Uncle J was told to change behind a makeshift screen in the room to the side, where he proceeded to remove his prison attire, adorning his civilian uniform of freedom once again. Instantly Uncle J started to feel like a human being. His clothes hung on him poorly, as Uncle J didn't realise but he had lost a certain amount of weight during his time inside. But unperturbed by this less-than-trendy look, Uncle J started to take his first steps toward freedom in many a year.

It took thirty minutes for Uncle J to complete the prison release process. The smile on his face was immeasurable when the final door opened and the great outdoors majestically appeared before his eyes. It was dark outside, sultry, and Uncle J could hear the familiar roar of city traffic in the near distance, but this time it wasn't from the prison exercise yard.

To the right of Uncle J, a medium-sized prison van was parked up. Uncle J was ordered to walk over to the van as this was to be his transport to Precinct twenty-seven, the place where he was going to be finally released back into the community.

The journey to Precinct twenty-seven took around fifty minutes. Never had Uncle J been so happy to be in the noise and commotion of city traffic. Through a porthole-type window in the back of the van, Uncle J absorbed the heavy traffic jams, the constant blasting of car horns, the frequent verbal volleys of abuse from reckless road-raged drivers, admiring the plethora of wandering cattle and goats that infiltrated the busy carriageways adding to the street bedlam; it was great to be on the outside again.

In no time, they had arrived at Precinct twenty-seven. Uncle J was bustled inside the building entrance by the two guards who had shared the ride with him in the back of the prison van. He was then ushered to a side office to sign his release papers and agree to his release conditions. Uncle J finally and jubilantly dropped the cheap plastic biro on the desk in front of him. With all signatures completed it was over, he was again free.

It was a twenty-minute walk from the Precinct twenty-seven police station to Uncle J's house, so Uncle J decided to walk the final part of his release journey, to take in the local ambience, to stretch his free legs and maybe pick-up a bottle of something along the way to help with the celebration of his liberty, as he was amazed to discover that there were a few surprise dollars in the pockets of his civies.

Uncle J knew exactly where to obtain a bottle of banished liquor from, so made haste to his favourite underworld shopkeeper to fulfil his long-awaited desire. Armed with a bottle of his favourite tipple, Uncle J was soon at the gates of his home. The sturdy prominent steel gates were unlocked so Uncle J pushed them open and walked into his front yard.

"Uncle J!" shouted a voice from the dark. "It's you."

It was Uncle J's loyal servant, Faisal. He had served Uncle J for decades, the only trusted and loyal person in Uncle J's life. Uncle J teared up as he approached Faisal.

"My friend," sobbed Uncle J as he consumed Faisal with the biggest of genuine hugs. "You are still here, the authorities didn't arrest you and take you away?"

"They did, sir," replied Faisal, "but they released me after days and days of questioning. They realised I was just a humble servant and not a warlord or activist, and that I knew nothing about the kidnapping, or any other activity that went on here, so eventually, they let me go. I did have to take a lot of beatings during questioning, but I held my nerve, maintained my loyalty, and convinced them that I knew nothing. So, they must have concluded that I was a nobody, so they let me go."

"Thank you for your loyalty, Faisal," said a grateful Uncle J, "and sorry about the beatings you had to endure. Unfortunately, that is the way of the authorities here, there is nothing I can do to influence that."

"I know that, sir," responded Faisal. "It is what it is, sir. I have kept the place maintained and tidy in your absence, sir. I have kept the business ticking over but I am sad to tell you that many of your tuk-tuk drivers have moved on to new ventures or bosses. However, your bed is clean and waiting if you feel tired and want to sleep now, sir."

"I know what I want right now," said Uncle J brandishing his bottle of whiskey like a league winner's trophy, "and I want you to join me, Faisal. We can catch up on business matters tomorrow as I have better things to do right now."

"How kind, sir," replied Faisal. "Just this once, sir, I will join you as it's a special occasion."

"Now, tell me, Faisal," continued Uncle J, "what gossip and events have I missed since I have been on my government-sponsored holidays?"

Uncle J and Faisal made their way to the main lounge where they devoured the bottle of whisky, as Faisal did his best to get Uncle J up to speed with the last decade of events which was no mean feat in itself. Conversations went on long into the night with Uncle J learning about the fate of his fellow gang members and

Faisal shared the news coverage broadcast on local TV showing the outcome of the failed kidnapping that Faisal had recorded for Uncle J just in case. The coverage showed Mansoor as a hero, boosting his reputation and popularity within the community to heady heights which enraged Uncle J, fuelling his desire for revenge.

By the time, a second bottle of whiskey taken from stock had been consumed, Uncle J and Faisal decided to call it a night and retired to their rooms tired, blind drunk but still elated.

The following late morning, a totally hungover Uncle J appeared in the kitchen. Faisal was busying himself and spotted Uncle J, so instantly began to prepare a much needed pot of strong, black coffee and something to eat to soak up the overindulged alcohol.

"Faisal," muttered a lifeless Uncle J "did we speak about the reserves last night? For some strange reason, my memory is somewhat sketchy at the moment."

"We did, sir," chuckled Faisal, "all is in order, sir, the authorities didn't locate it, so everything is as you left it. I used earnings from the tuk-tuk business for running costs, for the upkeep of this place and food for myself. I was careful though, sir, very careful."

"Fear not," responded an understanding Uncle J, "a man has to eat, and I thank you, kind sir, for your efforts with the maintenance of my home in my absence. How much do I have in my account right now?"

"Around one hundred and twelve thousand dollars, sir," responded Faisal. "U.S."

"Excellent!" replied Uncle J. "I need to put some of that to good use. For starters, a new computer with some decent internet speed."

"Laptops are all the rage now, sir," responded Faisal, "not computers. Laptops are portable and more flexible; might I suggest a new laptop for sir?"

"Right, you are, Faisal," said an enlightened Uncle J. "There's work afoot so I need to make myself busy."

"Work, sir?" quizzed Faisal.

"Revenge work, my friend," replied Uncle J with the look of the devil in his eye, "big, juicy revenge."

"I see," replied Faisal. "I guess the Mansoor family have left a sour taste in your mouth, sir. I hope it is not down to the news footage I saved for you?"

"Faisal," said a resigned Uncle J, "for eleven years, my friend, I could think of nothing but revenge. The sight of the news footage just put the cherry on top of the tart for me, giving me good reason to convince myself that my plan for revenge is the right thing to do. I have already been in contact with The Cell, and I already have an accomplice on board, courtesy of The Cell. This time, failure is not a consideration."

"A new team member?" asked Faisal. "Recruited from the inside, I take it?"

"Indeed," replied Uncle J, "he seems to be a bright cookie, trustworthy, and he claims he has close connections with The Cell, so much that they appointed him to work with me on my revenge plans. He may be released from prison soon, he will come here as a houseguest to help with the initial plans and maybe take part in the execution of the plans, so make up a bed in one of the guest rooms in readiness."

"Certainly, sir," replied Faisal. "I will do that immediately. It's great to have you back and even greater to have some activity in the house. It's been a long time on my own here, at last, that time is over."

Chapter Three

It was a glorious warm sunny day, not a single cloud blighted the clear blue sky which stretched out to the distant horizon. Uncle J, having had an excellent night's sleep, was in a chipper mood. Full of the joys of freedom, he took his breakfast on the patio on the back terrace of his home. Uncle J invited Faisal to sit and join him so that they could get up to speed with the latest state of Uncle J's tuk-tuk business.

Faisal had kept impeccable books in Uncle J's absence. The impressive paperwork was broken down by year, then by month, followed by a summary detailing each of the tuk-tuk renters' ability to pay their monthly dues.

Most of the drivers who had signed up with Uncle J were under his spell of being an ex-warlord and paid their monthly tuk-tuk rent as agreed. However, Faisal's accounts clearly showed Uncle J who he needed to visit to retrieve his rent arrears.

Uncle J was extremely pleased with Faisal's loyalty, dedication, and application of duties.

"This is exemplary, my friend," said an overjoyed Uncle J.

"It is my pleasure, sir," replied Faisal. "It was the very least I could do. I wanted to make sure you had some cash around you when you were released. After all, you have spent many long years building up your business. I didn't want all of your hard work to come to nothing."

"Thank you, my dear friend," said an emotional Uncle J. "I will take stock and reward you suitably for your admirable efforts in due course. However, we need to focus on other matters in the immediate future. My rent cheats will have to wait for their comeuppance, which, I assure you will come to them very soon."

"I was convinced that you would not let this missing rent go without due punishment," chortled Faisal. "It will be an opportunity for you to flex your muscles of power with these underlings announcing that Uncle J is back in town!"

"Indeed," smirked Uncle J, "but first I want you to go on a shopping trip for me, I have made a list and against each item, I have noted the names of who I want you to obtain these items from. I want to get use out of my network for a change. I haven't built up my reputation and contacts for the good of my health; it's payback time for Uncle J!"

Uncle J handed an A4 sheet of paper over to Faisal. Faisal studied the list for a few moments before nodding his head at Uncle J.

"It all looks pretty straightforward," said a confident Faisal, "leave this with me."

With Faisal busy with Uncle J's shopping, it was now time for Uncle J to see if he could determine if he was being tailed and if so, by whom. Uncle J disappeared into his house to change into some clothing suitable for a trek up the Baluchistan Hills. After all, Uncle J had let it be known to the prison staff that he was to take up a new angle in life, a more active and outdoor lifestyle.

Once changed, Uncle J jumped into his pick-up truck and made his way to the Baluchistan Hills. His journey would take him due west for around an hour. The majority of his trip would take him on busy city highways which would provide cover for any vehicles trying to keep tabs on Uncle J. However, later in the journey, the less busy suburban roads contained fewer vehicles which might allow Uncle J to identify any potential watching members of the authorities. For once, Uncle J drove his truck making sure he observed all speed limits, traffic signs and traffic lights. Uncle J didn't want to give the authorities a soft win just because Uncle J was breaking the rules of the highway. Three potential suspect vehicles had caught the eye of Uncle J that could be following him. A white Suzuki saloon car, a two-up moped and a large silver pick-up truck. All three had been in Uncle J's rearview mirror for some time now.

As Uncle J drew closer to the hills, the white saloon had branched off into a suburb side road taking it out of the potential threat equation, but the moped and pick-up truck were still present in the ensuing line of light traffic. Uncle J spotted a food outlet about two hundred metres ahead of him on the left hand side of the pothole-strewn road. If Uncle J was, in fact, being watched by the authorities, this was a chance for Uncle J to send out a message that he was aware he was being tailed.

Uncle J pulled up to the makeshift car park in front of the outlet and jumped out of his vehicle. He closed the driver's side door and leaned his back-up against it. Uncle J reached into his tunic and removed a packet of cigarettes and a lighter, facing the road as he did so that he could watch the reactions of his suspected tails.

Sure enough, the silver pick-up truck and moped passed by the food outlet, but as they had barely travelled three hundred metres from the outlet, both pulled over and parked up at a line of roadside market stalls selling fruit and vegetables.

This was sufficient evidence to confirm Uncle J's suspicions; Uncle J had flushed out some of his stalkers.

Uncle J now knew his movements were being watched and had also managed to identify a black Honda moped and a distinctive silver pick-up truck to keep watch out for in the future.

At the food outlet, Uncle J sipped on a warm cup of chai from a plastic cup and quickly chomped down a sugary snack. He wanted his hunters to think that he was taking a legitimate comfort break rather than attempting to flush out any trackers. Once the chai and snack had been consumed, Uncle J returned to his truck and pulled back out on the narrow highway to the hills. He made sure that he didn't look at the two suspected tails as he passed the market stalls, but from the corner of his eye, Uncle J did notice that the suspect vehicles were still parked up.

Uncle J's vehicle made light work of the steeper, rougher tracks once at his hilly destination. It was a hostile and arid landscape, a plume of dust trailed behind Uncle J's truck as his ride bounced over the rough, rocky terrain as he ascended the hill. Once Uncle J had reached what he considered a suitable elevation, Uncle J stopped the engine of his sturdy truck and opened the driver's side door. As Uncle J removed himself from his vehicle, he became immediately in awe of the vista in front of him. Although he was only part-way up the hillside, there was still an impressive view facing him. He could make out the distant residential and commercial city buildings to his right, and to his left, the flat, featureless countryside spread out to the Arabian Sea on the horizon. It was impressive. Uncle J thought to himself that his false statements concerning his new life of healthy living weren't actually a bad idea.

As the area was remote and sparsely populated, Uncle J took this opportunity to scan the foothills for the would be trackers. His disadvantage was that the followers would be able to keep an eye on Uncle J from a distance as there were no places where Uncle J could conceal his activities. The Baluchistan Hills were not clad with rocky outcrops or boulder formations and were relatively free from trees. Uncle J scoured the foothills for a few minutes but was unable to locate the pick-up truck or moped which he suspected had been following him.

Enthused and invigorated by the stunning views, Uncle J decided to climb up to the hill summit. After all, he was dressed for the occasion, and he intended to trek.

It took Uncle J about forty-five minutes to clamber to the top of the hill. Standing at the summit, Uncle J took a big lung full of fresh air. The view was breathtaking. Uncle J had never been to the Baluchistan Hills before in all his life in the city and was suitably impressed. Turning around from the panoramic view of the city and the sea, Uncle J cast his eyes north, looking up country towards the sandy flats in the foreground which made their way into the rocky hills and mountains that penetrated the skyline on the horizon. The sheer expanse and magnitude of the view made Uncle J realise that he was so lucky to live in a vast country full of glorious landscapes and beauty spots.

Uncle J gleefully absorbed the panorama in front of him for another half an hour before returning to his truck. The descent back to the metalled roads was a simple one for Uncle J's powerful pick-up, making light work of the uneven dry, stony environment. Once Uncle J had reached the relatively flat roads of the suburbs, he again observed the presence of the silver pick-up and black moped that had tracked him to the hills. This was not a problem for Uncle J. He guessed he knew what their likely objectives would be, and the fact that he was not breaking any laws set Uncle J's mind at rest, for the time-being. Having company on his back was not going to make any difference.

Within the hour Uncle J had reached his home. Faisal greeted him as he made his way to the kitchen area to get a much needed bottle of beer.

"Sir, you have a visitor in the lounge," said an official-sounding Faisal.

"Really?" replied a surprised Uncle J. "Who has come to visit me, Faisal?"

"He is sitting in the lounge, sir," responded Faisal. "I have given him some food and drink; he looked hungry."

"No bother," said Uncle J. "Let's see who is here."

Uncle J rushed to the lounge and threw open the door.

"Umar!" exclaimed a jubilant Uncle J. "My friend, you are out."

Umar rose from his chair and greeted Uncle J with a huge and friendly embrace.

"I told you," said a happy Umar. "Cigarettes all the way to grease the wheels of freedom."

"I'm starting to worry about you, Umar," replied a playful Uncle J. "Everything that you say will happen, actually happens, and exactly how you say it. I need to watch my back, you might be after my position of influence."

"There is only one Uncle J!" exclaimed Umar. "I have no chance of outshining and replacing the legend."

"Ha ha!" chortled Uncle J. "So, how long have you been out? Seeing you in front of me suggests that your release hearing went well."

"There was no hearing," replied Umar. "Guards showed up at my prison cell door this morning and told me to follow them. They took me to the release area, threw my belongings at me, ordered me to take off my prison uniform and leave. No release conditions, no ride into town, they just opened the front door and pushed me out."

"Well, I never," said a surprised Uncle J. "As simple as that. You are either a very lucky man or you have a sponsor lurking in the shadows looking after your interests."

"I've told you," said Umar with a beaming smile filling his face, "it's all down to the cigarettes."

"Anyhow," interrupted Uncle J impatiently. "I have been out to the Baluchistan Hills today and I am one hundred percent sure I had company."

"The authorities?" asked Umar.

"I'm pretty sure," replied Uncle J. "A silver pick-up and a black moped. I flushed them out on the way to the hills, so from now on just be mindful that whatever we do, the authorities will be in wait, watching our every move."

"I guess that's OK for now," replied Umar, "what can they pull us in for if we are not breaking any laws?"

"Exactly," agreed Uncle J. "So, I have made a shopping list containing things that we need to get the revenge plans underway, Faisal my manservant is looking after that for me, so I guess we need to talk to The Cell as soon as possible and get them involved."

"And the plan is to…?" quizzed a cautious Umar.

"Kidnap the children of Mansoor, of course!" boomed an irritated Uncle J.

"Exactly how?" asked a tireless Umar.

"I have been thinking," responded a more confident Uncle J, "we ask The Cell to get some surveillance on Mansoor's children, understand where and how they live their lives in San Francisco, monitor their regular movements, where they go for work, what they do in their spare time, who they meet with, who they socialise with, in short, build up a picture of their lives. I also need The Cell to arrange some false papers and passports for you and me; new and clean identities, so that we can travel to California. Once there, we can look for a suitable place to hold the kidnap victims once we have them and make Mansoor pay the ransom money he owes me from our previous attempts. This time he will pay, I will make sure he does."

"Hang on a minute," snapped Umar. "False papers, false passports, travel to the States. Who do you think you are? The Cell is not a bottomless pit, they are businessmen, they won't do a single thing for free, have you considered that?"

"They will get their fair slice," responded an agitated Uncle J. "That goes without saying. However, The Cell owes me, I am a known brave and decorated warrior, I have served The Cell well in the past, for many years, and won many bloody battles in their name, they can't refuse. Just wait, when I talk to them, they will not reject my request."

"You need to understand this, Uncle J," replied Umar with a look of stern seriousness on his face. "You won't get anywhere near The Cell, they have issued their orders already, and it will be me and me alone that will have direct contact with The Cell. You are high risk, they know the authorities will be watching so there is not a chance in hell of you getting anywhere near them. I am trusted and respected in the higher ranks of The Cell. So, cease with your illusions of grandeur, leave all negotiations with The Cell to me, end of."

"You cannot be serious?" exclaimed an irate Uncle J. "I am number one around here, this is my plot, my revenge, if I want to meet with The Cell then I will meet with The Cell."

"Then just forget about The Cell and their backing," said Umar walking towards the door of the lounge.

"Wait!" shouted Uncle J. "Don't leave. Let me think for a moment."

Uncle J walked across the lounge to a sideboard. He opened the right hand drawer and took out a wooden box. Uncle J stared down at the box for a short while, pondering the quandary that faced him. He then walked over to Umar with the box and opened the lid. The box was half-full of good-looking cigars.

"Smoke with me, friend," said a calm Uncle J. "I understand, you are right. I am a security risk for The Cell, I know, as I have seen it with my own eyes. The authorities are keeping tabs on me, I would be a fool to lead them to The Cell. But tell me one thing, friend, as you have been seen in my company, how do you know that you are not being watched as well by the authorities and you might lead the authorities to The Cell?"

"This worries me not," replied an arrogant Umar. "I can shake off these fools with ease, even if they are following me, I am an expert in such matters."

"Your over-confident manner worries me," responded Uncle J. "You have convinced yourself that you are some sort of super-human, capable of great things, but all I recall you telling me is that you got caught running an illegal side-line at the port. Your track record doesn't exactly smell of success, does it?"

"Look," said a ruffled Umar, "all the time I spent behind bars I was dealing covertly with The Cell and evaded detection. I helped out so many prisoners while I was inside, and The Cell is very much aware of my capabilities. So, I did get caught, I did get thrown in prison, but that was before my allies in the reformed Cell got hold of me and made me what I am today."

"We shall see," said a less than convinced Uncle J. "Anyhow, let's smoke these fine Cuban cigars and map out what you are going to talk about during your first meeting with The Cell."

The pair lit up their fine cigars and sat down in, what seemed, a more pleasant ambience.

"I too have been thinking," said Umar confidently. "This is what I envisage. I agree with your proposals concerning getting to understand the daily routines and contacts of Mansoor's children. I can talk to The Cell and see if they already have boots on the ground in the States or even California. Getting hold of false and clean identities for both of us is also a no-brainer so again I will get my contacts in The Cell to get working on that. You need to think about timeframes. When do you want to strike and take the targets hostage? How long are you prepared to hold the hostages? Think about what demands you want to issue to Mansoor? This time you will need a better plan to get hold of the ransom cash as we all know what happened last time."

"OK, OK," said a resigned Uncle J. "I can learn from #the previous attempt, it will make me a stronger person. I am well aware of what happened before, but I was surrounded by incompetent fools and petty street criminals."

"Maybe," replied Umar, "but it was also a different Cell back then, as I have told you many times now, The Cell operates differently now."

"As you keep bleating," said Uncle J resentfully.

"I will go back to my place now, Uncle J," said Umar. "If I am to be your guest, I will need to collect some of my belongings. I will return in a couple of hours. Is there anything you need while I am out?"

"I'm OK," responded Uncle J. "Faisal will see to my needs, but thanks for asking. Take my pick-up if you want to, it will spare you the dusty and noisy delights of a tuk-tuk ride across town, plus my truck has aircon."

"Try stopping me," said a smiling Umar.

With Umar occupied with the collection of his belongings, Uncle J wandered into the kitchen to understand how Faisal was getting on with the procurement of the items on the shopping list.

"I have the laptop," informed Faisal, "a new router, extra PC monitor and mouse, plus I have managed to get you three external hard drives to store data on. We can hide two of them just in case we get a house visit from the authorities."

"Excellent work, Faisal." replied a happy Uncle J. "What about the other stuff?"

"I have just focussed on the electronics today," responded Faisal. "I will set all of this up in your office tonight, then I will work on getting the rest of the items on the list tomorrow — there's only so much I can carry, sir."

"No worries," responded Uncle J. "I am off for a bath now, I have been looking forward to a bath for eleven years and I intend to enjoy this one. Keep an eye out for Umar when I am bathing, he will be back in a few hours. Is his room ready?"

"All ship shape, sir," replied Faisal.

The following morning, Uncle J summoned Faisal and Umar to his office.

"Faisal," demanded Uncle J, "fetch me the books and the list of my business debtors, it is time I showed the local community that Uncle J is back, and he is no soft touch."

"I'll get it right away," said Faisal scurrying out of the office.

"What do you have in mind?" enquired Umar.

"I'm going to pay my debtors a house visit," continued Uncle J. "I don't want my reputation sullied by these low life tuk-tuk drivers. They owe me. They are my vehicles and the contracts have been signed. If they choose to break the terms of our agreement, then they must pay the consequences.

Faisal returned with the business ledgers. All three meticulously checked the records just to make sure there were no glaring mistakes. Uncle J didn't want to perform a show of strength only for the victim to be on the right side of debt.

After lengthy deliberation, the handful of targets for home visits to recover the debts was made. Uncle J decided that dawn visits would be the best course of action as if they tried to recover the debts during the day, it was likely that the intended target would be on the streets chasing fare-paying passengers. One raid per day as the target households were spread across the city.

"We start tomorrow," said a confident Uncle J. "We will start with Javed as it would give me great pleasure to squash that felon's head like a melon."

"Won't that give the authorities good reason to arrest you?" asked Umar.

"Figure of speech," snapped Uncle J. "I will just put the frighteners on Javed if he can't pay his debt. If he doesn't have money, then we will take back my tuk-tuk and bring it back here to the compound. That is why you will come with me, Umar, my friend; you can drive the tuk-tuk if the need arises."

"I am here to work on behalf of The Cell, Uncle J," responded an arrogant Umar.

Uncle J leapt over to Umar and grasped his throat aggressively.

"You will do as I say, laddie," growled Uncle J. "Is that the thanks I get for giving you free board and lodgings, and the chance of a significant cut of the ransom money?"

"Chill man!" exclaimed a cowering Umar. "OK, OK, I'll come along with you."

Uncle J released his vice-like grip and backed off.

"What about the authorities?" asked Faisal nervously.

"What about them?" responded Uncle J.

"They will be watching and more likely following you," responded Umar.

"Let them," snapped Uncle J. "Are they going to arrest me for going about my business?"

"You are right," responded Faisal. "My mistake, sir."

The trio spent the remainder of the day mapping out the five intended debt-collecting dawn raids they were going to carry out. The remaining debtors were considered worthless as their debts were small and Uncle J knew that their tuk-tuks were old and in poor condition, not worth the recovery effort.

The following morning, Uncle J, Umar, and Faisal were parked in the ghetto in the deep south of the city. The streets were void of human activity of any kind. Scruffy street dogs patrolled the litter-strewn dusty streets; it was worlds apart from Uncle J's relatively comfortable suburb in the north of the city.

"Are you sure that is Javed's place?" asked Uncle J pointing towards a run down small ground floor dwelling in front of them.

"Certain," responded Faisal.

"Right, let's go," said a confident Uncle J. "The sun will rise soon, I want to catch Javed in his bed."

The debt-collecting posse clambered out of Uncle J's pick-up and crept across to Javed's front door. Uncle J gently probed the front door to Javed's home to try and get a feeling of how strong the door was. Grinning, Uncle J backed off a few metres to shoulder charge the door.

"No!" shouted Umar. "Not like this! The authorities will pull you in for breaking and entry. We have to knock on the door to get an answer."

"You are kidding me," exclaimed Uncle J. "How does that display a show of strength? I might as well have brought along a bunch of flowers."

"Trust me," continued Umar, "you can be sure we are being observed right now. Is that what you want? Your revenge plan finishing up at a small debt collection exercise?"

Uncle J held his ground.

"Damn it!" said an irate Uncle J. "You are right."

Uncle J then bashed the door with aggressive ferocity, nearly causing the door to come off its fragile hinges.

Moments later Javed answered the door with a look of terror on his face.

Uncle J rushed at Javed knocking him to the ground, pinning his shoulders to the floor with great force.

"Uncle J!" said a confused and frightened Javed. "You are out. What are you doing here?"

"Silence," barked Uncle J aggressively. "You owe me tuk-tuk rent. Why didn't you pay your dues to Faisal when I was away? Answer!"

Uncle J lifted his left hand from Javed's shoulder and landed a slap on Javed's cheek with the back of his hand.

"OK, OK," begged Javed. "You don't need to resort to violence, I will pay you what I owe."

"When?" demanded Uncle J.

"Give me a few weeks, Uncle J," said a flustered Javed. "I can get some money from my brother; he keeps my money, he has a bank account and all that."

Uncle J landed another blow to Javed's cheek. Uncle J knew it was unnecessary, but he had not been in this position of power and influence for many years, and it was giving him a buzz.

"Two weeks," demanded Uncle J. "We will come back in two weeks. If you don't have the money then you will pay dearly in other ways, do I make myself clear?"

Uncle J raised his left hand again but held it above his head, threatening another painful blow.

"Agreed," said a cowering Javed. "I will have your money."

"I am taking my tuk-tuk back as a form of hostage," continued Uncle J. "Just in case you get ideas of making a run for it."

Uncle J rose to his feet.

"Give me the keys to my tuk-tuk!" demanded Uncle J.

"They are on that chair," said Javed pointing across to a forlorn-looking chair next to Javed's threadbare sofa.

Uncle J retrieved the keys, then kicked out petulantly at the chair sending it tumbling into the corner of the room. He wanted to show Javed that his aggression was flowing and that he meant business.

Uncle J threw the keys to Umar who caught them.

"Don't cheat on me again," snapped Uncle J. "You get your wheels back when the debt is settled."

The three visitors then confidently departed.

Umar drove Uncle J's tuk-tuk back to his compound; it was Umar's first time behind the controls of a tuk-tuk for many years, so it was an enjoyable and novel experience, despite the now heavier city traffic and arduous road conditions.

Once back home, the trio assembled in Uncle J's office. Faisal had prepared chai and handed out overflowing mugs to Uncle J and Umar.

"See," said a smug Uncle J. "I have still got it! Did you see Javed cower like a frightened baby?"

"Why did you even have to do this?" asked Umar. "It's not like they owe you a small fortune?"

"All part of the act," responded Uncle J. "It gives the impression to the authorities that I am attempting to rebuild my legitimate tuk-tuk business. It sends out a message to the city community that Uncle J is back and is not taking any messing, plus it puts a few dollars into the kitty when he pays up. Simple."

"I see," replied Umar. "You are lucky the authorities did not intervene and arrest you for common assault. That aside, when do we actually get down to the matters at hand? The Cell will want some action soon, if you don't show willingness, they may pull their offer of support."

"I want you to meet with The Cell this week," said Uncle J. "We will sit down together for the next few days and map out a more detailed plan, then you can take it to The Cell and start to arrange the help and support that they will be giving us."

"About time!" exclaimed Umar. "Acting as your debt collection agent is not pleasing for me; it's small time and bad for my image."

"We all have to start somewhere," quipped Uncle J.

"I can assure you," replied a vexed Umar, "I am not starting anything. I am well-respected already by The Cell. Why do you think they trust me and agree to meet with me? And not you? So, give me the respect that I deserve."

Uncle J was not impressed with the upstart's attitude, but he bit his lip and did not respond with a counter-insult. Uncle J knew that he needed Umar because of his connection with The Cell, without which, he could not instigate his revenge plot and benefit from the riches that would bring.

Uncle J and Umar sat together and proceeded to map out their initial detailed plans. Umar was adamant that great thought and attention to detail were paramount. The new Cell would not tolerate half-cocked ideas. All plans that Uncle J makes must have a backup plan, contingency seemed to be the buzzword banded by The Cell, this being the mainstay for their alleged undeniable new success. This irritated Uncle J as it doubled the workload, however, Umar had convinced him that if Uncle J did it his own way, he would lose the backing of The Cell.

Over the next three days, Uncle J and Umar dedicated themselves to their planning tasks. There was not a single thought of trekking to the local hills to play out the healthy lifestyle pantomime for the benefit of the authorities — that could wait. The pair were determined to create the best possible plans and Uncle J in particular, recognised this as an opportunity to help alleviate the bad press from the previously failed kidnap, to restore his reputation with The Cell and the wider underworld.

Three days later, it was time. The plans had been checked and double-checked, plus all had a contingency plan. In a way, Uncle J was happy with this new way of working. The methods seemed to come with a sweet smell of success, something absent from his historic partnership with Zaheer.

Chapter Four

Uncle J and Umar sat in the kitchen of Uncle J's home taking breakfast. Today was the day. The day that first contact was to be made with The Cell post the drawing up of their initial revenge plans.

"So," said Uncle J, "what are you going to do about the authorities that are bound to be tailing you when you go and meet with The Cell?"

"Simple," replied Umar confidently. "The main railway station. My meeting with The Cell is arranged for two p.m. this afternoon. I will go to the main railway station at noon. The station will be busy with many trains coming and going, which will make it easy to slip away in the crowd. I might board an outgoing train and then jump onto an incoming train, it just depends on the circumstances. I will assess my options once I am there. One thing for sure though, the station will be full of people, that I know."

"What if they keep tabs on you?" responded a concerned Uncle J. "Even though you may think you have lost them in the crowd."

"I will go from here to the north ghetto first," continued Umar. "I will probably lose them in the ghetto in any case, well before I make my way to the railway station. I am fleet of foot and as sly as a fox. I know all the hidden rat-runs and obscured passageways. Slipping the authorities will be as easy as a walk in the park."

"You had better be good to your word," responded a nervous Uncle J. "You will have to answer to The Cell if you expose them to the authorities, that I do know."

"Worry not, man," replied a comforting Umar. "I've got this."

With breakfast done and dusted, a keen and enthused Umar set off on his quest to meet with The Cell. In order to throw a predicament at the authorities, Uncle J decided to pay another visit to the Baluchistan Hills to keep up the healthy lifestyle façade and to give the authorities two targets to monitor and worry about.

Sure enough, with Uncle J over halfway to his trekking destination, he spotted the silver pick-up tailing him, it was following him three cars back in the same lane. Uncle J smiled to himself as he pressed on to take his exercise. However, there was no sign of the moped. Maybe they were busy tailing Umar?

Once at the splendid foothills of Baluchistan, Uncle J managed to spot the holding place of his followers. There was a derelict wall belonging to a long gone fabric factory acting as their shield. However, the regular breaks in the less-than-perfect retaining wall gave away the less-than-imaginative hiding place of the authorities.

Uncle J marched confidently up the slopes of the Baluchistan Hills, confident that the next chapter in his life commenced today and praying that Umar's meeting with The Cell was to result in a positive outcome.

Later that day, just as the shimmering amber sun began to sink over the horizon, and Uncle J was relaxing after his healthy trek, Umar returned to Uncle J's house following his rendezvous with The Cell. Uncle J could not contain his excitement, jostling Umar to the lounge for an immediate de-brief. Clambering nervously over to the sideboard to muster a bottle of scotch and two glasses, Uncle J then sat down in a broad armchair opposite a smiling Umar.

"Well?" exclaimed Uncle J. "How did it go? What did The Cell have to say? Did they agree to our proposals? When do we start?"

"Hang on, dude," said an overalled Umar. "Let me get comfortable, I will tell you all, just let me speak."

An impatient and frustrated Uncle J threw himself back in his armchair like a spoilt teenager, he wanted all the answers, and now.

"Did you manage to shake off the authorities?" asked Uncle J.

"No problem, man," replied Umar confidently. "They didn't stand a chance. I reckon I had lost them well before I got to the railway station."

"Excellent," answered a jubilant Uncle J. "So go on then, spill the beans."

"OK," said Umar taking a sip of scotch and a deep breath. "The Cell seems to be reasonably happy with our initial plans. They already have contacts on the ground in San Francisco. The Cell is going to make contact and get observations started straight away. They will compile extensive and comprehensive accounts of both targets' daily lives. Work, play, social, family duties and so on. The Cell has also already carried out background checks, so they know exactly where Rayan and Talib live, so that's a win already."

"Rayan and Talib?" quizzed Uncle J. "Who the hell are they?"

"You idiot!" responded an exasperated Umar. "Rayan and Talib are the targets you so passionately want to kidnap. They are Mansoor's children."

Uncle J slapped his forehead firmly with his right hand in disgust.

"Can I continue?" begged Umar.

"Please continue," replied an embarrassed Uncle J.

"The surveillance will determine where and when we choose to carry out the kidnapping," continued Umar. "The Cell is undecided at the moment. They want to take both men at the same time but cannot decide if this is coordinated at separate sites or when they are physically together. The final decision will be made once they have more surveillance evidence to ponder over."

"What about a suitable place to keep the hostages safe while we wait for the ransom money?" asked Uncle J impatiently.

"That, my friend, is still under consideration," responded Umar.

"Do I get to choose?" begged Uncle J. "Or do The Cell tell us where the hostages will be held?"

"Like I said, dude," replied Umar "The Cell is still looking into that. They do have several established and previously utilised safe houses. They are just running through some scenarios to determine what is the likely best option. So, the bottom line, I guess, is that The Cell will decide."

"So, when do I get to go to the United States then?" asked a boisterous Uncle J.

"Not for a while, man," responded Umar. "The Cell wants at least three months of surveillance before they will even consider making their first moves."

"That is rather conservative, don't you think?" replied Uncle J. "At this rate it will be years before anybody gets their hands on any loot."

"The Cell is also well aware of your criminal past, Uncle J," continued Umar. "So, as you have indicated to them, you want to be at the coalface when the kidnapping goes down. The Cell has to make sure your travel papers are credible and will pass the stringent tests that the U.S.A. immigration people will complete. They don't just let anyone into their country, so our stories for being there have to be believable and our identities need to be squeaky clean, with no criminal history."

"And how are we going to do that?" asked Uncle J.

"The Cell likes your idea," replied Umar. "They want you to keep trekking locally on a regular basis, build up a picture that you are serious about your new healthy approach to life. In fact, you do need to lose some weight, that's plain to see!"

"Easy, tiger," replied Uncle J playfully.

"When you are told you can travel," added Umar, "you will do so on the premise that you are on a combined city break and trekking holiday. Trekking in the Californian mountains combined with spending a few days in San Francisco, Monterrey, Los Angeles, and San Diego. Using the exploration of Highway One as the core theme for the visit. The Cell will find suitable identities to travel under, so that's one we don't have to worry about."

"How can they create a false history for the fake identities?" asked Uncle J. "Surely that won't be good enough to endure the strict immigration enquiries that will be run."

"The identities won't be false," replied Umar. "The Cell will carefully select suitable targets, then take them out of the equation for a while, while we carry out our actions in America, I guess."

"Kidnap them?" asked Uncle J.

"I assume so," responded Umar. "That is for The Cell to decide and not us."

"Who does The Cell want to travel to the States?" requested Uncle J.

"The Cell wants to keep it manageable," replied Umar. "So it will be just the two of us, on separate flights as well."

"Flights?" said a shocked Uncle J. "We are flying out there?"

"Yes," replied Umar abruptly. "How did you think we were going to get there? Swim?"

"I just thought we may be smuggled over there," Said Uncle J, "on board a ship stowed away. I didn't even consider that we would fly on a scheduled flight."

"We will fly from the capital," continued Umar. "Our faces are known in the city and by the authorities. I am sure the city airport is being monitored, and I bet your name is on any list they are working from. If anyone spots you in the city airport and you are found to be carrying false papers, it's game over. However, if we fly from the capital, our faces are not known so we can hopefully travel on our false papers unchallenged."

"I like the idea," replied Uncle J. "Good, sound reasoning."

"So, in the short term," added Umar, "we just need to keep our noses clean and out of trouble. The Cell recommends that you rebuild your tuk-tuk business to maintain a front of good behaviour, carry on with your hill-based exercise and keep signing in at Precinct twenty-seven police station as requested by the authorities."

"When do we meet with The Cell again?" asked Uncle J.

"We?" mused Umar. "I am sure you meant 'I'. There will be a second meeting in a month to discuss the surveillance progress and to update me as to any changes to the plans. I already have a time and date arranged for this meeting."

"I am getting somewhat tired of The Cell already," said a disgruntled Uncle J. "I am supposed to be the brains and leadership behind this plan. It turns out that I am no more than a pawn, operating almost like a puppet for an overpowering master. I don't get to choose the hostage-holding location, I don't have a say concerning the timing of the kidnap, and I don't even get the opportunity to meet with The Cell."

"Come on, man," replied Umar. "Let's be honest here. You don't have the funding, contacts or resources to carry out a kidnapping in the States. You have been tucked away for eleven years, out of circulation and out of the know. For goodness sake, you didn't even know the names of your intended targets! Without The Cell this is just failure staring you in the eyes, so start manning up and accepting the fact that The Cell will pull the strings, but the strings are connected to your dreams."

"I suppose so," said a resigned Uncle J. "It's just not an easy pill to swallow."

"Just swallow, man up and get on with it!" said an animated and frustrated Umar.

With his tail between his legs, Uncle J retired to his bedroom for a much needed nap and to give him a chance to self-pity and lick the wounds inflicted on his now shrinking ego.

The following day, having shaken off the mental shackles that The Cell was going to call all of the shots, Uncle J summoned Umar and Faisal to his office. Operating now with a more positive mindset, Uncle J wanted to enlist the help of his two friends to start implementing the wishes of The Cell. Uncle J needed Umar and Faisal to help with the continuation of recent activity, with Uncle J's roughing up his outstanding tuk-tuk business debtors. In addition, Uncle J required candidates to take over the vacancies left by any non-payers, taking on their tuk-tuk-related duties, serving Uncle J to help him rebuild his business to its former glory.

Both agreed to assist. It was Faisal's task to compile a full and up-to-date list containing suitable candidates. The list would include names, addresses and current candidates. Umar was tasked with rounding up Uncle J's preferred contacts to determine their willingness to co-operate with Uncle J's proposals. Uncle J gave them both a week to get their tasks in order. In the meantime, Uncle J was going to spend his time leading the authorities on a daily goose chase. Making sure they followed him to Precinct twenty-seven police station for his sign in and for his refreshing daily trek to the Baluchistan Hills. It was just like a game for Uncle J.

The week passed quickly. Umar and Faisal did exactly as Uncle J had asked. Faisal had completed his accurate list as ordered and Umar had managed to persuade five local henchmen from Uncle J's network who were willing to join this latest Uncle J venture.

All were briefed by Uncle J and set about their tasks with single-minded purpose. Each debtor was paid a visit, threatened and told to pay up. Any who refused to co-operate were roughed up and told to have the money within the next seven days. In addition, any non-payers had their tuk-tuks stripped away from them, returning them to Uncle J's compound as hostage until any money was handed over. None of the five debtors who were visited to-date had any cash for Uncle J, so each violent visit caused much blood to flow.

Uncle J had careful decided not to be present when any retribution was handed out; he delegated that pleasure to the five hired hands, who had been told in no uncertain terms that, if needs be, any connection between the violence and Uncle J was to be completely denied. Faisal and Umar were now also kept at a distance from any violent scenes for the same reasons. Uncle J needed to get the money he was owed, and in this part of the world, the only way to get what you want is either with a bundle of crisp currency or the use of extreme force. However, Uncle J needed to distance himself from any illegal violence so that the authorities would have no just reason to arrest him so soon after his release. Trusting his hired hands to do his dirty work was a risk Uncle J was prepared to take.

At the end of the second week, Uncle J was discussing progress in his office with Umar and Faisal. The five debtors had failed to pay the full amounts owed. So, with their tuk-tuks already confiscated and willing replacements already recruited, Uncle J was happy that the completion of two beatings to each debtor and the recovery of his tuk-tuks was a good time to move on. Uncle J negotiated new terms with his five recruits, obviously in favour to himself, which had boosted the business to a much healthier position compared to when he was immediately released from prison.

Activities completed during the previous few weeks were now starting to fill Uncle J with a sense of achievement. He hadn't missed a day signing in at the police station. He had started to rebuild his tuk-tuk business. Umar was proving to be a more than competent ally and the violent capture of his tuk-tuks had been accomplished without appearing to cause a single ounce of reaction from the authorities. Add to that the fact that he was losing weight due to his regular exercise which also carried with it the elation of conning the authorities even more that Uncle J was following a new healthy lifestyle. Life was good and working with the new Cell was equally as good.

Time had passed by quickly. It was the day of Umar's second meeting with The Cell. Three months had elapsed and The Cell had contacted Umar to confirm that their arranged meeting was to go ahead as planned.

Uncle J sat nervously in his office, biting on his fingernails.

"I'm off now, man," said Umar confidently.

"You know what our requirements are for this session, don't you?" demanded Uncle J.

"Yeah, bro," replied Umar, "take it easy, man, I won't let you down."

"And make sure you shake off any tails," continued Uncle J.

"Stop fretting, man," responded Umar. "I've got this, just relax and have a few whiskies."

Umar was away, with the mindset of a secret agent trying to evade MI5, he disappeared into the distance.

This was the worst time for Uncle J. Firstly because he was not a party to the meetings with The Cell and secondly, the fear that Umar may lead the authorities to The Cell and his dreams for revenge would be over.

The sanctuary of an unopened bottle of fine Scottish whiskey became Uncle J's immediate target. He picked up a cut glass tumbler from his sideboard, raised it above his head and admired the beautiful form of the cut glass as the bright sunlight poured through it.

"If all this works out," said Uncle J out loud, "my whiskey glasses will be the finest in the land!"

A bottle and a half later, Umar had returned from his meeting with The Cell. Spotting that Uncle J was somewhat worse for wear as he lay fast asleep and snoring like a bull in his armchair in the lounge, Umar decided to tip-toe to the kitchen for some much needed sustenance with Faisal. After a brief chat and a tasty snack, Umar retired for the night. He didn't want to face off with a drunken Uncle J; that was a fate worse than a severe telling-off from a furious wife.

The following morning, a really grumpy Uncle J nursing a sore head, was slumped over a mug of hot black coffee, prepared for him by Faisal.

"Why didn't you wake me, fool?" growled an angry Uncle J at a smiling Umar who was sitting opposite Uncle J at the breakfast table.

"You seemed to be out with the fairies," sniggered Umar. "I didn't want to wake you from your cosy, whiskey-fuelled dreams."

"Anyway, stuff all of that," replied Uncle J. "So how did the meeting go?"

"At first, not well," responded Umar. "I had a few problems shaking off the authorities, there were three of them this time and they were difficult to shake off. They managed to stay with me through the ghetto. I had to take a cab to the port area and then another to the central market. By the time I arrived at the railway station I had managed to lose them all, but it took effort this time."

"Are you sure they were not following you at the railway station?" requested Uncle J. "How can you be sure?"

"I am sure," replied Umar. "When I left the railway station I went to the main park then to the south end of the park, where the public gardens are located. I hid in the foliage for half an hour and there was no sign of the authorities who were following me. I am certain."

"Good," responded a satisfied Uncle J. "So how did the meeting go?"

"Eventually, very well," replied Umar. "The Cell's contacts in the States have been performing very efficiently. They have built up a good picture of the targets. Work routines, social routines, shopping routines and so on. The Cell is now working on simultaneous interception places at slightly staggered times of day for the kidnappings. They still want to take out both targets on the same day. In addition, The Cell have reduced the potential safe houses to hold the hostages to a shortlist of three. All three are in Yosemite National Park and all three are remote cabins. Once they have chosen the safe house and agreed on the timing and places for the kidnapping, The Cell wants us to travel over to the U.S.A."

"Great news!" shouted a jubilant Uncle J.

"There is, however, a catch," replied Umar nervously.

"Catch?" growled Uncle J. "What catch?"

"The Cell has identified two suitable people whose identities we are going to assume for the trip," replied Umar. "We have to learn all about them before we leave these shores. Like everything, man."

"How the hell are we going to do that?" asked Uncle J.

"With these," said Umar dropping two dossiers on the kitchen table.

"Which one is mine?" said Uncle J playfully.

"You are Rashid, and I am Hanif," responded an equally playful Umar. "It's all here in these files prepared by The Cell. Everything we need to know. Where we work, our families' names and details, our birthdays, our favourite foods, everything."

"Well, I never," said an amazed Uncle J flicking through the Rashid file. "They have taken so much trouble preparing this data, the attention to detail is indeed impressive."

"We have to be studious," continued Umar. "We need to learn the contents by heart, and I mean the entire contents. I suggest we call each other Rashid and Hanif while we are in the house, to practice and to help us avoid mistakes when we are in the U.S.A."

"Good idea, Hanif!" joked Uncle J.

"I like it, Rashid!" replied a light-hearted Umar.

"How long do you think it will be before we get the call to travel?" asked Uncle J.

"The Cell has arranged a third meeting in a month from now," responded Umar. "I think we should get a better idea by then."

"Excellent!" said a jubilant Uncle J. "This is whetting my appetite for sure."

"The Cell does, however, still have a few areas of concern," added Umar.

"Concern?" responded Uncle J nervously.

"Yeah, bro," continued Umar. "The Cell is nervous about the money transfer process. Cash is cumbersome, trackable, and easy to replace with paper replacements as you know to your own cost. The Cell wants a digital transfer, but they are working on protecting the transfer, so the authorities can't monitor the account or accounts that the money goes to."

"All that sort of stuff is way above my head," responded Uncle J. "I am old-school, give me hard cash any day of the week."

"The Cell refuses to operate in that way now," replied Umar. "We live in a digital age now, Uncle J, so you had better accept that fact."

"Mumbo, jumbo if you ask me," said an irritated Uncle J. "So much has changed while I have been inside. Internet this, digital banking that, I've heard your boarding pass for a trip on an aeroplane is on your mobile phone now!"

"Ha ha," tittered Umar. "You old stick in the mud! Get with the times, Uncle J, because if you don't, you will be left behind."

"I'm alright back here in the past!" quipped Uncle J with a big smile on his face, only there to hide his embarrassment.

"So, to summarise," continued Umar. "In a month, we should know the time and place for the kidnap, we should know the location of the safe house, we should know how the ransom money is to be transferred and we should know the dates we will be flying to the States."

"And the ransom amount?" asked Uncle J.

"One million U.S. dollars, as agreed before," replied Umar sheepishly.

"And what cut is The Cell going to get?" requested Uncle J.

"Sixty percent," replied Umar with his head bowed.

"You must be joking!" shouted an irate Uncle J. "This is my baby. The Cell is not walking away with sixty percent of the bounty, that's for sure. I just don't accept these terms."

"The Cell is bearing the high costs," responded Umar nervously. "They are funding the surveillance in the States, they are sorting and funding the safe house, they are sorting out the ransom money transfer, they are providing me to assist you here. What is it costing you?"

"It cost me eleven years of freedom, laddie," shouted Uncle J aggressively. "Now you go back to your pals at The Cell and tell them that Uncle J says fifty-fifty split or the deal is off, final, non-negotiable."

"Fifty-fifty?" replied a shocked Umar. "I can speak to them and let them know your side of the deal, but don't hold your breath. As I said, The Cell is out of pocket already funding this deal."

"Hogwash," growled Uncle J. "They already have people working for them in the U.S.A., they probably already have suitable bank accounts to accept the ransom money, and, if truth be told, they probably own the three safe houses in the running. And what's more, I have you. Who do you think is paying to board and lodge you? 'Cos The Cell certainly ain't paying me a dollar for your upkeep. Now go back to your pals and renegotiate the deal. Pronto."

Uncle J was incensed. In his eyes, The Cell was taking liberties. Uncle J had suffered the pain of eleven years of prison life and was going to take all the risk at the coal face of the planned kidnapping; he wanted his full pound of flesh this time.

Uncle J retreated to his lounge with his old friend, a bottle of fine Scottish whiskey, to drown his sorrows and wallow once again in self-pity.

Two days had passed. Uncle J had continued with his new routine of a daily visit to precinct twenty-seven and a visit to the Baluchistan Hills, but Umar had been conspicuous by his absence. Uncle J sat in his office, fearing that his outburst concerning the offerings of The Cell had offended Umar which had sent him away for good. This troubled Uncle J as it filled his head with negative, conclusive thoughts that suggested that Umar's service had come to an end.

Just as Uncle J was in mid-thought, Umar appeared at the door of the office.

"Hey, bro," said a smiling Umar. "Did you miss me?"

"Where have you been, friend?" quizzed Uncle J. "I have been worried."

"I did as you said," replied Umar. "I went to see my 'pals' in The Cell. I told them that you were unhappy with the deal on the table and that you wanted an equal split. Considering the risks you will take in the States, the pain you have suffered already in prison, and all that."

"And?" requested Uncle J.

"Like I said, bro," responded a smiling Umar. "The Cell has changed. They are reasonable, they look at all scenarios. On this occasion, they feel your pain and sympathise, so they are willing to compromise. A split now of fifty-five, forty-five in favour of The Cell."

"Wow!" exclaimed a jubilant Uncle J. "I never expected that, goodness me, I've still got it! I never thought they would budge."

"You are kidding?" said Umar angrily.

"Yeah," said Uncle J playfully, "just kidding."

"You had better be!" exclaimed an irritated Umar. "This is not a game, you just don't joke with The Cell. They may be reasonable, but they still have a sinister side to them, they can be ruthless."

"OK, OK," replied a regretful Uncle J. "I have learnt a good lesson here, let's move on now."

OK," responded Umar with a stern look in his eye. "No more jokes though."

"Right!" said a more positive Uncle J. "Let's lighten the mood. Join me for supper, then we will lead our attentive friends on a different wild goose chase. Since my release, I have not visited the boardwalk and I do love a stroll along the boardwalk in the evening and there is still sufficient light remaining until my curfew. To the best of my knowledge, this is still legal and I am a free man to choose how I enjoy my evenings."

"I agree!" replied an upbeat Umar. "Let's do that, I've not been to the boardwalk for years myself."

The pair joined Faisal in the kitchen and feasted on a freshly prepared home made curry. When all had finished their sumptuous meals, they jumped into Uncle J's pick-up and made haste to the boardwalk, a concrete promenade that stretches for three kilometres along the Arabian Sea shoreline, often frequented by throngs of locals who collect to enjoy the delights of a sociable early evening coastline stroll, followed by a sumptuous local ice cream.

"Why would you want to live anywhere else?" asked a captivated Faisal, as he leaned on a wooden fence overlooking the splendid shoreline which was stunningly illuminated by a setting amber sun. "Such beauty on our own doorstep and we just take this for granted, seldom visiting this beautiful panorama in our grimy, busy, overcrowded city."

"Indeed, my friend!" responded Uncle J. "It is one of the final sanctuaries of beauty in our city, let's hope it stays like this, to be enjoyed for years by all, well into the future. And the fresh sea air down here is not as pungent and choking as the city."

"We can travel to places more beautiful than this when we finish our little project," sneered Umar.

"Silence!" said Uncle J as loud as he dared. "No talk like that in public, you never know who is listening."

"Sorry, bro," said an apologetic Umar. "My mistake, I was out of order."

"It is you who keeps barking on about how professional we must act, and here you are going against what you are preaching," preached Uncle J.

"OK, OK, man," responded Umar. "I've got it, I will zip it, OK."

"Let's just hope our followers are maintaining good distance!" added Faisal.

The three comrades wandered along the boardwalk for almost an hour.

"Let's go home," said Uncle J, "before we spill any more of our secret beans."

On the journey home, Uncle J and Umar started to test each other regarding their soon-to-be-adopted new identities. It was healthy preparation. It was one thing to read through the endless, well-compiled notes, but it was another thing to remember it all and reproduce the content precisely. So, many more oral tests would face them, to assist with the difficult preparation for the rewarding tasks ahead of them.

Chapter Five

It was another beautiful day. The bright sun was high in a clear blue sky and there was not a breath of wind. Uncle J sat in his office pondering and fanning himself to try and counteract the overbearing heat of the day.

Uncle J had a concern. If he and Umar were to fly from the capital, the reality was that their every move was being monitored by the authorities. So, if they were to travel up north, they would surely be followed every step of the way. Uncle J slapped his forehead with his left hand, he seemed to have had a light bulb moment.

"Got it!" exclaimed Uncle J.

Uncle J rushed around his house to round up Umar and Faisal to share his ideas. The three plotters gathered together in Uncle J's office, just as soon as Faisal had prepared a fresh pot of strong coffee.

"Right then, listen to this," said Uncle J slurping on his coffee mug. "We are to fly to the States from the capital, right?"

"Right!" confirmed Umar and Faisal in unison.

"The authorities are following our every move. Right?" added Uncle J.

"Right!" confirmed Umar and Faisal once again in unison acknowledging the obvious.

"So," continued Uncle J, "as soon as we get in my vehicle and drive up north to the airport, the authorities will be on our tails and will be watching our every move? Right?"

Umar and Faisal nodded their heads in agreement.

"Well, then," declared Uncle J, "our plans will be thwarted, I won't even get out of the country, let alone get near our intended targets. Watching us enter the airport, albeit to board separate fights, the authorities will prevent at least one of us from boarding a plane. The prison governor has told me that I need to inform the chief of police if I intend to leave the country, it was discussed when the governor informed me of my freedom."

"How are they even going to police that?" asked Umar.

"Our daily escorts will see to that, you fool!" replied an agitated Uncle J. "Are you not listening to what I am saying here?"

Uncle J slammed his palms firmly down on the desk in front of him causing nearby papers and stationery to fly in all directions.

"It's happening again!" ranted Uncle J. "I am surrounded by incompetent fools, why don't people listen?"

"Look, Uncle J," replied an embarrassed Umar. "I made a small mistake, man, you've got my full attention now, don't get all stressed out, it's not worth it."

Uncle J rose from his chair, wandered over to the office window and stared in silence through the grubby glass. He pondered for a minute, considering his idea further, before returning to his chair.

"Faisal," said a sterner Uncle J, "I want you to park my pick-up in the carport every day from now on, starting from right after this session. Each time I want you to reverse the vehicle into the parking spot so that the rear body is tucked away under the roof of the carport, as far as you can."

"I will do that, sir," responded Faisal.

"Then," continued Uncle J, "tomorrow, remember the dealership gave us a free cover as an incentive to buy when I picked out the vehicle. It should be somewhere in the carport, so you need to find it and fit it. Once you have fitted the load space cover, I want you to drive to the supermarket on the Northern highway, the one on the edge of the city. It's not as busy as the supermarkets in the city. I want you to start getting our groceries from there from now on. Plus, I want you to form a new shopping routine. I want you to go to the supermarket daily and at exactly the same time, without fail."

"Why do you want me to do this if you don't mind me asking?" replied a curious Faisal.

"I want to know if the authorities are also following you," added Uncle J. "Then, if they are, I want to know if they wish to continue wasting time following a servant just shopping for his master. Either way, I have a backup plan. When we are ready to travel up north to catch our flights, Umar and I will creep under the load space of my pick-up which will be concealed in the carport, under the cover, and then you drive us up north. If the authorities are following, you go shopping, as usual, if they are not following, we travel outside the city limits to a suitable spot, and then Umar and I can join you in the cab.

"And if the authorities are following?" asked Umar.

"Then we use the skills of Umar," responded a confident Uncle J. "Umar takes me on a maze-like trip into the ghetto, the railway station, the market, wherever it takes us, until we lose our escorts. Then, when we are free from the gaze of the authorities, we meet up at a predetermined place where Faisal will be waiting with my truck and our baggage."

"And what if Faisal is being followed?" requested Umar.

"I will arrange a convenient roadblock," replied Uncle J. "I will use my network to fabricate a situation to stop the authorities in their tracks. Maybe use an oil tanker or a cotton transporter to pull out and block the road."

"And the mopeds?" asked Umar. "They will have mopeds and trucks, we have seen them with our own eyes."

"The moped riders will be easy to knock from their saddles," responded Uncle J. "I can arrange for them to meet with an 'unfortunate accident', again using my local network of contacts."

"I'm not so sure this is foolproof," questioned Umar. "I may have to take this idea to The Cell and get their take on it."

Uncle J immediately jumped out of his chair, reached across the desk, and grabbed Umar by the throat.

"Oh no, you won't, laddie!" growled Uncle J. "This is my call. It is my ass I am trying to protect and ship up country and not The Cell's. In any case, my three-month probation period will soon be over. The authorities will likely stop following me so closely. I have given them no signs that I am up to my old tricks again. Plus, they probably have better things to do."

Uncle J released his grip. Umar spluttered and slouched back in his chair rubbing his throat. Uncle J was a formidable man in every way. Confrontation with his strong, muscular frame combined with a hot temper was to be avoided. But this type of bullying did not sit well with him. At that moment instant thoughts of quitting were going through Umar's mind. Going through this regular pantomime was starting to get tedious. Uncle J was a hot head, a bully and a control freak, and Umar was beginning to get tired of being Uncle J's punch bag. But, at the end of the day, Umar was trying to impress The Cell to rise in their ranks, he was not here to impress Uncle J, far from it.

The thoughts of quitting slowly diminished, as Umar resigned himself to the fact that this was all part and parcel when working with Uncle J and had to be tolerated.

"OK, man," said a resigned Umar, "let's give your ideas a go. As you said, you probation period is up soon, so it's likely that the authorities may back off and let you live your life, let's just suck it and see for now."

"Excellent!" exclaimed Uncle J. "Then we will start immediately. Faisal, go and sort out the pick-up. Pop it in the carport and fit the load space cover. I'm starting to get excited."

The following day at exactly ten thirty in the morning, Faisal did as Uncle J had requested and drove Uncle J's pick-up to the prescribed supermarket. With a sharp wit, Faisal mentally noted as many vehicles as he could which appeared in his rearview mirror during his outward and inbound journeys to the supermarket.

Faisal had reached the supermarket. The large car park was scantly populated which was as Uncle J had briefed. Any tailing vehicles could easily be spotted as there were no realistic places to hide. The supermarket was as good as in the middle of nowhere. The nearest domestic dwelling was a hundred metres away and there were no industrial buildings in the locality. It was perfect for what Uncle J wanted from this exercise.

Faisal sat in the pick-up for fifteen minutes keeping a careful watch on any movement or activity in his line of vision. Not a single vehicle had arrived or departed during that time and neither had any shoppers entered or departed from the supermarket. It seemed that Faisal had not been followed, but Faisal didn't want to count his chickens just yet.

Faisal took around forty minutes to complete his groceries shop. Returning to the car park, to his vehicle, Faisal looked covertly all around to determine if anybody was watching him. The scene before him was unchanged, all seemed to be escort free.

Faisal returned home, vigilantly keeping an eye out for potential tails but there was nothing whatsoever to report. Having arrived home, Faisal imparted his fresh shopping news to Uncle J and Faisal, which greatly pleased both allies.

Faisal continued his shopping duties for a week, making sure he departed at exactly ten thirty each morning and making sure he followed exactly the same route to and from the supermarket.

On each occasion, Faisal scoured for tails but there were none. Faisal was in the clear as it appeared that he was of no interest to the authorities.

Uncle J had called another get-together in his office. With Faisal and Umar in attendance, Uncle J began the meeting.

OK, then," said a jubilant Uncle J. "It looks like we are set fair for when we travel up north. It appears that Faisal is not on the authorities' watch list, which is great news. I still want Faisal to keep up the daily shopping trips at ten thirty each morning just in case."

"Will do, sir," said Faisal delivering a salute in Uncle J's direction.

"I still want you to reverse park the pick-up in the carport each night, Faisal, and I still think we should travel in the rear body of my pick-up, under the body cover, until we are well away from the city limits as previously discussed."

"Agreed!" chanted Umar and Faisal in unison.

"Any questions?" asked a cheerful Uncle J.

Umar and Faisal shook their heads in silence.

"OK," added Uncle J. "If you will excuse me, I am now off to Precinct twenty-seven to sign in for the last time. My parole time is now over so I can get on with the next chapter of my life. Let's hope it's a rewarding chapter!"

With Uncle J preoccupied with fulfilling his parole requirements, Umar had other business to attend to. He had arranged an impromptu meeting with The Cell, to take them through Uncle J's proposal concerning how to get out of the city and up north, despite Uncle J's demands to the contrary.

Umar slipped out of the front gates of Uncle J's abode, headed towards the ghetto to start his process of shaking off his pursuers. But today was different. He checked the usual hiding places for the usual faces, but today, the hideouts were unoccupied. Umar decided that he would change tactics and decided to walk briskly down the main thoroughfare to make his way to the railway station, rather than dodge and weave his way through the ghetto. En route, Umar was sure to regularly check all around him for any signs of his suspected escorts.

Umar arrived at the railway station in good time. To his great pleasure, there appeared to be nobody following him, so he continued on his way to the prescribed meeting place with The Cell.

Three kilometres from the main railway station, Uncle J was leaving Precinct twenty-seven police station with a broad smile across his face. He had signed in for the last time and he was adamant that was the last time he would visited a local police station ever again. Uncle J had met all of his conditions of release and was well pleased with himself, hoping that if ever the news of Uncle J's exemplary release reaches the ears of the prison governor, it will cause the governor to think that Uncle J's release was, in fact, the correct decision. But would it be going forwards?

Later that evening, Uncle J and Umar sat comfortably in Uncle J's lounge, sipping audibly on glasses of fine scotch whiskey.

"The Cell contacted me today," said Umar. "They have news and new orders for us."

"Orders?" questioned Uncle J. "For me? Were you expecting contact from The Cell?"

"The Cell has started the ESTA application process," added Umar. "They have used the online process so there will be no need to attend any U.S. Embassy for face-to-face interviews, or anything like that."

"Well, they would have a shock if we did have to go to the Embassy!" replied Uncle J light-heartedly.

"The Cell has come up with specific signatures should we need to sign any documents or paperwork in the future," added Umar. "The Cell has sent us a sample of the signature they have come up with and want us to perfect these signatures."

"Fine," replied Uncle J, "let me see mine."

Umar handed over a laminated strip of paper containing a squiggle.

"I'll get on it," confirmed Uncle J. "It is good thinking by The Cell, it does look like they try and cover every minute detail. How long will the ESTA application take?"

"Between two weeks and a month," replied Umar. "You never know with applications from this part of the world."

"So," added Uncle J, "we could maybe start our journey in a month?"

"Not necessarily," responded Umar. "The Cell will tell us when the time is right. It's not just the ESTA that turns on the green light for travel."

The following day, Uncle J was sitting at his desk in his office. He looked troubled. He was strumming the ends of his fingers on his right hand incessantly on the desktop while staring vacantly into space. Being told what to do all the time was alien to him. In the past, Uncle J had served as a fighter in the Northern territories, leading his loyal troops to battle against several invading forces that tried to take away the land located in the 'disputed zone.' But in Uncle J's eyes, there was no dispute, the land belonged to him and his countrymen.

Uncle J just needed to do something on his own, not something that The Cell wanted him to do, the constant stream of demands from The Cell was starting to stress out Uncle J.

"Got it!" exclaimed Uncle J.

Uncle J rushed to his bedroom, changed into his trekking gear, and made his way to a small storeroom located at the rear of his house. After ten minutes of frantic searching, Uncle J found what he was looking for.

"Here you are!" said a jubilant Uncle J clutching a pair of dusty binoculars.

Uncle J made his way to the kitchen, cleaned the dust off his binoculars and gave the lenses a good clean.

"I'll be out for a while," shouted Uncle J as he trotted out of the house and jumped into his pick-up.

Uncle J headed towards the coast in the north of the city. He parked his pick-up in a side lane off one of the main city throughfares. Uncle J got out of his vehicle. He flópped a hood over his head to hide his face; he didn't want to be recognised in this district. He then made his way to the foot of a dusty, rocky outcrop in the near distance. Uncle J started to scale the relatively steep rocky hill in front of him. The sound of waves breaking on rocks could be heard, and the unmistakable smell of the sea was all around.

It took Uncle J about thirty minutes to clamber his way to the summit. Once at the top of the slope, a breathtaking vista presented itself to Uncle J. Sipping on a bottle of mineral water, the majesty of the Arabian Sea filled Uncle J's gaze, stretching away to a cloudless defined horizon. The sultry city air had been replenished with a fresh, clean sea breeze. Uncle J filled his lungs with this most rare of local commodities.

Uncle J turned his attention to his left, to the entrance of the estuary that made way to the mangrove swamps and the port of Qadim. For Uncle J knew that the target for his revenge plans lived in a mansion perched above this estuary. Uncle J just wanted to set his own eyes on Mansoor's house before his plan for revenge reached the implementation stage.

Uncle J trekked to his left for twenty minutes over the tricky, rocky terrain; it was not as easy-going as the simple grass-covered Baluchistan Hills. Uncle J reached a giant boulder perched precariously on the cliff edge. Peering around the boulder, he spotted what he had come to look at.

"There you are, my beauty," said Uncle J out loud.

Uncle J trained and focussed his binoculars on a large house across a small bay in front of him. It was the house of Mansoor. It looked impressive with its imposing walls surrounding a luxurious-looking mansion of fair size.

Uncle J didn't want to invade and take ownership of this house or take on the privileged lifestyle that Mansoor lived, he just wanted to see the spoils that Mansoor had earned.

Although it was Zaheer's baby, the initial failed kidnap attempt of Mansoor still caused Uncle J a considerable amount of distress. Not only was he imprisoned for the part he played, but Uncle J also still felt a modicum of responsibility for the men who lost their lives operating for the cause, doing their best to deliver Zaheer's and Uncle J's dream of wealth and riches.

Uncle J took a good look around the property using his binoculars while he had the opportunity. Two imposing outer steel gates protected the entrance to the property, a void area and then another two equally strong inner steel gates. Uncle J spotted at least three security guards at a multitude of vantage points. It appeared that the authorities were still sympathetic to Mansoor and were providing him with more than suitable security.

"Good job I'm not trying to take Mansoor's home away from him!" said Uncle J out loud to himself.

Uncle J remained tucked behind the boulder for another ten minutes. He had fulfilled his need to be spontaneous and do something for himself away from the tethers of The Cell. Uncle J felt a lot better for doing so.

The next few weeks passed by slowly for Uncle J, with no events transpiring out of the now-new norm. Uncle J split his time between his regular exercise, running his now robust tuk-tuk empire and regularly learning the facts associated with his soon-to-be-adopted new identity. Uncle J was itching to get to the States and get his hands on the long over-due riches he had been promising himself.

Today was the day that Umar had arranged another meeting with The Cell, to get word on the ESTA's, to see if a hostage-holding location decision had been made, to see if the timing had been set for travel to the States and to take on board any further demands or orders that The Cell wanted to impart on Uncle J and Umar.

A weary Umar returned to the house and sat with Uncle J in his office.

"Our escorts have certainly stopped following us," said Umar with confidence. "Not a single sign of them at all. I still took precautions, just in case, but I am convinced they have lost interest in us."

"The prison governor doesn't appear to carry much weight with the authorities these days," replied Uncle J. "It's not surprising, he has been in the backwater of the prison for over ten years now so has lost what little influence he had back in the day when he was the chief of police's blue-eyed boy. What good has it done them following us for this time? Just a lot of wasted time, effort, and fuel with no returns. Fools."

"Fools indeed," responded Umar.

"Now then, laddie," interrupted Uncle J, "what news do you have from The Cell?"

"It was a good meeting," replied Umar. "The Cell is happy to continue to back your revenge plans. They indicated that they still feel indebted to you, in honour of your history of courageous and legendary service and takes pity on you for your involvement in the failures associated with the previous kidnapping of Mansoor."

"Enough of all the political bullshit," snapped Uncle J. "What did they actually have to say?"

"OK," continued Umar. "So, the ESTA applications are still in progress. The Cell estimates that they will be delivered here in the next two weeks. Obviously, The Cell has used the addresses of the victims to be used for our new identities, to keep matters in order, so The Cell will 'take them out of circulation' this week. Both live alone so there is no immediate family or friends to concern ourselves with. Their being businessmen living alone was one of the main criteria for their selection as targets, it keeps things simple."

"So do we kidnap them or does The Cell take care of matters?" asked Uncle J.

"The Cell will see to this," replied Umar. "They have been watching the pair and have a suitable plan to take them out without causing too many ripples."

"Of course, they have a suitable plan," said a petulant Uncle J.

"Look!" exclaimed a frustrated Umar. "Uncle J, if The Cell can take care of all the periphery details, it leaves us free to focus on the main event. Try and look at this from a different perspective. The Cell is backing us admirably. They know our team here is small and there are many preparations to take care of to make sure our plan goes ahead without hitches. Ask yourself, why is The Cell even helping you? This revenge you have set in your head is your problem. It is small fry to The Cell, you are trying to settle a personal grievance, trying to reset your reputation in the underworld. Any benefit of success has real meaning for only you. You continually berate The Cell, trying to slay your gift horse, just man up, stop bellyaching and just get on with it."

Uncle J was taken aback by Umar's outburst. It hurt but it was the truth and a difficult pill for Uncle J to swallow. He was used to being the main man. After due consideration, Uncle J looked Umar directly in the eye.

"You are right, my friend," said a temporary more humble Uncle J. "I am very lucky to have the backing of The Cell, and I am very lucky to have you and Faisal around me, my new family. I will change. I will do as

The Cell wants and I will do it well, so please continue, my friend, with the remainder of your news."

Umar looked back across the table at Uncle J with astonishment; it was far from the reaction he was expecting. Umar feared that these sharp words would not go down well with Uncle J in his own home, Umar expected Uncle J to lash out violently.

"Right, dude," said a still shocked Umar. "So the ESTA's look to be sorted. There appears to be no reason why they would not be granted, Rashid and Haneef have no criminal records or convictions of any kind, and the reason to visit is on the applications.

"And what are the reasons?" asked Uncle J.

"The Cell will give us a full briefing before we travel to the States," replied Umar. "We will have a busy couple of weeks ahead of us after we are given the green light to travel."

"I see," responded Uncle J, "do continue."

"Concerning the hostages and where we will keep them while we wait for the ransom demands to be met," continued Umar. "The Cell has decided on a suitable cabin in Yosemite National Park. It is accessible by off-road vehicles and is situated off the beaten track. It is perfect for our needs. The Cell has rented the cabin from the forestry people for six months under the pretence of supporting the study of local bird life in the area as a practical module for a university thesis. Apparently, this type of rental goes on all the time across their national parks. The Cell wants to get in there and construct a

112

temporary but secure holding room in the cabin, suitable for the hostages."

"Sounds like a reasonable idea," said an impressed Uncle J.

"The Cell wants us to travel to the cabin," added Umar, "when we arrive in California. They want us to take a look at the cabin suitability, the holding area, the approaches, the surrounding terrain and all that."

"Well," said a surprised Uncle J, "at least The Cell is giving us some responsibility, nice to see."

"Which brings me round to timing," continued Umar. "The Cell wants assurances from us that we have completely absorbed our new identities before they will allow travel."

"Do we have to sit an exam?" joked Uncle J.

"Get serious!" snapped Umar. "Our word is good enough. Once we offer our assurances, The Cell wants us to travel two weeks after receipt of the ESTA's. The application has a spread of travel dates based on exhibitions and events taking place during their visit. We have to attend two exhibitions and visit three events while we are there, to keep up the façade."

"What?" bellowed Uncle J. "I'm not going all the way over to the States to attend some boring exhibitions."

"I thought you had changed, Uncle J?" said a bemused Umar. "Only just now you told me that you will do as The Cell says."

"OK, OK," responded a frustrated Uncle J. "Carry on."

"Anyhow," continued Umar. "The pre-travel brief will give us time to learn about our activities once we are at our destination. So, that aside, I think we are pretty much set. The Cell will let me know when Rashid and Haneef are out of circulation and then I guess it's game on!"

"It's all starting to feel a bit more real," said a happier Uncle J. "Bring it on. Let's go on our holidays. Do we get any spending money?"

"The Cell will give us a debit card to use while we are overseas," replied Umar. "They will top up the account regularly but have warned that any spending on the card will be added to our bill and have advised you to watch your spending as the ransom money is not guaranteed. If the ransom money doesn't arrive, The Cell expects you to settle this bill regardless; they want to be sure that you fully understand this."

"I understand and agree," replied Uncle J. "If the Cell is good enough to do this, the least I can do is pay my way."

"Well," said Umar stretching his body in tiredness, "that's about all I have to say. We need to get ourselves focusing on revising our new identities with more vigour. This is a potential weakness in the plan. If we get stopped and questioned at the U.S.A. border, we need to have all the answers, and convincing answers as well."

"Agreed," responded Uncle J. "I am confident with my knowledge but there is always room for improvement. I will make sure I dedicate more time to this most important of activities."

A further week had passed and Umar had been summoned by The Cell. Uncle J hoped that this would bring news of ESTA's and kidnappings. Sure enough, Umar's return brought with him news that the ESTA applications had been successful, plus The Cell had informed Umar that Rashid and Haneef were where The Cell wanted them. Umar also brought back from the meeting a final debrief pack. It contained the promised debit card, false passports carrying the identities of Rashid and Haneef, money to cover return air tickets for both Umar and Uncle J, two exhibition entry tickets for both travellers and flyer posters for three half-marathons to be held in San Francisco, Monterrey and Santa Barbara. Also within the pack was a separate itinerary for both Uncle J and Umar detailing hotel names and dates. It looked like The Cell had done their homework and provided a comprehensive package.

"When we arrive in San Francisco," said Umar, "we will be contacted in person by a member of The Cell who operates in the States on their behalf. They will provide more details face-to-face and then take us up to the cabin so we can take a look at it. The contact will meet us at the airport and take us to our hotel in the city."

"How do we know who will meet us?" asked Uncle J.

"They will be holding a board containing our names at arrivals at the airport," replied Umar. "Apparently, San Francisco immigration is a bitch to get through."

"Tough border police?" asked Uncle J.

"No, man," replied Umar. "Just massive queues, it's a really busy airport apparently."

"Well," laughed Uncle J, "as long as we get through, I don't care how long it takes."

Uncle J and Umar buried their heads inside the pre-travel packs provided by The Cell. The date was set; in two weeks the pair would be flying to the United States, but first, they had to travel to the capital. An arduous journey that would take four days on remote, dangerous and pot-hole-ridden roads and highways. Uncle J was not looking forward to the journey but knew it was a trip that had to be made.

Chapter Six

Uncle J had been blasting his final orders to Faisal for the past hour. Poor Faisal: it was a bombardment of instructions in no particular order, with Uncle J barely stopping for breath. Uncle J was excited. Today was the day that he and Umar started their journey to the United States. It was going to be a long, drawn-out affair including the stopover in their capital city before they carried on to their final destination of San Francisco.

Keep the tuk-tuk business going, inform Uncle J immediately if monthly rentals are not paid, keep the house clean, keep fit and active; Uncle J's demands on Faisal were endless.

Uncle J, Umar and Faisal assembled in Uncle J's office for a final briefing. There was a feeling of expectation in the air. Smiles on faces, jokes aplenty and a plethora of non-stop hugs, high fives and back-slapping.

"Umar," barked Uncle J. "Are you packed? Lightly I trust, I asked you to take the bare minimum."

"Yes, Uncle J," replied Umar in an ingenuous manner, "you are not my mother, for goodness sake."

"Just checking," continued Uncle J. "Faisal, did you gas up the truck and give it the once-over? Tyres? Oil? Water?"

"Yes, Uncle J," replied Faisal in an equally ingenuous manner. "I did it all last night while you and Umar were finishing off another bottle."

"Good," declared Uncle J. "Looks like we are all set. I still want to travel with Umar in the rear body, hidden under the load space cover. I want you to be one hundred percent sure that we have no escorts before Umar and I join you in the cab. Even if that means we are halfway to the capital."

"I fully understand," responded Faisal. "We are too close now. To make a simple mistake now would be foolhardy."

"Indeed," replied Uncle J. "But just remember, Umar and I will be unrestrained in the rear body, so don't start driving like Nigel Mansell and send us tumbling around the body."

"I will be very careful with my precious cargo," said Faisal with a broad smile on his face.

The three went their separate ways to make their final preparations. Faisal went to the kitchen to gather together provisions for their journey, Umar scurried to his room to collect his baggage, and Uncle J walked outside to collect his thoughts. Uncle J had a bulging stomach full of butterflies. He had been waiting so long now to strike revenge on Mansoor plus repair the damage caused by his involvement in the failed kidnapping. Uncle J lit a cigarette. As he smoked his thoughts returned to his time in prison, the beating he received from the governor's henchmen and the verbal abuse and heckling he endured. Uncle J smiled as he decided it was all worth it; he was now a free man, and his plans were in place to make him a richer man.

As the bright orange sun began to set in the darkening sky, Uncle J gave word for his partners to make their way to the pick-up truck. Faisal jumped into the driver's seat as Uncle J and Umar clambered into the load space area, tucking themselves neatly under the cover. Faisal inched the vehicle out of the carport, jumped out of the cab and locked the access door to the house. Once outside the perimeter gates, Faisal made sure both inner and outer gates were locked before proceeding carefully down the access lane from Uncle J's house. They were on their way.

Uncle J had decided to leave under the cover of dusk, just in case, the authorities were still watching. He wanted to use the half-light as his friend, as this was the worst light to use binoculars in Uncle J's experience.

Faisal was uncomfortable driving with his unsecured human load in the rear body. He was nervous that a hidden pothole may send his load shooting dangerously up in the air which would inevitably result in a roasting from Uncle J. Furthermore, there was the chance that the authorities were actually tracking Faisal's movements and could pounce at any moment to search the truck. Along with the evening humidity, beads of sweat were clearly visible on Faisal's worried brow. With his hands now starting to sweat, Faisal continued to navigate the crowded city streets to the best of his abilities. Not getting drawn into the cultural traffic light red light running, Faisal made steady progress. As they reached the outskirts of the city, the traffic was less congested with only occasional drivers passing the truck in a "do or die" fashion.

In the rear body, Uncle J and Umar were being bounced around like ragdolls. They dared not complain or shout out as they wanted to minimise the chances of being detected in their hideout. Occasionally they glanced across to each other with raised eyebrows, but, in the main, the pair remained silent as they endured their most unpleasant of journeys.

An hour had passed and the furious congestion of city traffic was now behind them. Faisal spotted a roadside stand that sold refreshments ahead on the left hand side of the road. It had ample parking and was poorly lit, so Faisal decided that this was a suitable spot to stop and transfer his load into the cab area. The pickup ground to a gentle stop on the loose gravel surface. Faisal mopped his sweaty brow, his pothole-dodging nightmare was over and he could now relax. He had parked partly behind the tumbledown refreshment shack to obscure their intended activities as best he could.

Uncle J and Umar scrambled out of the load space. Both stretched their arms above their head in unison, complaining about sore bones and joints as they did so.

"Well," uttered Uncle J, "that was a blast. I know what a load in a washing machine feels like now."

"Indeed." agreed Umar.

"I tried my best to make your journey as comfortable as possible," said an apologetic Faisal. "But the city roads are far from perfection."

"You did well, my friend," replied Uncle J. "It's not an everyday occurrence transporting people in the rear body like that. I commend your driving."

Faisal smiled.

"So," added Uncle J, "any tails? Did we have company on our trip out of the city?"

"Nothing," responded Faisal. "I was keeping a vigilant, watchful eye on the rearview mirror. I stopped here as there has been no vehicle behind us at all for over twenty minutes."

"The roads are quiet here," said an observant Umar. "Now, let's get some chai and a snack and get on our way. We still have a long way to go."

"Agreed," boomed Uncle J. "Faisal, line up the chai and snacks."

The trio spent fifteen minutes at the stall, taking chai and samosas, but all three were suffering from a strange sense of thinking they were being watched. All kept nervously looking around for signs of movement, shadows and vehicles; constantly listening out for footsteps or strange noises. It was a most peculiar and uncomfortable feeling. It appeared that some form of paranoia was setting in.

Having finished their comfort break, the group jumped back into the pick-up and set off on their long and arduous passage to the capital.

In Yosemite Park, U.S.A., an impressive jet black off-road pick-up truck pulled off the highway into a gated side entry. It was early morning and there was a hint of mist in the air. Two trendily clad gents jumped out of the truck and walked across to the padlocked five-bar galvanised steel gate. The taller of the two gents retrieved a key from his pocket, unlocked the padlock and swung the heavy gate open.

"Race you to the truck," joked a cheerful Bahir.

"Not again," responded a somewhat peeved Ramiz. "Every time we have to go through this pantomime. I'm driving. I've got the keys and that's that."

"Not if I get in the driver's seat first," replied a cheeky Bahir.

The pair started to jostle and wrestle for the upper hand. A play fight broke out as the pair play-fought their way to their vehicle. Being taller and stronger, Ramiz came out on top, pushing the hapless Bahir into a nearby bush.

Eventually, the pair jumped into the car and started to proceed down the rough track that was in front of them. Soon, they entered a dense tree line, populated by impressively tall redwoods, black oaks and pines which towered impressively into the morning sky.

"How far is it down here?" asked Bahir.

"About five kilometres I've been told," replied Ramiz. "One track, no turning off, just a simple, straightforward drive."

"Sweet," replied Bahir.

Ramiz was a sensible chap. He drove at a safe speed on the difficult terrain. He was a trusted member of The Cell with five years service; he was one to be counted on. He had been given specific orders and fully intended to carry them out to the letter.

Bahir was not so mature. Five years the younger, he had only been with The Cell for two years and was still under the watchful eye of Ramiz, who was attempting to mould and mentor him in the ways of the new Cell. It was a frustrating detail at times. Bahir was always looking to mess about and have a laugh, even when the circumstances were not appropriate.

"So, what do we need to do when we get to this cabin thingy?" asked Bahir.

"We check it out," replied Ramiz, "make sure it is clean and tidy, make sure there are no surprise guests, human or otherwise, try out the generator and make sure all the electrics are in order, check the water, make sure that's OK, you know, that sort of thing."

"Cool," replied Bahir. "Who's coming to stay? A V.I.P.? Someone important?"

"No idea," snapped Ramiz. "That's not our business. Our business is to do what is asked of us and check the place is OK, no more, no less. And not to ask stupid questions."

"Take a chill pill, man," responded Bahir. "I was just asking, no need to go off on one."

"This is what I've been trying to drill into your tiny mind," replied a frustrated Ramiz. "There are certain levels in The Cell. At our level, we operate on a need to know basis. If you start poking around in stuff that doesn't concern you, you'll get your fingers burnt, big-time."

"That's absolute bull if you ask me," responded Bahir.

"Then you know what you can do then," retorted Ramiz. "Look. It's your choice that you are here, working for The Cell, taking a generous wage each month. You are not on the streets, you have a good standard of living, as well as a future. Just toe the line and do as they ask. For once in your life."

Bahir slumped sulkily back into his seat, staring in silence out of the passenger window, he was clearly rattled. The remainder of the short passage was completed in an uncomfortable silence.

Back in the homeland, Faisal was starting to tire. He had been driving for eight hours and was in desperate need of a break. Uncle J and Umar had been asleep for the past three hours. Faisal pulled over at another roadside food stall that sporadically littered the highway. As the pick-up pulled up, Uncle J and Umar awoke from their slumber.

"What's going on?" asked a sleepy Umar.

"I need a break from driving," replied Faisal. "I've been behind this wheel all day. I need a rest and something to eat and drink."

"Fair enough," replied Umar., "I'll take over the driving if you like. I'll go and get some drinks and something to eat. You can come off duty Faisal, you have done well."

"Thank you," nodded Faisal.

"Let's get some food and drink here now," sparked up Uncle J, "then, when we get to the next town, I'll rent a hotel room if we can find one, for some proper shuteye. I'm exhausted, so I bet you are too, Faisal, with all that driving you have been doing."

"Music to my ears, sir," replied Faisal.

After a brief pit stop, the trio continued on their way. Forty five minutes up the highway, they arrived at a small, isolated town, where they managed to find a tatty hostel to take a rest. It wasn't the Ritz, but the call for sleep was strong.

In California, Ramiz and Bahir had reached their destination. It was a smart log cabin, located in a valley next to a clean, rock-strewn babbling stream. Surrounded by towering redwoods and a variety of shrubs, the secluded cabin was completely hidden from view from the access track.

The pair got out of their vehicle and walked up the gravel path to the entrance porch. Ramiz took out another key and unlocked the front door. They entered the cabin. There were white sheets thrown over all of the furniture, to the left was an open but empty fireplace, and to the right and straight ahead were closed internal doors. One by one the pair started to investigate the property, trying each internal door to peer inside the room behind each door. There were three bedrooms, a kitchen, and a roomy bathroom. The décor was sharp and clean and the place in general was very modern and tidy.

"Rather impressive or what," chirped Bahir.

"It's pretty much what I expected," responded Ramiz. "The Cell only works with the best. Now we need to go outside and find the generator. It's in a small shed apparently and there is also a master switch and fuse board there as well. I'll go and sort that, you try and find the stopcock and see if you can get the water running."

"OK," replied an intense Bahir.

They spent the next half an hour sparking the cabin into life. Bahir had no trouble locating and turning on the water stopcock, however, Ramiz took a while to fathom out the generator, eventually getting it running once he had realised he needed to open the fuel valve. Ramiz tried all of the lights and kitchen appliances to make sure they all functioned, which they did.

Once the cabin was considered fully functional, Ramiz and Bahir congregated in the smallest of the three bedrooms.

"We have to make this room secure," stated Ramiz.

"Secure?" questioned Bahir. "How secure and for who?"

"A visitor who must not be allowed to leave," replied a serious Ramiz. "By my reckoning, we need to fit a window bar on both the inside and outside of the window and get some sort of strong lock for the door. Right, we need to go to the hardware store and do some shopping. I've got tools in the truck, we just need the hardware."

"Sounds like a plan," replied Bahir.

Ramiz returned to the generator and turned everything off. Once finished, he then whistled at Bahir to indicate that they were leaving and then jumped back into their truck. The pair then set off for a shopping expedition at the hardware store located in a small town located around twenty kilometres north of the cabin.

A few hours later, the black truck again rolled up to a halt at the remote cabin, with a load space awash with hardware. Ramiz and Bahir took no time at all to unload and position the hardware adjacent to the cabin. Armed with a drill, screwdrivers and the like, the pair set about their reinforcement duties. Ramiz fitted some hefty black security bars to the inside and outside of the third bedroom window, testing the robustness by pulling vigorously on the bars once fitted.

Inside, Bahir had been tasked with fitting heavy-duty locks on the outside of the third bedroom door. He fitted three heavy-duty shoot bolts. Again, with the shoot bolts engaged, Bahir tested his installation by pulling energetically on the door handle. All was in order.

The pair stood outside the bedroom door.

"That's a tidy job if I don't mind saying so myself," said a proud Bahir.

"Not bad," replied Ramiz. "I suppose it will do."

"I guess it's your turn to make the chai," demanded Bahir.

"On your bike," snapped Ramiz "We are done here. I don't want to make a mess. If you want a drink, we can stop on the way home. We have a four-hour drive ahead of us and I want to get on the road."

"OK," replied a disappointed Bahir. "You can pay though."

Ramiz grabbed Bahir playfully around the neck and scrubbed the top of his head.

"Just this once," smiled Ramiz. "Now come on, let's get going."

The pair double-checked that everything was off, secured all the doors, and headed back to their vehicle.

Four days had passed and Uncle J and his team had arrived at the capital. They were tired, miserable, and totally fed up with travelling on substandard roads. They had to find the safe house and wait for their flights. The Cell had given Umar the address of the safe house

128

which was located about fifteen minutes from the International Airport. The main objective now for Uncle J and Umar was to maintain a low profile and make sure they were fully in character with their allocated new identities. When not in deep slumber, they had been practising all the way and were confident that they were up to speed.

With no trouble at all, they found the safe house. The directions sent to Umar by The Cell were spot on. Faisal asked Uncle J if he could spend a night at the safe house, so he could rest up before his long journey back to the city.

The safe house was a modest ground floor apartment close to a small shopping centre. The Cell chose this location as there were several escape routes if things went bad. It was also a very popular and busy area with the locals, which made "getting lost in the crowd" a simpler task.

The Cell had sent Umar the key to the apartment with the briefing notes, so there was no welcoming committee when they arrived.

Uncle J and Umar had separate bedrooms. There was a small bathroom and a living space with a kitchenette area in the corner. All very simplistic and minimalistic. Not really a problem, as Uncle J was due to fly the next day, and Umar the following day.

"We just need some food and water for tonight," commanded Uncle J. "Faisal, you go out and get provisions, I want to keep Umar's and my appearances outside to a minimum."

"I understand," replied Faisal. "I'll also get some provisions for myself, for my journey home."

Faisal disappeared through the front door on his shopping mission.

"Nearly on the plane," said a nervous Uncle J. "I am terrified that we will get rumbled in the airport at immigration, or check-in."

"Fear not, Uncle J," said a reassuring Umar. "The Cell is good at what they do. These adopted identities are watertight. The only reason we will get busted is if we act suspiciously or bring attention to ourselves. So, act as cool and as normal as possible."

"I feel like I need two bottles of whiskey to settle my nerves," added Uncle J.

"That's a big no-no," snapped Umar. "You need to be on your game tomorrow. That means bright, alert and sober."

Soon after, Faisal returned with provisions. The team feasted on a mixture of junk food before settling in for the night. It had been another long day and they all needed their rest.

After a restless night's sleep, it was D-Day for Uncle J. He was first up to run the gauntlet of the International Airport. Staring down at the third full bottle of whiskey positioned on his bedside table, Uncle J resisted the temptation for some last minute Dutch courage. He deemed that the whiff of whiskey at the immigration desk might not go down too well with the strict robots who manned these posts.

Uncle J dressed quickly and rushed into the living area. Umar and Faisal were in conversation, while sipping carefully on hot, freshly made coffee.

"I'll have some of that," barked an excitable Uncle J. "I'll get my breakfast in the airport, I don't want to get any food spillage on my tunic."

Faisal got up from his seat and poured Uncle J a cup of coffee.

"I reckon you have thirty minutes until the off," Said Umar.

"You bet," replied Uncle J. "Who's taking me?"

"We both are," responded Umar. "I want to get in the feeling of airport life. It's my turn tomorrow and I can't wait."

"Maybe just Faisal takes me, just in case?" said a nervous Uncle J.

"Why on earth would you say that?" snapped Umar. "It's not like we are well-known celebrities up here. We are pretty confident that we don't have any tails from the authorities with us, why not just let me come with you?"

"I just want to keep to the plan in my head," replied an irritated Uncle J. "Just be patient. In twenty-four hours you will get your turn. End of story."

A sullen Umar stared angrily towards Uncle J, then stormed into his bedroom, slamming the door petulantly behind him.

"Kids," japed Uncle J as he looked over towards Faisal.

Thirty minutes later, Uncle J and Faisal set off for the airport. There was clearly tension in the air and not a word was spoken on the journey to the airport.

On arrival, Uncle J gave Faisal a warm man hug and whispered his thank yous in Faisal's ear.

Once inside the airport, Uncle J was greeted by a colossal foyer with an impressive ceiling that reached up to the heavens. The airport was very busy. Travellers, workers and alike jostled their way through the throng of serious-looking faces.

Uncle J nervously approached the check-in desk queue. Trying his hardest not to keep looking around for tails or the authorities, Uncle J focussed his attention on his tickets and passport in his hand, attempting to look like a "normal traveller."

After queueing for twenty minutes, Uncle J was beckoned by the check-in lady. Uncle J was greeted by a smartly dressed lady with a broad smile. Uncle J handed over his documents.

"Direct to San Francisco, Rashid?" quizzed the check-in lady.

There was a momentary pause as Uncle J had not dropped into character, having been too busy looking normal while fighting off his overwhelming nervousness.

"Eh, yes, please," said a less-than-confident Uncle J.

"Nervous flyer?" again quizzed the check-in lady.

"Absolutely," replied a very anxious Uncle J. "I'm always the same, if we were meant to fly, then we would have been born with wings."

They both chuckled at Uncle J's attempted witty comeback.

The check-in lady processed Uncle J, handing over his documents and boarding pass.

"Gate forty-two, sir," stated the check-in lady. "Have a great flight, and try not to be too nervous, our staff will look after you well."

"Many thanks," uttered a relieved Uncle J.

Uncle J's heart was pumping out of his chest. Step one was completed without a hitch, but now he faced the first of two massive immigration trials. Had The Cell done their job well enough? Was Uncle J going to be a convincing Rashid? Were the false papers going to hold up? Boy, did Uncle J need a swig of something alcoholic right now, but he knew he had to remain focussed and sober.

Uncle J battled his way through the crowd to the immigration queues. They were lengthy as always, but the efficient staff ensured that the queue flowed well. In no time, Uncle J was ordered to approach the immigration desk. This was it, his plans rested partly on this very moment.

Uncle J handed over his passport and boarding card. He looked assertively at the border guard, making sure he made confident eye contact.

The border guard started to flick through the passport with the sternest of looks on his face. Uncle J's heart was now in his mouth, which was totally dry. Uncle J could feel his palms clamming up, and beads of sweat were also starting to run down his back.

The border guard gestured for Uncle J to look directly into the security camera to the right of the immigration station. Uncle J stared into the lens as if his life depended on it.

After what seemed an eternity, the sounds that Uncle J was praying for emanated from the desk. The border guard aggressively stamped and closed Uncle J's passport, stamped his boarding card and handed them back to Uncle J, and cried "next" to the awaiting travellers in the queue.

He was through. It was like a firework display was going off in Uncle J's body. Praise be to The Cell, they had done Uncle J proud, very proud. The border authorities here were usually not easily fooled and took their jobs extremely seriously. This was the biggest test to be applied to the paperwork thus far, and there were no hitches. All Uncle J had to do now was stay calm, then convince the San Francisco border police that he was a Rashid not to be concerned about.

Uncle J grabbed some breakfast, sat down in the public dining area, and let out a huge sigh of relief. He grabbed his mobile phone in readiness to send a text message to Umar to share the great news about being airside. However, after a brief moment in contemplation, Uncle J decided against sending the text, just in case his mobile phone activity was being monitored. Uncle J didn't want to give the game away, even before he had set foot on the big silver bird to the States.

Umar was pacing up and down in the living area of the safe house. His nervous state was etched on his bearded face. Anxious to know about Uncle J's airport activities, Umar was unable to settle.

"It's going to be alright, you know," said a calming Faisal.

"How can you be sure?" snapped back an agitated Umar.

"Well, it's down to you and your new Cell," continued Faisal. "It was you who ordered the false papers and passports. So have faith in your Cell's abilities. If you think they are good as you say they are, then there will be no issues."

"Fair enough," sighed Umar. "I guess you are right. The Cell is experienced in such matters, they leave no 'i'' without a dot, and no 't' without a cross. It will be fine."

"Come on now," added Faisal. "Let me sort you some food, then you can take a rest. It's your big day tomorrow."

Two hours later, Uncle J's flight was called. Uncle J vigorously sprang from his seat, checked he had left nothing behind, and strode confidently to his gate. After yet another time-consuming and lengthy queue to get onto the aircraft, it was time for Uncle J to pass through the threshold towards revenge. As his feet touched down inside the aircraft, it was like a weight being lifted from his shoulders. He had done it. He was on his way to get what was his, and this time with the backing of a far more efficient team.

Uncle J sorted out his luggage in the overhead locker and sat back comfortably in his aisle seat, halfway up the fuselage. He started to thumb through the array of magazines on offer when his confident state of mind was suddenly shattered.

Looking up to understand what the fuss and noise were about, to his horror, Uncle J's attention was focussed on the three uniformed and armed officers that had just boarded through the aircraft door.

Uncle J's mood hit the floor at top speed. Busted at the last hurdle with the finishing line in sight would be the cruellest of outcomes.

The officers muscled their way towards Uncle J, barging past any innocent passengers that blocked their way. Uncle J stayed seated but braced himself for the inevitable.

To his total surprise, the officers went straight past Uncle J, stopping three rows behind him to remove a suspect passenger. In an aggressive flash, the suspect passenger was in handcuffs and being escorted from the aircraft unceremoniously.

Uncle J could not believe his eyes. Total despair to ecstasy in ten seconds. His nerves couldn't take much more of this. Did he need a full-fat cigar and large tumbler of whiskey right now!

Once all the passengers had settled, in no time, the aircraft started its long journey to San Francisco with a relieved and elated Uncle J in seat 42G.

Umar had an equally restless night at the safe house. He tossed and turned, worrying about the plight of Uncle J, along with consuming thoughts of the stressful airport experience that awaited him.

The night dragged slowly. Umar watched as his bedroom began to light up with the sunrise, flooding into his room like fresh hope. It will go well today, thought Umar, Uncle J is safely onboard his flight, all is on plan, it has to be.

There was a knock at Umar's bedroom door.

"Time to get up, Umar," said a sprightly Faisal. "You have a flight to catch."

Umar vigorously jumped from his crumpled bed, dressed with speed and burst into the living area.

"I'm going to follow the same process for you as I did for Uncle J," said a superstitious Faisal. "You just get coffee now, you can get your breakfast at the airport, just like Uncle J."

Umar smiled and took the cup of coffee offered by Faisal.

"What would we do without you, Faisal?" said a thankful Umar.

"Come on, drink up," interrupted Faisal. "We need to leave for the airport in half an hour, and you need to get yourself together."

Umar methodically readied himself for his journey. Double-checking his documents, Umar nervously closed his bedroom door behind him. He sidled over to Faisal and gave him a warm hug.

"Thank you, sir, for all you have done," whispered a modest Umar. "Take care on your way home. I hope to see you soon, a very much richer man."

"What do I do with the apartment key?" asked Faisal.

"There are instructions on the dining table, they are simple, just follow them," replied Umar.

The embrace was over, it was time to go. Faisal looked up for divine intervention as he closed the safe house door firmly behind him.

Chapter Seven

Umar's state of mind when he entered the airport main entrance was far more relaxed than Uncle J's had been on the previous day. Uncle J considered Umar to be a minnow swimming in a great lake, so this indicated that there was scant chance of Umar attracting much attention from anybody at the airport, let alone the authorities.

Sure enough, Umar's mission to board his aircraft to the States was a seamless, uneventful breeze. When you peel back the elements of jet setting, it's dominated by queue after queue, with endless obtrusive checking of personal belongings and personal paperwork, usually followed by hours of boredom waiting for airport milestones to transpire once you are airside.

This was the case for Umar. His prompt check-in, immigration and security adventures had gone without a hitch or delay, which had him airside in less than thirty minutes. Now he had the problem of time to kill while trying to maintain a low profile. Not being a great fan of phone-based activities such as social media or gaming antics, Umar searched the concourse for a bookstore. He wanted to sink into a best seller to wane away the three hours of probable boredom that faced him.

Having located a suitable bookstore, Umar armed himself with a bestselling novel and found himself in a quiet corner of the airport to start his inconspicuous wait for his flight.

Eventually, three hours later, Umar's flight was called to board and he was soon on his way.

On the other side of the Pacific Ocean, a somewhat flustered Uncle J was fast approaching the next stress-loaded challenge of his journey. To convince the border guards of the mighty U.S.A. that Rashid was a fine, legal, upstanding businessman and there was absolutely no need to question him intimately or even consider refusing him entry.

For almost the entire flight, hidden inside a copy of a lifestyle magazine, Uncle J had his head covertly buried in his brief, swatting every paragraph, every sentence, every letter, to ensure Rashid's story was completely absorbed.

With the aircraft on the ground, Uncle J walked down the airbridge, following his fellow passengers towards his dream. Once on the main thoroughfare, passengers from the other flights that had landed in San Francisco at the same time mingled, swelling the numbers trudging towards immigration, making slow, uncomfortable progress. In no time, the procession of travellers had ground to a halt around forty yards short of the immigration signage recently spotted by Uncle J.

This only inflamed Uncle J's already anxious state of mind.

Uncle J could hear a border guard barking directions at the logjammed passengers in an attempt to free up the tailback, but Uncle J was too far away to understand what was expected.

"Don't worry, man," said an adjacent local, "this is normal. 'Frisco airport is a nightmare, the two runways put too many people on the ground at the same time, and this is the result."

"Yeah, I bet you," responded Uncle J, reluctant to get into any form of communication at this time.

"I hope you ain't in a hurry," continued the local, "'cos you are gonna be here for at least ninety minutes or more."

"Great," replied Uncle J desperately trying to retreat away from the conversation.

As the queue of impatient travellers started to shuffle forwards, Uncle J changed his direction as best he could to get away from the clutches of the unwanted chatterbox. He managed to politely push his way into a small gap that had conveniently opened up in front of him. With the effort of trying to establish a new position in the queue along with his overall plight, Uncle J could feel himself starting to sweat. This was a disaster. Uncle J wanted to portray a calm, normal and controlled appearance at the immigration booths, so as not to attract unnecessary attention to himself; having a covering of sweat on his forehead was definitely not on his agenda.

Maintaining as much eye contact with the floor as possible, Uncle J made slow but steady progress. Forty minutes later, he was positioned in the doorway to the main immigration hall. His eyes were greeted by a vast official-looking space, crammed full of people, miles of cordons to segregate the now aggravated travellers who were desperate to hear the dulcet tones of the immigration stamp on their passport, so they could get away from this noisy and longwinded process.

Uncle J joined yet another huge dawdling queue for non-nationals. When would this end? He had been on the ground for well over an hour and didn't seem to have made any progress at all.

Ironically, as the non-national's queue snaked its way towards the immigration booths, Uncle J spotted the unwanted chatterbox in the national's queue which followed a similar path. Not wanting to restart the previous conversation or sweating process, Uncle J snapped his head to the left to be one hundred percent sure that there was to be no more contact with this unwanted pest.

A further fifty minutes had passed. Uncle J had shuffled and weaved his way to within twenty feet of the immigration booths. Uncle J scanned the booth to reveal that his test would be with a woman immigration officer. He didn't know if this was a good or bad omen. He hadn't really pictured the moment of interrogation as he had just been set on getting the detail accurate and delivered in a confident manner.

"Next," barked the immigration officer eventually.

This was it, the big moment, again, Uncle J's success or failure may hinge on this very moment! Inside he was shaking, his nerve ends were frayed, and he could feel his body temperature rising with the stress.

Uncle J handed over his passport and immigration documents. He was mildly quizzed as to the nature of his visit, where he was residing and when he intended to return home.

Uncle J responded to all questions with composed answers delivered confidently, then, the sound that signified another victory as the immigration stamp came down with vigour. He had done it, Uncle J was in — The Cell had delivered the goods.

Uncle J was mindful that he had to muffle his elation, after all, he was just a travelling businessman, doing what he does week in, week out. He calmly walked to the baggage hall to collect his stowed luggage.

Fortunately, the time spent in the immigration queue allowed sufficient time for the baggage to find its way to the carousel. Uncle J immediately spotted his suitcase because of the red sock that he had tied to the suitcase handle which made it stand out from the surrounding luggage. He only had customs to negotiate and his stressful ordeal would be over. Dragging his wheeled suitcase behind him, Uncle J marched through the 'nothing to declare' channel. Fortunately, as Uncle J briskly proceeded, the attentions of customs officers were busy with a family of three, with at least two of their suitcases clearly open and under scrutiny. At last, a stroke of good luck.

With a spring in his step and a smile on his face, Uncle J assuredly strode out of the arrival hall. Greeted by yet more cordons, Uncle J focussed on the array of welcome boards being displayed by the waiting crowd. Momentarily baffled that there was no board displaying 'Uncle J', he realised that he should be trying to locate a board for 'Rashid'.

Towards the left of the gathering, Uncle J spotted his waiting host. Uncle J shuffled out of the arrivals cordon and made his way to the board.

"Rashid?" quizzed an expectant host.

"You bet," replied an excited and relieved Uncle J.

"Hi, I'm Jez," responded Jez offering a friendly handshake.

Uncle J firmly took up the handshake offer, but he really wanted a man hug as was the scale of Uncle J's utter relief.

"How was the flight?" continued Jez. "I bet the immigration queue was huge; it always is here."

"The flight was ok, thanks," replied Uncle J. "You are right, the queues were horrendous. I've never arrived at an airport with so many people trying to get through immigration at the same time."

"Well, you are through now," said Jez. "Let's get you to your hotel as I bet you need to freshen up."

"Don't you know it," responded Uncle J.

Jez took Uncle J's suitcase and led him away to his vehicle. Once out of the airport they joined a busy three-lane freeway leading towards San Francisco. Travelling in a four-by-four, the raised driving height gave Uncle J the advantage of taking in the novel stateside vistas as they hurtled towards the city.

"You are staying in the Fisherman's Wharf area," said Jez breaking the silence. "It's a great place to stay; lots to do, lots to see, lots going on."

"Nice," replied a fragile Uncle J. "How far is it?"

"It will take around an hour, depending on traffic," replied Jez.

Noting Uncle J's reluctance to participate in small talk, Jez backed off and concentrated on the task of delivering his passenger to his hotel.

Their journey took them through downtown San Francisco, where the office buildings towered into the cloud-filled sky. Uncle J was in awe of the impressive buildings, along with the relative calmness of the busy traffic that was negotiating the streets around them. At home, in this sort of area, there would be the deafening orchestra of vehicle horns, there would be an 'every man for himself' driving mentality, and many vehicles would not be following the rules of the road, some travelling in illegally, random directions to make progress in the bedlam. But what Uncle J was witnessing was novel but a good novel. Busy streets, but relative careful and courteous driving.

"Here we are," said a happy Jez. "Let me help you check-in, then I will be on my way. I'll let you settle in and freshen up."

"Thanks," replied a grateful Uncle J. "Thanks for the ride as well."

"No problem," responded a smiling Jez. "My pleasure. I'll leave you to your own devices today, then tomorrow, I have to pick-up your friend from the airport. I'll bring him here. I've been told to travel to the airport alone, so don't ask to come with me, OK?"

"I guess so," replied a disappointed Uncle J. "So, who told you to travel alone?"

Jez ignored Uncle J's question as he took Uncle J's suitcase from the load compartment.

"Follow me and I'll help get you checked in," said Jez.

Uncle J checked himself in and was escorted to his room by Jez. Jez started to arrange Uncle J's luggage and show Uncle J around the room. Once sat on his bed, Uncle J began to feel a tad apprehensive. Not being allowed to meet Umar at the airport was trivial, but it again made Uncle J feel like he was far from in control of events here, almost to the degree that he felt like a small fry pawn in a game of chess. Uncle J couldn't contain himself any longer.

"So, level with me, Jez," demanded Uncle J. "Why can't I go to the airport tomorrow? Who is behind telling you what I can and can't do?"

"Look," whispered Jez. "We all know why you are here. You know that The Cell is calling the shots; you know you are placing me in an awkward position with these unnecessary questions. We must make sure you keep a low profile. We don't want any unwanted attention on you while we are preparing for the operation. Just keep your head down, keep your nose clean, and do as The Cell asks. Why create unnecessary risks now? It's a no-brainer."

"I understand," replied Uncle J. "But this is my baby. Yes, The Cell is helping me, but I feel powerless and not in control of events."

"Believe me, you would not be here if it wasn't for The Cell," responded Jez with a slightly raised voice. "You really think you have the skills and resources to compile the papers and documents needed to get convincingly through U.S. immigration? No, you don't. The Cell has been instrumental in getting you to this very spot, safely through your homeland immigration, safely through U.S. immigration, safely from the airport."

"OK, OK," replied Uncle J. "Don't turn this into a lecture. I am grateful, I really am. It's just frustrating not being involved in the decision-making process. I am used to leading, not following."

"I appreciate that," replied Jez. "But you are in an alien environment. Just trust me and do as I say, it's for your benefit and the benefit of the wider cause."

Uncle J paused for thought.

"Am I allowed out of my room at all?" asked Uncle J.

"Just maybe freshen up and rest tonight," replied Jez. "Maybe in the morning, you can take a walk and have a look around, just like a tourist. Maybe take a few photos?"

"Be rude not to," responded a smiling and calmer Uncle J.

"Right," said Jez. "I'm off now. I'll see you tomorrow, hopefully with your friend. Take this mobile; it has my number in the contacts under 'Jez', use it if you need me or you need anything."

Jez handed over a simple black mobile phone to Uncle J.

"Thank you," said Uncle J. "Can I phone home on this?"

"No," snapped Jez, "just local calls, please."

Uncle J rolled his eyes in disappointment. Jez bid his farewell and left the hotel.

Uncle J finished unpacking his belongings, took a shower, and took a brief look at U.S. TV on his impressive forty-eight inch plasma television, before giving way to the ever-building travel tiredness that was now bearing down heavily.

As with Uncle J, Umar's head was covertly submerged in his character brief, revising each and every detail, mentally testing himself periodically. The seat belt sign was illuminated in the aircraft, quickly accompanied by the aircrew's advanced warning of the impending landing that will follow in around forty minutes. For the first time, Umar could feel butterflies in his stomach. Umar's need for success was not as strong as Uncle J's, but there was still the background fear of being caught by U.S. immigration with false papers and what that would bring.

Once the plane had smoothly touched down at San Francisco airport, Umar had to endure an identical fate as Uncle J. Once again there were huge queues of passengers battling towards the immigration hall. It took Umar the best part of two hours to be processed through to baggage reclaim. The immigration stamp in his passport was achieved without a hitch and Umar was off to find his host in the arrivals area.

Almost immediately spotting his named board, Umar rushed over and gave Jez a huge man hug.

"How are you, man?" asked a delighted Jez.

"Really good," responded an equally elated Umar. "I'm so pleased that airport nonsense is all over with. Those immigration queues don't get any shorter."

"Too right," replied Jez.

"Are we going straight to the hotel to meet Uncle J, I mean Rashid?" said Umar putting his hand to his mouth in recognition of his schoolboy error.

"Enough of that already," said a slightly angered Jez. "Act professionally, you have to remain in character at all times, otherwise this is going south pretty quickly."

"Sorry, man," replied an apologetic Umar. "It won't happen again."

"OK," responded Jez, "it's alright, just be careful, I know it's easy to slip up, but just don't. So, we are not going straight to the hotel, The Cell wants to see you and make some finite modifications to the plan, they want to give you a final briefing."

"Sounds interesting," replied Umar as the pair made their way to the car park.

Uncle J had tucked away a hearty breakfast and was walking towards the waterfront. He wanted to take in the sights and sounds of Fisherman's Wharf before concentrating his efforts on his revenge quest. Having read some of the pamphlets in his room, Uncle J was making his way to Pier thirty-nine, to enjoy the congregation of seals that populate this natural tourist attraction. Uncle J could hear the unmistakable baying call of the seals well before he arrived at the pier. Once by the water, Uncle J gazed at about fifty fat, smelly and noisy seals that were basking on the wooden platforms in front of him. He was in a crowd of around sixty tourists, also there to witness this free, natural phenomenon. A strong, pungent smell of fish saturated the air as Uncle J walked to the end of the pier. Once against the sea wall, the impressive Golden Gate bridge came into view to his left. Panning around the bay to the right, eventually, the island that houses the Alcatraz prison came into view. A most cold and inhospitable island accommodating a bedraggled set of run down buildings which straddled the island. Uncle J could see several boats shipping tourists to and from the rock. Uncle J averted his gaze away from Alcatraz, the thought of looking at a prison sent a shiver down his spine.

Uncle J spent another three hours wandering around Fisherman's Wharf, enjoying the numerous restaurants, shops and bars that littered the area. He also took a long walk towards the Golden Gate bridge so that he could take a more impressive photograph for the archives.

Thinking that it was beyond the time for Umar's arrival, Uncle J returned to his hotel room to greet his companion. To his surprise, when Uncle J returned to the hotel, the receptionist told Uncle J that 'Haneef' had not arrived yet. Uncle J was particularly proud of himself for asking for the whereabouts of Umar's false name rather than his real name.

Uncle J had been in his room for nearly an hour when there was a gentle knock at the door. Uncle J rushed over to open the door.

"Hey!" said a jubilant Umar.

Uncle J shuffled Umar into his room and closed the door firmly behind him.

"What's up?" quizzed Umar. "Why the cold reception? You should be delighted to see me."

"I am, I am," said a jubilant Uncle J as he administered a giant man hug to Umar. "I didn't want to greet you in the hallway, in public."

"Oh, I see," replied Umar. "Just being careful."

"We have to be," barked Uncle J. "All good through immigration?"

"Not one single issue throughout the journey," replied a smug but relieved Umar. "How about you?"

"Apart from thinking I had been rumbled while still parked up before the plane had even taxied to the runway, nothing," responded a slightly flustered Uncle J, briefly reliving the torrid event.

"What?" exclaimed Umar.

"Yeah," continued Uncle J. "Some soldiers came on the plane, came right past me and removed some fall guy a few rows behind me. I thought my time was up, but thankfully it was someone else who had to take a rap."

"How bizarre," replied Umar. "What are the chances?"

The comrades spent the next thirty minutes catching up and sharing their experiences of their journeys to the States.

"Just one more thing," said Uncle J. "According to my calculations, your plane landed over four hours ago, I don't think it took you four hours to get through the airport and travel by car to the hotel?"

"It sure did," replied an apprehensive Umar. "Where else could I go?"

"You tell me," snapped Uncle J.

"The flight was delayed a bit," continued Umar. "The queues in immigration were huge, my bag was not on the carousel, so I had to claim it from the airline's lost baggage area, and the traffic in downtown San Francisco was a nightmare, it all adds up you know."

"Yeah, but not over four hours," questioned Uncle J. "You better not be going behind my back with The Cell."

"What?" bayed an agitated Umar. "What the hell are you implying? Do you really want to work together on this? I can go home right now if that's what you want?"

Uncle J aggressively looked Umar directly in the eye.

"You had better be acting above board," snarled Uncle J. "I've eaten people like you for breakfast."

"People like me?" replied Umar. "What the hell is that supposed to mean?"

"Like I said," uttered Uncle J. "You better be on my side."

"I'm going to my room to rest," said a disappointed Umar. "I hope you will be talking more sense the next time I see you. Thanks for such a warm welcome."

Umar stormed out slamming the door behind him, leaving an angry, wary, and confused Uncle J in his wake.

Uncle J slumped on his bed. His mood was steaming. He was really starting to have trust issues with Umar. Uncle J had himself recently been through the rigours of the U.S. airport process and knew how long that took. Combined with the journey time from the airport to the hotel, there was just too large a timeframe for Umar to have taken from landing to arriving at the hotel.

As he was deep in thought, the phone located on the bedroom sideboard discharged a loud and unruly blast, causing Uncle J to bolt upright. He dashed to the phone and picked up the receiver.

"Hi, Rashid," boomed a familiar voice. "It's me, Jez."

"What do you want?" replied Uncle J dismissively.

"I am going to pick you and Haneef up in the morning," continued Jez. "I'm going to take you on your first mission."

"Should you be saying words like 'mission' over an open phone line?" questioned a somewhat bemused Uncle J.

"Ah, sorry," replied Jez. "I'm going to pick you up to take you on an exciting excursion."

"That's better," responded Uncle J. "I thought this new Cell had all bases covered and never made any mistakes. Where are you taking us?"

"Just on a sightseeing tour of the city," replied a rattled Jez. "There are so many sights to see in San Francisco, we'll have a blast."

"Ok, what time?" asked Uncle J abruptly.

"Let's say nine-thirty a.m.," replied Jez. "That will give you time to have your breakfast."

"Do I need to bring anything with me?" asked Uncle J. "Or do I need to wear any specific clothing?"

"Just wear something comfortable and warm," replied Jez. "After all, we are going on a sightseeing trip. So why would you need to bring anything else with you?"

"I don't know?" continued Uncle J. "Maybe we are going near the coast and might try our hand at trying to spot some wildlife? Perhaps I need some binoculars to help with my wildlife spotting?"

"I see what you mean," said a resigned Jez. "I think that's a good idea. Bring along your binoculars, just in case. It's whale-watching season and we might get lucky."

"What are we really going to be doing?" snapped Uncle J. "I'm not here to play games, I am an adult, it's my plan, now tell me what the hell is going to happen."

"Uncle J," replied Jez. "What have you said about conversing on open phone lines? We are going to downtown San Francisco for a tour around the sights, we will grab some lunch, then we might go to the headland past the Golden Gate and try and spot some whales."

"What about the fun runs we have been entered in?" quizzed Uncle J. "Then there are the exhibitions that we have tickets for? When are we starting to discuss arrangements for these events?"

"We can discuss our full itinerary in the car tomorrow," replied a completely flustered Jez. "I haven't forgotten, I just assumed you would leave arrangements to me and trust that I will deliver as promised. You've only just arrived, you will probably have the effects of jet lag, that's why I haven't raised the subjects with you yet. Give me some credit."

"I imagined this trip to be watertight, run like clockwork," continued Uncle J. "I have been told by your fellow members that every 'i' will be dotted and every 't' crossed. To be frank, it doesn't appear to be that way so far."

"Give it time, Uncle J," said a sympathetic Jez. "It's early days, I've got everything in hand, don't worry."

"You better have, matey boy. See you tomorrow then," said Uncle J abruptly returning the phone to its receiver.

At last, a mission, thought Uncle J. He didn't want to wait for weeks until something started to happen. An excitement filled his bones, deflecting the negative trust issues momentarily to the back of his thoughts, despite the apparent lack of 'on the ground' briefing so far from The Cell.

Uncle J decided to visit Umar just in case Jez had not called him to discuss the planned events for the morning. Uncle J tapped Umar's hotel room door.

"Just a minute," came a muffled call from within.

Moments later, a flustered-looking Umar opened the door. He looked surprisingly scruffy. He was usually impeccably presented, however, his shirt was hanging out, he had an obscure gilet over his shirt that looked like it had been thrown on at speed in the dark, and his hair was all over the place.

"Blimey, what have you been up to?" sniped Uncle J. "You look like you've been dragged through a hedge backwards."

"Ignore this look," replied a somewhat embarrassed Umar. "I was messing about in the bathroom with a new 'American' look, to blend in. What do you think?"

"Just make sure the fashion police are off duty when you go out," japed Uncle J.

The pair smiled at each other as Uncle J wandered into Umar's hotel room.

"So, to what do I owe this pleasure?" asked Umar.

"Did you get a call from Jez?" quizzed Uncle J.

"Nah, nothing," replied Umar shrugging his shoulders.

"OK then," continued Uncle J. "We are out on a mission tomorrow with Jez. No details, but at least it could be the start of U.S. operations."

"Where are we going?" asked Umar.

"Don't know?" replied Uncle J.

"What are we going to be doing?" asked Umar.

"Don't really know for sure?" replied Uncle J.

"So why did you come and see me then, if you know nothing?" said an irritated Umar.

"To tell you we are going out with Jez at nine-thirty in the morning, that's why," said a very disgruntled Uncle J.

"Great, thanks," replied an aloof Umar. "I'll be there."

Umar's current arrogant and remote manner did not bode well with Uncle J. In all honesty, he wanted to throttle Umar. The constant lacklustre attitude that Umar showed towards Uncle J was becoming overbearing. This made Uncle J assume that Umar had little real commitment to Uncle J's cause, re-igniting the now burning fires in Uncle J's head concerning the trust issues he had mounting up with Umar.

After pondering his plight, Uncle J decided against the use of violence; he needed to be away from Umar's company. Instead, Uncle J bid Umar a good evening and returned to his room.

Once in his room, Uncle J became restless. He was agitated and felt like he was trapped inside his own plan. Here he was, in a foreign land, with a relative stranger he met in prison, working with a new Cell he had never met. In his mind, Uncle J was vulnerable, and he didn't care for that feeling.

After some considerable thought, Uncle J prepared himself to go outside. He adorned a hoodie so that he could try and obscure his identity as best he could. Once out of his room, Uncle J made his way to the swimming pool area, using it as his exit route. There was a passage off the swimming pool patio that led to an adjacent shopping mall. This tactic ensured that Uncle J did not have to go through the busy hotel reception area, which would increase the possibility of Uncle J being seen leaving the hotel.

Soon in the mall, Uncle J started to look for his target shop; he was trying to find a mobile phone outlet. He didn't trust, so didn't want to use the mobile phone that Jez had issued earlier. Uncle J had cash on him, cash that Umar and Jez knew nothing about. After scanning the ground floor of the mall with no success, Uncle J used the escalator to continue his search on the first floor. After a short time, Uncle J spotted what he was looking for.

He entered the shop and started to browse the displayed models. Uncle J needed the smallest sized phone he could find, as he wanted to try and get a phone that he could tuck away on his person undetected. In addition to the phone, Uncle J wanted to buy a local SIM card and charge it with plenty of credit, as Uncle J had international phone calls on his agenda.

After around twenty minutes the transactions were complete, and Uncle J headed out of the mall towards the seafront. He made his way to the edge of Fisherman's Wharf, to a small bay below the chocolate factory, a less busy area where he could make a private phone call.

Uncle J took a good look around before he started to dial. He was still wary that his location was open to prying eyes, so he decided to move.

Thirty minutes later, tucked away at the back of an empty coffee shop, Uncle J dialled a number into his mobile phone.

"Faisal? Is that you?" asked an apprehensive Uncle J.

"Yes, it's me," exclaimed a joyous Faisal. "Are you safe and sound? Did you get through to the States OK?"

"Yes, we both did," replied an equally joyous Uncle J. "How was your journey home? Did you get back hassle-free?"

"It was absolutely fine, sir," replied a comforting Faisal. "Is that why you are calling me? Was it playing on your mind?"

"No," commanded Uncle J. "I need you to do me a favour."

Chapter Eight

Uncle J did not sleep well. He was tossing and turning all night with excitement about the planned events but mixed with deepening worries concerning Umar's commitment and attitude. Breakfast with Umar was an awkward affair. Sadly, Uncle J's attitude and commitment concerns were beating his feelings of excitement. Barely a word was spoken as the pair tucked into their hearty breakfasts. The atmosphere was heavy with tension.

Eventually, the atmosphere lightened for the better when Jez appeared in the breakfast room.

"Are you two ready to go?" chirped Jez. "The truck is out front, I'll go and wait for you. Just hurry up as we've got a fair distance to travel today."

Jez disappeared as quickly as he had appeared, which left Uncle J and Umar staring at each other in silence over the breakfast table."

"Right," barked Umar. "What is your problem? You've barely said a word this morning, and you are looking at me like you are about to kill me. What's going on?"

Uncle J picked up a convenient spoon from the table and gave his mug of coffee an extended stir.

"Let's go outside," replied a stern Uncle J.

Uncle J and Umar made their way to the car park at the front of the hotel. Instead of making their way to Jez, who was standing next to a black truck with the driver's door ajar, Uncle J guided Umar over to the left hand edge of the car park.

Uncle J turned to look at Umar face-to-face, positioning himself just a few inches from Umar's nose.

"Attitude and commitment," stated a resigned Uncle J. "That's what's wrong with me. From the start, even when we were inmates, you always seem aloof, disrespectful, and secretive to me. Plus, when I speak to you, you treat me with scant respect. I am a legend up north back home. People idolise me when they are in my presence. My name stands for courage, commitment, and leadership. What do I get from you? Secret meetings with The Cell, drip-fed bits and pieces of information, never the full story. You seem to have taken control of my revenge project and have been in cahoots with The Cell, behind my back. In doing so, you show no remorse. You never consider how I feel about losing my grip on this operation. It is me who feels the pain of the previously failed kidnapping. It is my name that was tarnished with failure. It was me who served time. Can't you try and understand why I am conducting myself in this way? Then maybe you might adjust the way you behave in front of me."

Feeling uncomfortable with the close positioning of their faces, Umar took a step back.

"Look, Uncle J," replied Umar. "This is me. This is how I am. It's nothing personal, I have had to harden my exterior as, in the past, I have been taken advantage of, and I don't want to be treated like a fool again. If you take a step back, I have introduced you to the new Cell. I convinced them to take up your cause and assist you. Look at how your prison release hearing ended up. Look at how you managed to get through our airport customs and immigration without a hitch. Look at how you got through San Francisco customs and immigration without a hitch. It's partly down to me. It is down to how I have dovetailed with The Cell to help your quest succeed. How can you now accuse me of being uncommitted? I have done more than you so far to get us where we are, and all I get in return is accusations and cutting comments. If you really feel this way, just tell me to leave and I will be on my way out of here."

As he delivered his response, Umar looked Uncle J directly in the eye. There was a look of determination and honesty about Umar's look. Uncle J immediately began to sense a strong feeling of guilt enveloping him. Of late, Uncle J had been selfish in his outlook with Umar, not completely considering how he had allegedly assisted with Uncle J's release from prison, along with the countless meetings that Umar had untaken with The Cell, at great personal risk, which resulted in all meetings having positive outcomes that helped Uncle J with his mission.

After a short period of rational thought, Uncle J stepped forward and embraced Umar.

"I'm sorry," whispered an apologetic Uncle J. "It must be the stress of the situation. I am grateful for all of your help, honestly, I am. I will try and act with more dignity and professionalism, and above all, treat you like the friend you have become."

"That's OK," responded Umar immediately. "I understand. I appreciate the pressure you are putting yourself under. I will also work on my attitude, plus I will treat you with the respect you deserve."

The pair embraced for a while longer.

"Are you two lovebirds ready?" quipped Jez. "We need to get going, right now."

Uncle J and Umar released from their embrace and made their way into the truck, both with a smile on their faces as they did so. It is exactly what was needed, a 'clear the air' confrontation, followed by a positive move forward.

Jez plotted his way out of San Francisco. Jez needed to avoid unnecessary traffic jams as they had the best part of two hundred miles to negotiate to their intended destination. As the rush-hour traffic subsided, they soon found themselves on the freedom of the freeway. The traffic was fair but light enough to make good progress. As part of his brief, Jez was under strict instructions not to exceed speed limits or traffic controls. The attention of the traffic police was to be avoided at all costs. The mission was well and truly underway, nothing trivial should be risked jeopardising success.

Once out of the city limits, the vista soon changed to a more pleasing panorama. The concrete jungle gave way to vast green, rolling hills, littered with space-aged-looking windmills. There was a feeling of liberty given off by the clean, uncorrupted open spaces. The horizon to both sides of the freeway seemed to be endless. This lifted Uncle J's spirits even more. It was far removed from the heat, humidity, and squalor of his homeland. There was order here; a sense of freedom, cleanliness and of being at one with nature.

Soon, they were out of the hills and the terrain became less undulating. The hills had given way to what appeared to be limitless fields and plains. The horizon looked even further away so much so that Uncle J could not comprehend this feeling of vast openness.

For the first hour or so there was pretty much silence in the truck. This was mainly down to Uncle J's and Umar's overwhelming appreciation of the landscape. Never before had they witnessed such a succession of beautiful but constantly varying views.

"I'm going to pull off at the next exit," said Jez breaking the silence. "We are around halfway and I need a break from driving."

"No problem," replied an understanding Uncle J. "Do me one favour though."

"What's that?" said an inquisitive Jez.

"It's a bit silly really," replied Uncle J. "It's been a wish of mine since I was young. I've always wanted to eat at a McDonald's in America."

"What?" barked Jez in response. "You come over here, with all it's got to offer, and your biggest wish is to eat fast food?"

"When did I say it was my biggest wish?" replied a disgruntled Uncle J, whose grin widened as the unmistakable golden arches sign was visible from the off-ramp.

Forty minutes later, the trio were back on the road, fed and watered. Plus, Uncle J had ticked off an item from his culinary bucket list.

"I've booked a motel in Mariposa for tonight," announced Jez. "We need a full day tomorrow at the cabin to check it out and the surrounding area. I've already talked to the people at your hotel in San Francisco. They are OK to let you leave your room as we will only be away for tonight, so you don't need to worry about that."

"This is news," said a slightly disgruntled Uncle J. "I wasn't expecting an overnighter. Why didn't you mention this earlier?"

"I just assumed you would expect an overnight stay," replied Jez. "After all, it's over eight hours on the road for a return journey, that doesn't give us much time at the cabin."

"I guess not," responded Uncle J. "Look, in future, please give us the courtesy of letting us know what's going on. I thought this new all improved Cell had all bases covered, including communication."

"I'll take this on board," replied Jez. "I will try and make sure you are fully briefed in future. I just didn't think it was a big deal, that's all."

Uncle J slumped back in the passenger seat of the truck. The last thing he wanted right now was more evidence that he was not in control of his mission. The apparent lack of communication from Jez just inflamed Uncle J's doubts. Uncle J remained silent for the remainder of the journey, deep in thought, his head was once again full of suspicion and doubt.

Just under three hours later they reached Mariposa. It was a small town that had a wild west, frontier town feel to it. The main street was lined with wooden structures containing shops, restaurants and the like. The town was surrounded by rugged tree-laden hills. Uncle J felt like he was suddenly in the middle of nowhere.

Jez turned off the main route into the motel. They drove through a triangular-shaped entrance canopy into the motel car park. All three got out of the vehicle and were feeling the effects of the journey, stretching their limbs as they cast their judgemental eyes over the motel.

"Not a fancy place then Jez," said a disappointed Umar.

"It's OK," replied Jez. "It's clean and it's in the right place for us. It's only for one night."

"We have no change of clothes," moaned Uncle J. "What am I supposed to do for nightwear? How am I going to clean my teeth? This is exactly why you should have warned us."

"Look!" shouted Jez. "You are big boys now, it's for one night. We are not here to model your pyjamas. We are here for an important phase of the plan. Your constant petulant behaviour is worse than bringing my kids along."

Uncle J and Umar bowed their heads in shame, following Jez as he made his way to the motel reception to check-in. Jez had booked three rooms. He was not the only one who needed space after the awkward journey and accompanying hissy fits.

Once checked in, Jez told Uncle J and Umar to meet him in reception at seven in the evening. Jez wanted to take them for an early dinner as they had a prompt start in the morning.

That evening they dined at a pizza restaurant. It was another uncomfortable experience as there appeared to be evidence of cracks appearing in the team's morale. Few words were exchanged, mainly because Jez warned against open conversations in public regarding their reasons for being in the Yosemite region. Being strangers, the locals would probably be watching them closely and would try to listen into conversations where possible to get the low down.

Once dinner had been endured, the three travellers returned to Jez's motel room for a short briefing.

"We leave at eight in the morning," demanded Jez. "I will take care of checking us out, so just come to the car park just before eight a.m. The cabin is around an hour from here. We can grab some breakfast on the road so that we don't have any delays in the morning. Once we are at the cabin, we need to check out the suitability of where we are going to hold the captives. That is the main objective. We are checking the work of the set up team, so any issues at all, make sure you flag them up, we need the site to be perfect and fit for purpose."

"Why are we checking something that should have been signed off already?" asked Uncle J.

"Because that's the way the new Cell works now," responded a confident Jez. "Our sign-off will be checked by another separate team as well before The Cell gives the go ahead to go to the next phase. This is a very important element of the overall plan. We need a workable and secure cabin, otherwise we can't hold our target captives with full confidence."

"Captives?" snapped a surprised Uncle J.

"Yes, captives, plural," replied Jez.

"Like whom?" responded Uncle J.

"We are targeting both siblings," continued an assured Jez. "The Cell considers the chances of success greater if we have both sons kidnapped."

Uncle J violently slammed his open palm down with vigour on the bedside table.

"Here we go again," exclaimed an irate Uncle J. "Why was I not consulted about this dual kidnapping? How the hell are we going to kidnap them both? I'm just about ready to pull the plug on this mess and go home."

"Empty-handed again?" teased Jez. "Look. I'm sure we have discussed this before. You have just got so much on your mind, it's probably escaping you right now."

Uncle J sprang from the bed and grabbed Jez around the throat. Jez had finally pressed Uncle J's buttons, he was riled.

"Don't make fun of me, laddie," roared Uncle J. "You know who I am and what I am capable of. One more remark like that and I will snap your neck."

Almost immediately, realising his overreaction, Uncle J released his grip. There were visible signs of harm to Jez's neck area, Uncle J had used enough force to leave a raised imprint on Jez's throat.

Jez equally realised his inappropriate comments and also backed off. Jez wanted to try and convince Uncle J not to give up but should not have used sarcastic humour to make his point.

"Let's call it a night," interrupted Umar. "It's getting a bit spicy in here. Let's all retire for the evening and get some rest. We have a busy day tomorrow."

Uncle J issued a final death stare in the direction of Jez before leaving the room, petulantly slamming the door behind him.

With Uncle J out of the room, Jez approached Umar.

"Are you OK, man?" asked a concerned Umar.

"Sure. Do you believe this guy?" said a visibly agitated Jez. "The bloke's mood is up and down like a roller coaster on speed. I've heard great things about him, but boy is he high-maintenance. We are supposed to be on the same team."

"Yeah, right," exclaimed Umar examining the damage around Jez's throat. "I've had to endure this for weeks now. Uncle J is well aware that we were targeting both kids, maybe it's his current state of mind that is clouding his memory. I'll talk to him and calm him down. Do you need anything for that wound?"

"I'll be OK," replied Jez. "I just want this whole escapade done and dusted so I can move on to more worthwhile causes."

"You and me both," responded Umar wearing a broad smile.

Umar gave Jez a small embrace and retired to his room. Being around Uncle J was starting to annoy Umar. He was not used to working in this manner. Uncle J was headstrong, but just couldn't come to terms with the fact that he was not in a position to pull all of the strings, and this was affecting team morale. Things had to change.

The following morning, the three gang members assembled in the car park. Jez had taken care of checking out, so they were ready for an immediate departure.

The fallout from the antics of the previous evening was still evident. There was still a noticeable awkwardness in the air and none of the three was entering into eye contact with anyone. Not the best start to the day.

In silence, the team hit the road. Once out of Mariposa, they started to enter the delights of Yosemite Park. They were surrounded by immense forests populated with towering trees. The road meandered its way through the sensational vista leaving Uncle J, Umar and Jez in awe of the park's beauty. There was almost a scene transformation around each sweeping bend they took. A spectacular waterfall, a break in the trees revealing a clean, babbling mountain stream, another opening in the trees revealing a view towards soaring mountain tops that penetrated the horizon. It was just nature at its beautiful best.

"Wow!" exclaimed Uncle J breaking the silence. "Have you ever seen such a beautiful environment?"

"Never," responded Umar immediately. "It is just sensational, stunning."

This mutual admiration of their surroundings had broken the stifling tension. Upbeat conversation then flowed between the trio, even raising gasps when the vista presented them with eye-watering scenery.

Not only was the mood upbeat, but they were also all distracted from the journey and the passing of time.

Before they could enter into another bout of mutual appreciation, Jez activated his left indicator, turning off the road into a gated side road.

Jez negotiated the locked gate, double-checking that it was locked once they were past the sweep of the gate.

Jez started to pull away.

"So, how far is this cabin from here?" asked Uncle J.

"Roughly three miles," relied Jez. "I've not been here before, but I have been briefed that it's about three miles."

"Fine," replied Uncle J. "Does the road surface get any better?"

"Nope," chuckled Jez.

The truck made its way steadily down the forest track. It was a reasonable, dry surface, but the undulations, constant sharp bends and overhanging branches prevented rapid progress.

It was clear that the further they drove away from the highway, they were entering a very remote and unpopulated area. Uncle J started to understand why The Cell had chosen such a location and started to come to terms with the superior local knowledge of The Cell.

Twenty minutes later, having negotiated yet another right hand bend between two redwoods, a log cabin came into view. The truck came to rest and the three colleagues stared towards the wooden structure.

Once out of the truck they walked down the gravel path, taking in their surroundings as they walked. There was a fresh smell in the air, just like a natural pine-scented air freshener. Uncle J filled his lungs with the delightful aromas.

Jez produced a key ring populated with a variety of different-sized keys. Looking at the lock, he selected what he thought was the right key.

Jez opened the door and ushered his companions into the cabin.

Walking into the living area, the three separated to take a look around. Uncle J immediately spotted the shoot bolts fitted to the door frame to his right and made his way over to the door.

"This must be the holding area?" said Uncle J. "I guess these shoot bolts are the giveaway."

With the shoot bolts in the lock position, Uncle J pulled vigorously on the door handle. The structure remained solid and didn't budge an inch.

"That'll hold for sure," commented Umar. "Looks like a fine job to me."

Uncle J nodded in approval towards Umar, unlocked the three shoot bolts and opened the door.

Inside was a small empty room. There were two mattresses on the floor covered by some very basic bedding. There was a single window that appeared to have bars fitted. There was no other furniture in the room and there was a sole light bulb fixture fitted to the ceiling, with no light bulb in situ.

"Leave me and Uncle J in here and lock me in," asked Jez. "I want to see what the security is like."

Umar did as he requested locking Jez and Uncle J in the room.

Uncle J heaved rigorously on the window bars as Jez tried to escape through the locked door. Both remained sturdy, giving the impression that they were impenetrable.

"Let me get on your shoulders," requested Jez standing under the light bulb. "I want to see if they can do anything with this light fixture."

Once on Uncle J's shoulders, Jez took the light bulb fixture apart in no time. Soon he had freed the live wires to the fixture.

"Just as I thought," said a proud Jez. "We need to do something with these live wires; we don't want them used in any way by our captives."

"I wouldn't have even looked up," said Uncle J. "Great call."

Jez was returned to the floor. We need to cover that fixture somehow. Leave that with me, I will get it sorted."

Uncle J and Jez called Umar to release them from the bedroom.

"That all looks secure," stated Jez. "Just need to sort that light fixture. Can you see now why we have triple checks, Uncle J?"

Uncle J bowed his head in embarrassment. Jez was right, the installation team hadn't fully considered the light fixture.

The three subsequently checked out the remainder of the cabin. Checking each room thoroughly, thinking outside of the box to try and unearth issues that may cause problems when holding their prisoners. Once all interior rooms had been checked, Jez face the group.

"We need to check outside as well," said Jez. "Let's take a look at the generator to make sure it's in good working order."

"You guys do that," interrupted Uncle J. "I want to take a look at the surrounding areas, just to get a feel of the place. I also need some fresh air after being in this stuffy cabin."

"Great idea," replied Umar. "I'll come with you."

"No," snapped Uncle J. "I'll go by myself. I need some alone time. It's all starting to get real again. I just need to collect my thoughts."

Umar and Jez looked at each other in amazement, not really expecting such a reaction from Uncle J.

Uncle J smiled and calmly left the cabin. Jez and Umar went immediately to the window to watch Uncle J leave to try and see which direction he would go and to try and understand why.

"What's got into him?" asked Jez.

"Just Uncle J being Uncle J, I guess," replied Umar.

"What's he going to gain by looking out there?" quizzed Jez.

"Beats me," replied Umar. "Just let him be and get on with it. Maybe it makes him feel more important if he owns being the periphery team leader?"

"Whatever," continued Jez. "Come on then, let's go and take a look at that generator."

Jez and Umar made their way down the side of the cabin to the generator, scanning the surrounding forest to see if they could see Uncle J and what he was up to.

Jez and Umar had long since checked the generator, as well as all the remainder of the property, but there was still no sign of Uncle J. Had he done a runner? Had he got lost? Had he been eaten by a passing, hungry bear? Jez and Umar were starting to show signs of concern.

"So, how did you get mixed up in Uncle J's affairs?" asked Jez.

"I met him in prison," replied Umar. "I was instructed by The Cell to make his acquaintance, then oversee his actions inside, making sure he stayed out of harm's way as best I could."

"By The Cell?" quizzed Jez. "Directly?"

"Kind of," responded Umar. "It's a bit complicated. The prison governor was involved; he has direct contact with The Cell. Prison is a very useful place to control people and keep a close eye on them. The governor is an obvious choice as he sees all and gets told all. Uncle J has been on The Cell's radar for some time."

"Really?" said a surprised Jez. "Why was that then?"

"I can't say too much," replied Umar. "I don't want to start talking out of turn. The Cell has ways of flushing out loose tongues, it's as if they are everywhere."

"So, what does The Cell really want with Uncle J?" continued a persistent Jez.

"I've said enough," snapped Umar. "Let's talk about something else, this is getting boring. Let's talk about how you became involved in The Cell."

"Now that is boring," replied Jez. "My father was following a similar cause to Uncle J. Back in the day he fought against the authorities in the disputed area, he wasn't a big shot like Uncle J, but he did his bit. He was shot in the leg and had to dilute his fighting activities on the front line. He became more an adviser than a fighter, as he just wasn't fit or mobile enough to fight, so he stayed in the shadows, helping with the cause more indirectly. I guess as a thank you for his service, The Cell took him on board which eventually passed onto me via my father."

"Cute," replied Umar. "Like a family business passing down the generations."

"You could say that," laughed Jez. "But it certainly isn't a family business like a butcher or hardware store."

Another hour passed. Through the foliage, the unmistakable gait of Uncle J appeared before them. Uncle J casually strolled up to the cabin.

"Where the hell have you been?" yelled a frustrated Jez. "You've been hours; what on earth have you been doing?"

"My job," replied Uncle J assertively. "I've been checking the surrounding area; for authorities that may be spying on us, for other cabins or holiday homes that could become involved involuntarily, for potential escape routes should our captives break out of the cabin, and stuff like that."

Jez looked at Uncle J with his mouth open, he was speechless.

"I bet your Cell didn't think of that?" quipped Uncle J.

"How do you think they selected this cabin?" replied Jez. "They have checked out this area time and time again, along with countless others. Do you think that The Cell would jeopardise this mission, just because they couldn't be arsed to check it out thoroughly?"

"I don't doubt that," replied Uncle J. "But I thought we were here to double-check what the initial team had done?"

"OK, I'll give you that," replied a frustrated Jez. "Come on, we need to get back to San Francisco. I don't like driving at night, so I want to get off now."

They all played their part in making sure the generator was off, the cabin was secure and there were no signs of recent activity around the cabin.

Jez carefully guided the truck back down the forest track. Once they arrived at the main road, Jez double-checked that the gate was properly locked, then jumped back in the truck. They turned back onto the road.

"What do you think then, Uncle J?" asked Jez. "Does the cabin meet your expectations?"

"Not bad," replied Uncle J, "not bad at all. It's remote, it's secure, and we stand more chance of being watched by wild bears rather than the authorities."

"Indeed," chuckled Jez. "So, I can inform The Cell that you are happy to proceed?"

"What?" said a startled Uncle J. "The Cell want my blessing?"

"Absolutely," replied Jez. "After all, it is your mission. The Cell is just doing all it can to make it a success. Let me be totally clear; if at any stage you don't feel happy, you let me know and I'll talk to The Cell."

"This is ludicrous," said Uncle J shaking his head. "Why have I felt like a passenger all this time, bowing down to the demands of The Cell, and then you come out with something like this?"

"It's of your own making, Uncle J," continued Jez. "Your involvement in the leadership of this operation has never been in doubt. You are creating issues in your head yourself. The Cell just wants to help you deliver your revenge plot. I'm not sure where you are coming from?"

Uncle J didn't answer, he was as confused now as he had ever been since starting to plot his revenge. It was like Jez was messing with Uncle J's head, playing mind games.

"Uncle J?" asked Jez again. "Are you OK?"

Again, Uncle J remained silent. He was concerned and needed to think about events up until now just in case he was making up issues unnecessarily with the part he was playing in this plot. Uncle J's brain felt like it was made of mush. To say he was confused was an understatement.

The remainder of the journey back to San Francisco was completed mainly in silence. Umar fell asleep shortly after leaving the Yosemite area, and Uncle J spent the journey staring out of the passenger's side window with a vacant look on his face. Not wanting to spend more time in this company, Jez didn't even suggest a comfort break. He headed back home as fast as he dared.

As the unmistakable profile of the Oakland Bridge appeared in the distance, Jez decided to break the silence.

"Gents," said Jez in a louder voice than usual.

Umar stirred from his slumber and Uncle J reconnected with the world.

"We have another task to work on tomorrow," continued Jez. "Tomorrow is the day that you get your first look at one of our targets. We have been watching him for some time now and The Cell feels confident enough that the target's routine will put him in Union Square tomorrow at ten in the morning. I will take you to a vantage point where you can see the target for yourself for the first time, exciting?"

"Excellent," said Umar. "This is great news, eh, Uncle J?"

"Super," replied a sarcastic and subdued Uncle J. "Can't wait."

"Come on, Uncle J," said Jez trying to reassure and motivate Uncle J. "It's going to be a great couple of days. You've seen the cabin and now you are going to see one of the intended occupants."

"I'm tired," replied a grumpy Uncle J. "What time are we meeting in the morning? I need a night of sleep. I promise I will be more connected in the morning."

"I get it," responded Jez. "It's been a busy few days and I bet the jet lag is hitting as well. Let's meet in the hotel car park out front at eight thirty a.m., which will give us enough time to get downtown."

Chapter Nine

Following a good night's sleep, it was another morning and another hotel breakfast for Uncle J. His mood appeared lighter today as he sat down opposite Umar. The previous evening, as he was again feeling down, Uncle J turned to his burner phone to speak with his loyal manservant, Faisal. This was not only Uncle J's safety net but also his opportunity to gain back some perceived control. The political game-playing since he had been in the States had driven Uncle J from excitement and elation to confusion and depression, with a fair few other levels in between. Something that Uncle did not appreciate and was not used to.

Uncle J bounced the unfolded events off Faisal to try and obtain an impartial second opinion. To try and justify his feelings of anxiety and frustration with the only person in the world who give him a straight and honest answer. Based on Uncle J's more affable look at the breakfast table, his contact with home appeared to be serving its purpose.

"So, what do you think we will achieve today?" asked Uncle J.

Almost coughing into his cereal, Umar looked up with great surprise at a cheerful-looking Uncle J.

"We should get a good look at one of our targets," replied a still-shocked Umar. "I'm not sure we will be able to piece together a movement trend after the first sighting, but all in all, it should be a positive and useful day."

"Agreed," stated Uncle J. "If nothing else, it gives us something constructive to do, plus it's a day closer to the actual events that we are pursuing. Has The Cell actually agreed on D-Day?"

"I'm not sure," replied a nervous Umar, looking around him as he responded. Umar was not comfortable with the conversation subject matter in the breakfast room.

"I wonder what's keeping them from making a decision?" continued Uncle J. "I thought their planning process was second-to-none. Surely they have an end date in mind?"

"Well, if they have, they haven't shared it with me," whispered Umar with his head lowered to almost table height.

"I think we need to raise this with Jez this morning," said Uncle J confidently.

"I agree," responded Umar. "But let's talk about something else in the 'public' breakfast room."

Uncle J received Umar's coaching loud and clear, immediately changing the conversation subject matter to discussions around what the weather would be like back at home.

Thirty minutes later, Jez arrived to transport Uncle J and Umar to their downtown lookout post. Within five minutes of them congregating in Jez's truck, Uncle J could not contain himself.

"Mr Jez," boomed an upbeat Uncle J. "Has your beloved Cell arrived at a date yet when we implement our kidnapping duties? It appears that the cabin is ready to go, when are we going to populate it?"

"Soon," replied Jez. "Very soon, just be a little more patient."

"I am always in the dark," continued Uncle J. "I feel like I am being treated like a child, almost like I don't have the maturity to deal with key information, maybe The Cell thinks I can't keep my mouth shut, which will jeopardise operations?"

"Uncle J," snapped Umar. "Enough. It's like listening to a broken record. You persistently bleat about your treatment by The Cell. For goodness sake, man up and get on with it. The Cell is on your side. Please stop going on and on about feeling like a child, it's starting to grate my nerve ends. Please, rest assured, we are on the same team, fighting the same cause, sharing the rewards."

An immediate veil of silence fell over the truck. Jez was inwardly smiling as he completely subscribed to Umar's observations. Jez was also tired of fending off Uncle J's feelings of being a victim of The Cell.

185

The remaining thirty minutes of the journey were awkwardly completed in total silence. Jez had manoeuvred his truck into an ample parking space in a downtown multi-storey car park.

Jez walked over to the parking metre and paid for two hours.

"Right, follow me," said an apprehensive Jez.

Uncle J and Umar shuffled behind Jez and followed him to the elevator like obedient sheep. Once outside, Jez led his followers to Union Square where their lookout post was located. Entering Macey's department store, Jez took another elevator and selected the top floor. When the elevator doors opened, the group was greeted by the reception area of a cheesecake restaurant. Uncle J's eyes lit up as he assumed Jez was treating Uncle J to lift his spirits.

Jez spoke with a receptionist, who soon led the trio to a more isolated table located in the open air, overlooking Union Square. All three took a seat at an oblong table which was positioned against a glass barrier at the edge of the restaurant.

"Great view of the square from here," said Jez breaking the obdurate silence.

"Great," replied Uncle J using a sarcastic undertone.

"Before you start," continued Jez while looking at Uncle J, "we are here to take our first look at Rayan, who is Mansoor's eldest."

Jez produced two separate files containing several A4 sheets stapled together. Uncle J and Umar immediately delved into the paperwork.

"This is Rayan's file," added Jez. "There is a clear photograph of him, along with a diary of his movements for the past month, regular and random. His home address is also listed, along with known friends and accomplices. He works at that office over there with the blue window frames."

Jez pointed across to the far side of Union Square.

"Looking at these notes, he is due to arrive any minute," stated a confident Umar.

"Let's hope so," agreed Jez producing two sets of binoculars out of his backpack. "Take these, but don't make your actions too obvious when using them."

Barely five minutes had passed when Rayan entered Union Square on a pushbike.

"There he is," commanded Jez. "Over there, look, on that bicycle. He should ride over to the office."

Uncle J and Umar immediately put the binoculars to their eyes. In silence, the pair watched as Rayan pulled up outside the office.

"I bet you he is folding his bike right now, before he goes in the door," said a confident Jez.

Sure enough, Rayan folded his bicycle and entered the office.

"We've made all this effort just for that?" exclaimed an angry Uncle J. "You could have taken a video and played it back to us over breakfast."

"Nonsense," replied Jez. "I wanted you to validate our observations to-date; how we knew exactly when Rayan would show up and tell you exactly what Rayan would do. You have seen for yourselves what has happened with your own eyes. If I had taken a video, you would have cast down on its authenticity. This way, you have witnessed events yourself; there can be no doubt."

Uncle J looked over to Umar and shrugged his shoulders.

"I guess The Cell is on point," said a resigned Uncle J. "Fair enough, whatever I have complained about so far, my trust in the Cell's intelligence gathering was never in question."

"Great," replied an upbeat Jez. "There is no point waiting here for six hours until Rayan leaves the office. Let's order coffee and cheesecake; it is just divine here, then I will take you to another part of the city for act two."

Once they had devoured their scrumptious treats, the three returned to Jez's truck for their next instalment.

In the truck, Jez produced another two files from his backpack and handed them over to Uncle J and Umar. Once they had left the car park and were battling moderate city traffic, Jez began to explain act two of the surveillance validation plan to Uncle J and Umar.

"We are off to show you the typical movements of Mansoor's youngest, Talib," explained Jez. "He works out of town at the football stadium. He works in the merchandise store as an assistant manager. As you will see from the notes, he works five days a week on a flexible rota, so his movements are not as straightforward as Rayan's."

"Football stadium?" quizzed Umar.

"Yes, the San Francisco 49'ers," responded Jez. "They are the NFL team I follow; it's American football, not soccer."

"I see," said a clueless Umar. "I'm not really into sport so I have no idea what you are on about."

"Let me explain," replied Jez. "It will help pass the time as we have an hour's drive in front of us."

Jez then started to explain in detail a potted history concerning the San Francisco 49'ers; how they moved from Candlestick Park, how many Super Bowls the team has won, and how Joe Montana is an all-time great of the sport, amongst other snippets. In reality, Jez helped pass the time as both Uncle J and Umar had dropped into a semi-conscious nap. Jez was aware of this but was not deterred, as he loved spouting off about his beloved 49'ers.

As the truck turned off the freeway fast approaching Levi Stadium, Jez coughed loudly to stir Uncle J and Umar from their slumber. Both immediately jumped out of their skins.

"There it is in all its glory," said a proud Jez, pointing at the impressive structure that was fast unveiling out of the misty morning California air. "We will park up and then go into the merchandise store. Talib doesn't know us from Adam, so it's fine to be this close to him."

"Are you sure?" asked an anxious Uncle J. "Has The Cell cleared this?"

"Yes, they have," replied Jez. "Don't be paranoid, they get thousands of people in the shop each month."

"I guess so," replied a somewhat nervous Umar. "After all, we could just be real tourists."

"One more thing," added Jez, "this is just so that you can see what Talib looks like. We are not going to kidnap him from work, that is just madness. I'll take you to the planned site once we have finished up here. So, for now, just browse in the shop with me and I will point him out to you."

"What's the point coming all this way if we are not actually using this site for an extraction?" asked an irate Uncle J.

"Two reasons," snapped Jez back. "To get eyes on the target, and to make your time here a bit more interesting. It's an impressive shop and an even more impressive stadium. We can take a quick look at the pitch when we have finished in the shop."

"Looking at a sports field is interesting?" said a bemused Umar.

"Just wait and see," replied a confident Jez.

Once parked up, the trio made their way into the large shop. It was certainly impressive. You could purchase just about anything from shot glasses to football jerseys, all emblazoned with the San Francisco 49'ers logo. It certainly wasn't Uncle J's or Umar's cup of tea. Not being sports fans, the trip to the shop was as useful to them as a chocolate teapot, both struggling to conjure up any interest whatsoever in today's activity, but they resigned themselves to the fact that they had to get a look at one of their intended targets.

Browsing deep in the home jersey aisle, Jez attracted the attention of Uncle J and Umar with a quiet hiss.

"That's him," said Jez. "The chap who has just come into the shop in the grey suit, white shirt and red tie. Don't both look over at once, he may get suspicious."

Thinking he had the divine right, Uncle J almost immediately looked across, staring in the direction of the suited gentlemen walking next to the aisle of 49'ers teddy bears.

"He's a bit young," whispered Uncle J to Jez.

"He's old enough and valuable to kidnap," responded Jez.

"Very smart," added Umar.

"Both of you stop staring," demanded Jez. "We are not in a zoo."

Both Uncle J and Umar looked away sharply in tandem.

"Look," said an angry Jez. "You are going to give the game away acting like this. Try and act naturally and less like a spying double-act. You stand a good chance of raising suspicions at this rate. Just split up and browse, take a look when you can, and for goodness sake make sure you buy something. Use the fifty dollars that was in the files I gave you."

The three split up, making their way to different areas of the vast store. Uncle J walked over to the impressive display of shot glasses, Umar made his way over to the teddy bear display, and Jez wandered over towards a mound of bathroom towels. All three tried to covertly follow the activities of Talib, which mostly involved walking between the till area and his office on a ten-minute rota.

Uncle J angrily glared in Talib's direction when Talib was not looking his way. Uncle J regarded this man as a real enemy. In Uncle J's mindset, it was Talib's family who had brought failure, disgrace, and deep reputational harm to Uncle J's door, and he wanted aggressive revenge. Uncle J had near uncontrollable urges to lash out and fire a round of insults at Talib, almost to the point where Uncle J had the inhospitable words in the back of his mouth. Fortunately, Jez had been keeping a watchful eye over his guests, realising that Uncle J was in a bit of a state and he breezed over to Uncle J and led him away to a quiet corner of the shop.

Noting that Uncle J was physically shaking, plus wearing a 'warrior about to go into battle' expression on his face, Jez decided to call time on their store visit.

Jez led Uncle J over to the till area where Umar was paying for a cuddly toy. Once the merchandise was inside the bag, Jez led his cohorts out of the shop and into the car park.

Uncle J was not in a good place. He was overcome by a hateful rage. He didn't realise how much the Mansoor experience had actually deeply affected him. Up until now, Uncle J thought he had been acting as the big man, on the revenge trail, happily participating in his accustomed criminal activities. Attempting to make large sums of money at a soft target's cost, was all like a game. However, the reality was that it was becoming really personal to Uncle J. Never had he wanted to see a plan through so much, at any cost.

Umar put his arm around Uncle J.

"Are you OK, man?" asked a sympathetic Umar.

"I'll be OK," replied Uncle J. "Just give me a minute to come to terms with eyeballing the enemy close up. It's all hitting home at the same time."

Staring into Uncle J's eyes, this was somewhat alien to Umar. Uncle J has a rich history of front line action up country back home. Uncle J was seen as a brave, fearless leader, so to see Uncle J off his game like this was a first.

After a few minutes of observing, Jez broke the awkward silence.

"Right," barked Jez, "let's get back in the truck, return to the city, and I'll show you the second intended extraction site."

Still not over his stressful meeting with Talib, Uncle J just gazed emptily back at Jez and fractionally nodded his head. They all returned to the truck and set off back to the city.

The journey back to San Francisco was again a silent affair. Jez and Umar were reluctant to open up any discussions, regardless of the subject matter, for fear of an avalanche of fallout reactions from Uncle J. They had never seen Uncle J in this mood, so they considered caution to be their friend.

Once back in the city, Jez took them back to the Fisherman's Wharf district. Parking up adjacent to a sea-fronted marina, the three jumped out of the truck. The Golden Gate bridge spanned majestically and impressively over the bay to their left, the top third of the bridge uprights obscured by a thick layer of low cloud.

"We go this way," said Jez pointing towards a small park on a hillside. The atmosphere was still strained. Uncle J was remaining sombre and silent, Umar was unquestionably nervous about Uncle J, and Jez was just making mental notes of what was going on.

A narrow strip of tarmac weaved its way up the park hillside, garnished by ample neatly mowed grass, with an occasional bizarre spiritual statue breaking up the open spaces.

Once at the top of the hillside, Jez stopped and sat down on the concrete barrier to the left of the tarmac pathway.

"This is where we take Talib," said Jez confidently. "He jogs along this section every evening. He reaches this point between ten and ten-fifteen every night, he's like clockwork."

"It's a bit public, isn't it?" said Uncle J breaking his silence at last.

"Not at ten in the evening," responded Jez instantly. "Tourists rarely frequent this area after dark. There shouldn't be anyone around to act as a witness."

"So, if we do take him here, it's a long way to the truck from here," said an apprehensive Uncle J.

"We take him through these pine trees, then around fifty yards over the hill where we can park the truck. There is another entrance to the park for service vehicles, so we don't have to manhandle him back to the car park."

"Show me," growled Uncle J.

The three walked between the tall pine trees and small shrubs, walking around fifty yards as Jez had indicated. The spot was behind a large bush that acted as ideal cover for the truck.

"I will get the truck stickered up with local authority livery," said Jez. "To make it look like the truck is allowed in the park. If there is anyone around, they will just think we are emptying the bins or something like that."

Uncle J appeared to be reluctant to agree to the plan. His face was screwed up, indicating that he was not impressed with the truck with stickers plan.

"Are you sure this will work?" questioned Uncle J after a short time pondering.

"I'm not saying it's foolproof, but we will only be in the park for ten minutes, tops," responded Jez.

Uncle J paced around nervously, occasionally looking around him, weighing up the surroundings. He just couldn't convince himself that this was a viable and foolproof kidnapping point. It was just too public, in the middle of a popular tourist thoroughfare from the wharf to the Golden Gate bridge; it just didn't make sense.

"I'm sorry," said Uncle J. "I'm just not on board with this. The site is too public. There could be plenty of witnesses around. Dog walkers, joggers, cyclists, tourists, I could go on and on. This is not a good plan and, for the record, I don't like it."

"OK," replied Jez, "let's take a walk up here tonight at ten, and again the following night. Then you can see how this is a good extraction point. Nothing better than seeing for yourself, Uncle J."

Uncle J stood in silence, looking all around him as he pondered.

"Let's do that then," responded Uncle J eventually. "I will reserve judgement until I have seen this place at ten in the evening."

"Great," replied an ecstatic Jez. "So now we need to take you to the planned extraction point for Rayan."

"I thought we are going to kidnap him near that cheesecake place?" quizzed Umar.

"That was just to show you Rayan," replied Jez. "Now Union Square is too public to attempt an extraction, that would be crazy. We are going to take Rayan from the Golden Gate Park. Like Talib, Rayan also jogs in the evening, and Rayan does not like a crowd."

"So how far is this Golden Gate Park?" asked Umar.

"Not far," responded Jez. "Let's go back to the truck and I can show you."

The party ambled back down the hill, along the marina boardwalk and back to the truck. The atmosphere between them was still tetchy, as Uncle J was still suffering from the effects of his visit to the football stadium, plus his doubt with the kidnapping site had deepened his bad mood.

Fifteen minutes later, Jez parked the truck in Golden Gate Park. Not far from the giant, white-framed botanical gardens, Jez walked his guests along a pathway guarded by tall, mature hedges.

"Here we are," said Jez confidently. "What do you think of this site, Uncle J?"

"Well, it's slightly better than the first site," grumbled Uncle J. "At least this place has cover. Are you sure there will be no witnesses when we carry out the kidnapping?"

"You know I can't guarantee that, Uncle J?" responded Jez. "These places have been watched by The Cell for some time now. I'm sure they are not just random, convenient extraction points. I can assure you that The Cell does their research very thoroughly. Mark my words that this extraction point will be totally suitable to carry out our plans. I am very confident of that."

"I just don't get it," replied a confused Uncle J. "The last place I would try and carry out a kidnap attempt is in a public park, and you are telling me that The Cell has planned this based on thorough research. It just doesn't make sense. If this was my plan I would avoid public places like the plague, I would never consider either of these two proposed sites. They are just nonsensical."

"OK," replied Jez. "Again, I hear where you are coming from. We plan to extract Rayan at nine p.m. on the day we execute the extractions, so let's come here tonight at nine p.m., see how the lie of the land is, and then make our way to the other extraction point. Then you will get a feel for the suitability of both extraction points."

Uncle J looked across at Umar and shrugged his shoulders.

"I guess we had better do that," responded a reluctant Uncle J. "Maybe my views may change once I see this place at the time of the intended kidnapping."

Jez blew out a huge sigh of frustration.

"That's great," added Jez. "Let's go and grab some food, I'm starving."

The three associates went off to grab some food. Jez knew of a great place towards the top of Highway One that sold great seafood.

After the food break, Jez took Uncle J and Umar back to their hotel so that they could get some well-earned rest. The reality was that Jez was up to the brimming point with the awkward atmosphere created by Uncle J's mood swings and resistance to the kidnap plans at every given opportunity. Jez just needed a bit of time to himself.

At eight-twenty later that evening, Jez sat in his truck in the hotel car park waiting for his guests to appear from the hotel. Eventually, they both appeared, looking somewhat drowsy.

"Going out at this time," complained Uncle J as he got into the truck.

Jez looked at Umar, who was rolling his eyes at Uncle J's constant complaining.

"Right, let's get this done," said Uncle J.

Jez drove quickly to Golden Gate Park, he parked in the same area as earlier; there were plenty of spaces available as indicated earlier by Jez. The three walked along the pathway to the intended extraction point, standing exactly where they had earlier in the day.

"There you go," stated Jez. "Absolute tranquillity. No witnesses, nobody here, what did I tell you?"

"Indeed," replied an arrogant Uncle J. "Not even a jogger called Rayan."

"Too early," responded Jez as he looked down at his wristwatch. "If you like, we can move over to that shrubbery and watch Rayan jog past. He should be here in ten minutes."

"Yep, let's do that," responded Uncle J instantly.

The group carefully wandered over to the shrubbery and tucked themselves out of sight. Jez maintained a watchful eye on his wristwatch. He really wanted Rayan to be on time. If he was early, late or didn't show up, this would play directly into Uncle J's doubting hands.

At nine o'clock and fifty seconds, a lean jogger came into view in the near distance, plodding along the pathway methodically but swiftly. Jez blew an inner sigh of relief and looked across to Uncle J. Fishing for validation, Jez smiled at Uncle J.

"See, I told you," whispered a relieved Jez. "Nine o'clock and no witnesses."

"I'll give you that," replied a scowling Uncle J. "Maybe you were just lucky this time."

"No way," Jez snapped back. "Like I keep telling you, The Cell takes their research very seriously. I wasn't concerned at all."

Uncle J huffed in the direction of Jez as he watched the jogger run out of view.

"Are you sure that was Rayan?" asked Umar.

"Absolutely," responded Jez. "Didn't you recognise him from the square?"

Umar just shrugged his shoulders and looked at Uncle J.

"If you say it's him, then it must be him," said Uncle J in a more accommodating manner. "You know what, when I was in my hotel room earlier, I had another epiphany. I've been grumpy, moody and against the plans, but that's going to change. From now on I'm going to be more positive, more amenable, more co-operative. This time, I mean it."

"Great news," responded Jez displaying a broad smile. "Now let's go to the second extraction point and show you its suitability."

Thirty minutes later, the three teammates were yet again huddled behind the shrubbery in the Black Point Gardens, waiting for Talib to come jogging by. Sure enough, almost exactly at the hour, a jogger appeared on the pathway in front of them.

Jez smiled and looked over at Uncle J, who was also smiling.

"No witnesses," said Uncle J looking all around. "Not one single person."

"I told you," replied Jez. "Nobody comes up here after dark, not even the locals. It's a social area all right, but only in the daytime."

"So, the plan is to grab him and bring him up here to the truck?" asked Umar.

"Pretty much," responded Jez. "After we've injected him to knock him out."

"No use of a decent cosh then?" asked an expectant Uncle J.

"Caveman!" exclaimed Jez. "No, we don't employ such tactics. The Cell has a great device for administering knock-out drugs. It's simple, effective and there's no risk of putting the target in hospital with concussion or even killing them with a blow from a cosh."

"Terror groups are going soft these days," joked Uncle J.

"Just think about it," continued Jez. "It's a means to an end. We wish Rayan and Talib no harm, they are just pawns, just the bait to get the ransom money. We must keep them alive and well."

"Do I have to wear health and safety apparel when we complete the act of kidnapping?" responded a sarcastic Uncle J. "Safety goggles and a high vis vest?"

"You can wear whatever you like," replied Jez. "As long as we don't get rumbled."

"It's all different these days," grumbled Uncle J. "No brutality, no threatening behaviour, nobody is scared these days, it's all gone soft."

"Maybe it's OK to act in that way in your home country," added Jez. "But over here we do it our way; no coshes, no aggression, no threats, and it works."

"I'm not going to get into a debate about this right now," responded Uncle J. "Each to his own, right?"

"More than one way to skin a goat," added Umar.

"That will do for today," stated Jez. "We can repeat our watch tomorrow if that gives you more confidence in the plan. What do you think?"

"Agreed," snapped Uncle J. "We do this again tomorrow, if it's a repeat outcome, then I am happy."

Jez took Uncle J and Umar back to their hotel. On the journey back Umar needed to get something off his chest.

"So, when is D-Day then, Jez?" asked Umar.

"Friday evening, this week," replied Jez.

"That's in two days' time," coughed Uncle J.

"Well worked out," replied Jez. "I thought you guys would be chomping at the bit to go for it."

"We are," responded Uncle J. "But we've barely watched the targets, we haven't signed off the cabin yet. It all seems a bit rushed to me."

"You have to consider all of the groundwork done by The Cell so far," added Jez. "They have tonnes of hours of reconnaissance, tonnes of research and plenty of meetings."

"Without us," exclaimed Umar.

"Why tie you guys down with all the dull stuff?" continued Jez. "Look, we all know that planning is boring, and the actual doing is more exciting. Why do you want to get involved in the boring parts? I thought you were men of action?"

"We are," replied Uncle J. "But these men of action are a bit in the dark at the moment."

"Nonsense," Jez snapped back. "I've taken you to the extraction sites, I've shown you the targets, I've shown you the cabin, what else is there to show you that will add value?"

Uncle J looked over to Umar who looked back with a confused look.

"I guess you have it covered," replied Uncle J. "I guess I just have to trust you guys."

"Exactly that," said a jubilant Jez. "OK, tomorrow. The plan is to go back to the cabin so that you can take another look around and give it the thumbs up if you are happy."

"This is all starting to feel real," said Uncle J with a buzz to his tone. "Sounds great, I can't wait for all of this to kick off, it's been a long time coming."

"Payback time," added Umar. "For all that prison time you served, Uncle J."

Uncle J nodded firmly in approval at Umar.

"Go and get a good night's sleep, it's going to be another long day tomorrow," said Jez. "Plus, we need to visit the extraction sites again after we have finished at the cabin."

Chapter Ten

That evening, Umar decided he wanted a scotch on the rocks, but he was out of rocks. Returning from the ice-making machine, Umar passed by Uncle J's room. He could hear a mumbled but animated conversation. Wanting to know more, Umar pressed his right ear firmly against Uncle J's door. This was not much use to make out the detail, but Uncle J was definitely in conversation with someone he was not happy with. After a few minutes, Umar lost interest and returned to his room for his awaited refreshment.

In the morning, Umar was sitting in the breakfast room tucking into another feast piled high on his plate. Uncle J arrived at the table looking tired and fed up.

"You OK, Uncle J?" quizzed Umar.

"I'm OK, but I didn't sleep well, to be honest," replied Uncle J.

"Was that because you were on the phone all night?" added Umar.

"What?" barked Uncle J. "Have you been spying on me?"

"No," replied Umar. "I was fetching some ice and I heard you on the phone when I walked past your door. Who were you speaking with?"

"None of your goddamn business!" shouted Uncle J.

A hush gripped the breakfast room, as the other guests taking breakfast were concerned and startled by Uncle J's outburst.

In total embarrassment, Uncle J looked around apologetically at his fellow guests and took a seat with his head bowed down opposite Umar.

"I was just talking to Faisal," replied a calmer Uncle J. "I just wanted to see how things were at home, how the business was running and to catch up on the gossip. That's all."

"But you sounded angry and hostile," continued Umar.

"It's that Khan family," responded Uncle J. "They are trying to muscle in on my patch. I told Faisal how to deal with them and gave him a few names of my contacts who will help stop the Khans in their tracks."

"Oh, I see," replied a now embarrassed Umar. "I thought, well, I thought, well, I don't really know what I thought."

"You idiot," snapped Uncle J. "Maybe this will teach you to keep your nose out of other people's business. You made me cause a scene in here, maybe you should apologise on my behalf."

"I'm sorry, Uncle J," said Umar. "It won't happen again."

Uncle J and Umar finished up their liberal breakfasts and made their way to the car park where Jez awaited them in his truck. It was cabin sign-off day at last.

"Morning, gentlemen," said a cheery Jez as he greeted his guests. "It's a beautiful California morning, the sun is shining, and the weather is warm."

"'Morning," grunted Uncle J. "Let's get this done and dusted, I'm chomping at the bit to get my hands on my cash."

"Easy tiger," replied Jez. "It's our cash, Uncle J."

"Whatever, let's just get going," responded a grumpy Uncle J.

As the truck pulled onto the road, Jez started his briefing.

"When we get to the cabin," added Jez, "I want you to leave no stone unturned. Again, look at every scenario possible and try and consider that whatever has been done to the cabin, will cope with all eventualities. There are two of our team up there right now adding some finishing touches as we speak. The light fitting has been sorted, the locks on all doors have been fully tested, and the latch bolts on the bedroom where the targets will be held have undergone extra testing, so we should be all good to go."

"Who are the two people at the cabin right now?" asked Uncle J. "What are their roles and backgrounds?"

"They are Ramiz and Bahir," responded Jez. "They are trusted members of The Cell. They are well-respected. Ramiz has been serving The Cell for over five years now, Bahir for two years."

"Two years?" growled Uncle J. "He's not even served his apprenticeship yet. Can he be trusted?"

"Completely," said a reassuring Jez. "He has served on many missions to-date, and all have been a resounding success. He's one to keep an eye on for the future of The Cell, as is Ramiz."

"We'll see," said a sceptical Uncle J.

Once outside the city limits, Uncle J and Umar sat back and started to again revere the diverse, breathtaking scenery that astounded them almost around every corner negotiated. The impressive giant pines that rose from the earth like natural skyscrapers. The rolling plains littered with space-age-looking windmills. The jagged mountains reaching for the sky that dominated the horizon. The endless vistas certainly made the journey time pass very quickly.

It seemed like in no time at all, the truck was pulling up to the cabin track entry gate. Jez leapt out of the truck and dealt with the gate. In a flash, the truck had navigated the forest tracks and was pulling up next to the cabin.

Uncle J and Umar could see another jet black pick-up truck already parked outside the cabin.

"Ramiz and Bahir I take it?" said Umar pointing at the black truck.

"Yep," replied Jez. "Let's get you introduced."

The three associates made their way up the gravel path to the cabin entrance. Inside, Ramiz and Bahir were sat at a large dining table drinking chai. They had prepared chai and cakes for the arrival of Jez, Uncle J and Umar.

As Uncle J and Umar walked through the front door of the cabin, Ramiz and Bahir sank into their chairs in terror.

Bahir leaned across to Ramiz.

"It's Uncle J," whispered a terrified Bahir. "Do you think he will recognise us?"

"I hope not," replied an equally frightened Ramiz. "We have these beards now, plus our hair is different. Try and use your baseball cap to obscure your face, but don't make it too obvious."

Jez escorted Uncle J and Umar over to the dining table.

"This is Ramiz," said Jez gesturing his right arm towards Ramiz.

Ramiz stood up and offered a handshake to Uncle J and Umar.

Umar shook Ramiz's hand, but Uncle J remained motionless.

"This is Bahir," added Jez, again gesturing his right arm.

Again, Umar accepted the handshake invitation, but Uncle J remained unmoved.

Uncle J looked closely at Ramiz and Bahir, eyeing them up and down attentively. After a minute or so Uncle J broke his stillness.

"Do I know you two?" asked Uncle J politely.

"I don't think so," replied Ramiz. "You might have seen us in a restaurant or bar in San Francisco maybe?"

"No," snapped Uncle J. "From the homeland, I'm sure I've seen you before."

"Not possible," replied Ramiz quickly. "We are the second generation. I've never been out of the States, I've lived here all of my life, and so has Bahir. So, unless it's a chance passing meeting, I don't see how we could have met before."

Uncle J looked totally puzzled. He was sure the two looked familiar, but he couldn't put his finger on exactly where he had seen them before. After a short pondering moment, Uncle J finally accepted the invitation and shook Ramiz and Bahir's hands. A sense of relief charged the cabin air.

"So, show us what's been done then," said Jez breaking the tense atmosphere.

"Let's have chai and cake first," Ramiz replied. "We've prepared it specially."

"Be rude not to," added an ever-hungry Umar.

The group found themselves a chair and randomly took their positions at the dining table. The awkwardness of the initial greetings had generated an air of mistrust. After all, they were a group of criminals gathered together, who could actually be trusted?

After twenty minutes of sumptuous cake and forced small talk, the group finally rose from the table to start their cabin tour.

Ramiz confidently led the group around the cabin, explaining what work had been completed and why. Not only had the cabin been reinforced, but Ramiz and Bahir had almost totally redecorated the entire inside of the cabin. It looked immaculate.

The party was then taken outside, where Ramiz showed them the generator refurbishment, the work completed to make the outer steel bars on the bedroom window look less obvious, and the pile of freshly cut firewood just in case the weather turned fresh.

The party returned inside the cabin, assembling around the dining table.

"More chai?" asked Bahir.

"Absolutely," replied Jez. "You can never have enough chai."

As Bahir departed to the kitchen area, Uncle J approach the group.

"I'm going for a private stroll, to clear my head," said Uncle J.

"I'll come with you," stated Umar.

"No!" snapped Uncle J. "I want some space, I'll go alone. I love this fresh mountain air, it lifts me."

"If you insist," replied Umar.

Uncle J checked his pockets for a suitable supply of cigarettes and drifted out of the cabin.

As the remaining group members started to sit around the dining table, Jez stared across at Ramiz and nodded his head in the direction of the door. Ramiz understood the gesture immediately.

"I'm going outside for a smoke, I won't be long," said Ramiz.

Ramiz took his coat from the back of the chair and darted out of the front door.

Umar looked around, he was very suspicious of Ramiz's actions, assuming that Ramiz had been sent out to keep an eye on Uncle J, but why?

As the second helping of chai landed on the dining table, Ramiz burst back through the front door, out of breath. He walked into the kitchen, staring at Jez as he did so.

"Are you OK, Ramiz?" asked Jez getting up from the table.

Jez walked into the kitchen where Ramiz looked angrily back at him.

"He gave me the slip," said Ramiz. "No sign of him anywhere. What the hell is he up to?"

"It's probably nothing to worry about," replied Jez. "Maybe he is actually going for a walk to clear his head?"

"That Uncle J is a slippery one," continued Ramiz. "He doesn't know the meaning of the word 'honesty'."

"Calm down," responded Jez. "Where could he go? He has no reason to escape our company or run off, he's on our side. He probably wants some alone time. He is a bit of a loner."

"I don't trust him," added Ramiz. "He's bound to be up to something fishy."

"Relax, Ramiz," said Jez. "Come back through and have some chai. I'm sure Uncle J will return soon."

Jez and Ramiz returned to the dining table to take some more chai. Umar and Bahir were completely baffled by recent events and wondered what on earth was going on.

"Is everything OK?" asked Umar.

"What do you mean?" inquired Jez.

"Well," continued Umar. "All this business with Ramiz apparently going outside to smoke, but in reality, it looks like he went after Uncle J."

"Nonsense," replied Jez. "Why would Ramiz want to go after Uncle J? Ramiz is a heavy smoker, he just wanted to have one, nothing more than that."

"Likely tale," said Umar sarcastically. "I've never come back from a smoke break out of breath like that and comment on Uncle J giving him 'the slip'."

"There could be many reasons for Ramiz's condition," replied Jez. "Maybe he has asthma?"

"Do you think I am some clueless child?" snapped Umar. "I've been around the block a few times, and I know when I smell a rat. Stop messing with me. Either tell me what's going on or keep your mouth shut, because it can't stop spilling lies."

"How dare you talk to me like that!" shouted Jez.

"Stop!" came a loud voice from an open front door.

It was Uncle J, back from his constitutional cleansing walk.

"We are a team, aren't we?" added Uncle J. "Now let's start acting like one. What's all this bickering about?"

"Umar thinks that Ramiz is spying on you," stated Jez. "And that's not actually the case. Ramiz just went for a smoke."

"Who cares?" responded Uncle J. "I've got nothing to hide, he can come and watch me drink another cup of chai if he really wants to. Where's the cake? Give me more cake."

False smiles circled the room. Uncle J had lightened the mood with impeccable timing. The group would hardly benefit from internal bickering so close to D-Day.

As the ambience lightened, the group set about agreeing if the cabin was ready for action as it stood. In no time at all the consensus was that there was no more work required on the cabin.

Having polished off the final cake, Uncle J looked over to Jez and nodded towards the front door. Uncle J was ready for the off.

"We'll head back to the city now," announced Jez. "Can you sort the gate out please, Ramiz?"

"Sure," replied Ramiz. "I'll make sure it's secure. We don't want any nosy tourist getting in the way now."

"Too right," responded Jez.

Uncle J, Umar and Jez made their way out of the cabin, while Ramiz and Bahir secured the cabin. Once Jez had driven his truck out of view, Bahir exploded into a fit of laughter.

"Wow!" shouted Bahir. "Do you ever believe that? Of all people to entertain it had to be Uncle J."

"Unbelievable," replied a shocked Ramiz. "My stomach dropped a foot when I first set eyes on our guests. He had to recognise us, no danger."

"Well, if he did or didn't, he kept his cards close to his chest," responded Bahir. "What do you think he would do if he recognised us?"

"Difficult to predict," said Ramiz. "As we are all involved in criminal activities, he's hardly going to involve the police or the authorities. At the end of the day, we are all on the same team, chasing the same goals. Why would he be concerned about who is or isn't on his side?"

"The first kidnapping episode didn't exactly go to plan, did it?" added Bahir. "Maybe he thinks that is partly down to us? Maybe he holds a grudge? He might do us harm if the circumstances are in his favour?"

"Nonsense," snapped Ramiz. "He would have made more of a scene if he was still angry with us, that's assuming he knows who we are."

"Just a crazy, crazy situation," continued Bahir. "Who would ever have believed it!"

"Let's move on," said Ramiz attempting to change the subject. "We have a final brief tonight at Jez's house. I guess we need to be on our A game now we know who else is involved."

"I didn't even consider that," said a shocked Bahir. "Does that ever change the picture?"

Ramiz and Bahir locked the cabin, double-checking the front door handle before they jumped in their truck.

Five or so miles in front of them, Umar broke the usual silence of the truck.

"Who do you think those guys were, Uncle J, back at the cabin?" quizzed Umar.

"I'm not one hundred percent sure," responded Uncle J. "But they sure look like two of the men that worked alongside me during the first kidnapping. Their names were Mohsin and Khalid. Word on the street was that they were executed by the authorities after an identity parade back home. So, I guess it's just my eyes playing tricks with me. They just looked familiar, that's all."

"What did the authorities do to them?" asked Jez.

"Shot them in cold blood apparently," replied a sombre Uncle J. "They didn't stand a chance. No warning, no trial, no discussion, just smoked them where they stood."

"That can't be right?" challenged Jez. "Surely that's illegal? If you have a situation where people are executed by the authorities without trial, then the only way forward is anarchy?"

"Tell me about it," sighed Uncle J. "It's all rumour, never been confirmed, but those lads just disappeared off the face of the earth, so what else became of them if they weren't executed? They had families, they were active and useful members of Zaheer's little gang. So where did they go?"

"I see," replied Jez. "It all sounds quite brutal."

"It's certainly no picnic," said Uncle J.

"Moving on," added Jez. "We will go to both extraction sites at nine and ten o'clock tonight for a final validation visit. Then, if you are happy to go ahead, we will extract the targets tomorrow night. We have to make haste as we aren't stopping overnight this time, and we have a distance to cover."

"Boom!" shouted a gleeful Umar. "About time."

"Let's see," added a cautious Uncle J. "As long as both targets are where they should be, and on time. And there are no witnesses to spoil our kidnapping theatres."

"Agreed," concluded Jez.

Jez drove Uncle J and Umar back to their hotel for some rest. After dropping his guests off, Jez returned home where Ramiz and Bahir sat in their truck outside Jez's house.

"Come on in, chaps," beckoned Jez.

Just as Ramiz and Bahir were out of their truck almost instantaneously and in unison, three more black saloon car doors opened, and the occupants followed Ramiz and Bahir into Jez's dwelling.

There appeared to be around four men in each car, dressed in similar dark suits and grey shirts.

Later that evening, Jez had collected Uncle J and Umar from their hotel a little earlier. Jez wanted to take them to a restaurant that he frequented on Pier thirty-nine. As it was 'kidnap-eve', Jez wanted to wine and dine his companions in a reputable restaurant. Before they even arrived at the restaurant, Jez lay the law down firmly. While they were in the restaurant, there was to be no talk of their plans for the next day. Risks of the plans being overheard and uncovered at this late stage were high, so lips had to remain sealed concerning the plans.

This embargo made the meal drag on painfully slowly. The three had little in common outside of the operation, and Uncle J and Umar were completely uninterested in the accomplishments of the San Francisco 49'ers.

Jez was totally reluctant to discuss Uncle J's and Umar's lives back home, suspecting that prison life might crop up in conversation, again a subject matter not appropriate for a fine restaurant.

As the service was good, the delicious fare was gorged in no time. Both Uncle J and Umar were wishing time away, as they just wanted to get the final observations done and dusted, so they could sleep. Then it would be D-Day.

With the restaurant ordeal behind them, the three made their way to the Golden Gate Park car park. From there, they once again took their places and stooped down in a mature shrubbery.

It was nine o'clock and no sign of the target jogger. Uncle J looked over to Umar and rolled his eyes in disappointment.

"Just wait," whispered Jez. "He'll be here shortly."

Sure enough, at one minute and thirty seconds past nine, the expected athlete appeared in front of them. He was carrying a small bottle of water.

The trio watched in silence as the jogger came and went.

"Satisfied?" asked Jez looking directly at Uncle J.

"I am," replied a happy and smiling Uncle J. "These people are boring. They do the same thing, at the same time every night. What are they? Robots?"

Umar and Jez laughed at Uncle J's uneducated analysis of San Francisco life.

"Let's get over to the marina car park now," said Jez. "We are good for time."

The three gang members returned to their vehicle. Jez drove them across to the seafront and the marina car park. From there, they climbed the hillside to where they took up their observation positions.

Again, as if by clockwork, the target athlete appeared at ten o'clock, almost precisely. Uncle J could not contain his excitement. It looks like The Cell had done an exemplary job. The research was spot on. The sites were free from any potential witnesses. The targets looked fit but looked slightly frail in build, which would make them easy to overpower.

Uncle J turned to Jez.

"Let's have a whiskey before we retire," demanded Uncle J. "Take us to a bar somewhere not too busy."

"OK," replied a jolly Jez. "I know a bar on one of the piers."

Fifteen minutes later, Jez parked the truck in one of the side streets off the main drag. Walking towards the sea, Umar spotted a subtly lit tower on top of the hill overlooking the bay.

"What is that place?" asked Umar pointing at the tower.

"Coit Tower," replied Jez. "It's cool up there. It's a favourite with tourists. You can go up the tower and enjoy fantastic views of the bay. If you are lucky, some days you can spot wild parrots flying around."

"Cool," responded Umar. "Maybe you can take us there when this is all over?"

"Why not," said Jez.

The group wandered across the main thoroughfare into the chosen bar. Sitting at the bar on stools, Jez ordered a round of double whiskeys. Once all three had a full tumbler in front of them, Jez grabbed his glass and raised it.

"Success," said a confident Jez.

Uncle J and Umar also raised their glasses, chinking them together as they collectively toasted for success.

An hour later, the three associates had staggered back to Jez's truck. Once inside, Jez began to brief them.

"OK," started Jez. "Tomorrow is the day that we've all been working towards. There will be two cars tomorrow as we are taking out the targets separately. Uncle J, you will come with me and Bahir to the Golden Gate Park. We need to be parked up by eight-forty-five p.m. latest. At nine o'clock or thereabouts, we will jump the target. Bahir will administer the injection as he's well-trained and experienced in this field. Once we have the target down, we will cover the target's head with a hood and take him over to the truck which I will bring as close to the extraction point as I can."

"So that means Bahir and I will carry out the jump?" interrupted Uncle J.

"Exactly," replied Jez. "Once we have the target in the truck, we will drive to the cabin."

"Hang on," butted in Uncle J. "What about Umar and the second target?"

"That's not your task," continued Jez. "You worry about your extraction, Umar will carry out the second extraction with Ramiz. We have modified Ramiz's truck to look like a refuse collection vehicle so that Ramiz can drive in the park. Ramiz will administer the injection as he is also skilled in this tactic. Once they have extracted their target, they will follow the same route to the cabin and meet up with us. We will then contain the captives in the secure room and then focus on the ransom demands."

"And what exactly are the demands?" asked Uncle J. "And who will be issuing the demands?"

"Leave that to The Cell," replied Jez firmly. "They have this all in hand. They have the contact number and the equipment to issue the demands. Any communication will be untraceable."

"Yet again, this is feeling less and less like my project," said an irate Uncle J. "The Cell might as well do the lot and take all the ransom money for all I care."

"Don't start, Uncle J," replied Jez. "There is no need for this type of reaction. The Cell has masses of experience in these matters. Nothing has gone wrong to-date, you have to start trusting them, they are on your side. You wouldn't be sitting here in this strong position without them. Just let go of this negative attitude."

"It's very hard," mumbled Uncle J. "I am a hero back home, in my gang, I call the shots. I am respected, and revered. I have hard conflict experience on the front line. I'm just not used to being controlled."

"So you keep telling me, however, you are being helped, not controlled," said a reassuring Jez. "We are on the threshold of getting you the revenge that you have yearned for years. To be honest, I really know that back home you are a hero, as you've told me so many times now."

Uncle J stared out of the window in contempt. He was sick and tired of absolutely everything. This whole revenge journey had been peculiar. From the outset, he had never felt like he had the reins. So many twists, turns and surprises. Plus, Jez clearly had zero respect for Uncle J's reputation. Uncle J was not happy.

"OK," said Uncle J "Let's see what happens."

"That's better," replied a more confident Jez.

"What about contingency plans?" drummed up Umar. "What happens if things don't go to plan? What then?"

"Good point," responded Jez. "If we have any problems with either extraction, there are backup teams at both sites. They are primed to move in at a moment's notice."

"Backup teams?" shouted an angry Uncle J. "You haven't mentioned this before. Who are these people that make up the backup team? Can they be trusted? Yet again, you drop another surprise. You are just making fun of me now."

"Uncle J," snapped Jez. "I'm telling you now as I suspected exactly this response. If I would have told you earlier, you would have insisted on looking at all of their CV's, and interviewing them individually, giving them a medical, and so on. Look, this is the way The Cell operates now. They have trusted employees and proven templates, and they work. Like I said before, just let go and trust your team, they will come through for you."

Uncle J returned to silently staring out of the window.

"What if there are witnesses at any of the sites?" added Umar. "What then?"

"If the targets are in the extraction zone and there are witnesses," responded Jez. "Then we pull the plug and try again the following evening. We can't afford witnesses. There should be nobody around at the extraction times. The Cell has chosen these extraction sites for good reason, including the risk of potential witnesses."

"Pull the plug?" snarled Umar. "We could be here for six months if dog walkers or tourists keep getting in the way."

"Did you see anybody hanging around tonight or last night?" asked Jez.

A silence fell over the truck.

"We have the upper hand physically over both targets," continued Jez. "Plus, we have the element of surprise. It's not like they have been in training to resist. Come on, guys, we are all good to go now, agreed?"

Uncle J looked over at Umar with a look of frustration. He was backed into a corner. He was in a foreign land and up to his armpits in a revenge plan that was way out of his control. As far as he could make out, Uncle J had two choices right now. Go with the plan or ship off back home. If he went home, there was no guarantee that The Cell would continue their protection, leaving Uncle J exposed and vulnerable to the authorities. How did he get himself into this position?

"Just be honest with me, Jez," said a humble Uncle J. "Why now? Why tell us about the details of the plan tonight? Why not sooner? It's all very much last minute. Umar and I feel unprepared."

"Say that again," bellowed Umar from the back seat of the vehicle.

"You keep telling me about the templates," continued Uncle J. "You keep telling me how good The Cell is, but why leave two of the main protagonists in the dark until the last minute? That's not very professional, is it?"

"I appreciate where you are coming from," replied Jez, "But to be totally brutal, Ramiz and Bahir are carrying out the extractions, you and Umar are just there to assist. As I've said time and time again before, you have been to both extraction sites twice, you are familiar with the cabin, and you have already met Ramiz and Bahir, what is there to be cautious of? What is there to complain about regarding the timing of the final brief?"

"So," responded Uncle J. "What you are basically saying, is that Umar and I are just ballast. Just here for the ride, support acts."

"Not at all," replied a frustrated Jez. "Valued and active members of the team, that's how I would describe you."

"Well, it doesn't feel like it," growled Uncle J.

"At the end of the day, it's your call, Uncle J," said Jez. "If you are so unhappy, then you have the option to call all of this off and call it a day. Or go forward with confidence, knowing that the plan is well-prepared with people in place to execute the plan successfully. Your choice."

"What have we got to lose?" said Umar as he broke into a yawn.

"Take me to the hotel," ordered Uncle J.

Jez cranked the engine and drove Uncle J and Umar back to the hotel. Not for the first time, not a word was said during the short journey.

Pulling up to the hotel car park, Jez turned off the ignition.

"Uncle J," said Jez calmly. "I have so much respect for you, as a man and as a warrior. I am proud to be on your team, working alongside a living legend. I know you are out of your comfort zone. All I can say is that the whole team and The Cell are behind you and want this to work out for you. Just trust in us, we are all pulling in the same direction."

"Talk is cheap, my friend," snapped Uncle J. "For all I know you could be spinning me a pile of garbage. Give me a good reason why I should trust you or your precious 'new' Cell?"

"Think about it," demanded Jez. "How come your prison hearing went so smoothly? How do you think your papers survived the rigours of two seasoned immigration officers? How do you think you have been able to wander freely around San Francisco without a single issue? I will tell you. The Cell has been looking out for you, all the way."

Uncle J looked over again at Umar.

"Well," replied Uncle J, "when you say it like that, I guess you are right. Looking at the bigger picture, we have managed to get over here without a hitch. Plus, we have enjoyed free movement in San Francisco. Even the hotel breakfasts have been divine."

"So, are you on board? Are we on?" asked Jez.

"Screw it, let's go for it!" yelled a jubilant Uncle J.

Chapter Eleven

Both Uncle J and Umar had restless nights. Thoughts of the excitement of the following day's activities amongst other factors was just overwhelming. Uncle J spent a considerable part of the night mentally going through his turbulent relationship with Jez since he had been in the States, while pondering his own role and influences in the bigger picture. As time had elapsed in the States, Uncle J was concerned about his loss of control of planned events. He was also nervous about how the participants of the extraction team were not completely transparent and discussed only at the last minute. In addition, Uncle J was suspicious as to how The Cell had chosen the cabin location, questioning repeatedly why the proposed site for holding the kidnap targets was so far from San Francisco. Was there a need to have such a distant and isolated location? Surely there were safe houses closer to the city? But, at the end of the day, Uncle J was confident that whatever the outcome, he would pull through as he was an experienced and slippery survivor. He may come across as a non-intellectual, a bit of a hot-head, knee-jerking his way through off-the-cuff criminal activities for personal gain, however, there was another side to Uncle J that was not revealed to his associates or partners in crime. A side that contained thoughts and actions for self-preservation, and this particular kidnapping plan was no exception.

Umar on the other hand was absorbed in running through each phase of the next day's planned activity step by step in his head. Mentally, he pictured himself from the drive from the hotel to the extraction site. He then moved on to the extraction itself, followed by the long drive to the cabin. Never questioning any phase or validity of the overall plan. In his opinion, it was deemed to be a simplistic and achievable kidnapping proposal, and never questioned the selection of the cabin as a prisoner-holding base. It appeared to be well away from the tourist trails.

Eventually, fatigue took over, with both Uncle J and Umar dropping into a deep sleep.

Several hours later, the morning sun shone through a narrow crack in Uncle J's curtains, casting a strong, thin line of piercing sunlight across Uncle J's face, raising him from his sleep. Uncle J sat up, yawned, and reached across to his mobile phone to establish the time of day. It was nine in the morning and there was still time for breakfast.

Uncle J quickly readied himself and rushed to the hotel breakfast room.

Sat in the far corner of the breakfast room, a weary-looking Umar was tucking into a large slice of buttered toast. Picking up a bowl of cereal, Uncle J wandered over and sat alongside his fellow countryman.

"Today's the day," whispered an excited Uncle J.

"It sure is," replied a somewhat deflated Umar.

"What's wrong with you?" asked a concerned Uncle J, expecting Umar to be full of energy and enthusiasm.

"I barely slept last night," replied Umar. "I just couldn't stop thinking about today's events."

"Me neither," responded Uncle J taking another mouthful of cereal.

"I have no concerns," continued Umar, "I was just full of apprehension. I kept running through my perceived view of planned events and how they would pan out."

"Me too," said Uncle J.

"I think we have a great plan, a great team and a great place to hold our prisoners while we wait for the ransom money." added Umar.

"I agree somewhat," responded Uncle J. "But I'm still concerned about the ransom part of the plan. We both have no idea how The Cell is going to approach this. I feel completely in the dark and at the mercy of The Cell."

"But is that an issue?" asked Umar. "At the end of the day, if we line our pockets with dollars, who cares who asked who for the ransom, as long as we get our share of the spoils."

"I appreciate that," replied Uncle J. "However, we've had no input into this part of the plan. Jez has been very defensive when we try to raise the subject matter. It all seems a bit strange that we are being kept at arm's length. There is even a possibility that we leave with nothing."

"I get that," added Umar. "But we are on their turf, they know how things work over here. It must be different to how we do things back home. Back home, life is cheap, plus violent or mortal actions are easy to carry out, with little comeback. Over here, we are going to kidnap people who are well-known and respected members of their community. If we blast away at them with revolvers there will be consequences. It's not the wild west here anymore. We need to tread carefully. The Cell knows how to get what they want, so I guess we just need to trust in them."

Again, Uncle J faced a rational defence of the plans laid down by The Cell. This time, not from Jez but from one of his own. So, the plan in its entirety could be right after all.

"OK," said Uncle J after yet another pause. "I finally agree. Let's go with what we have. I'm sure you are right. Just don't judge me for being cautious."

Umar picked up his glass charged with fresh orange juice and offered it towards Uncle J.

"Here's to a great day," announced Umar as he and Uncle J touched glasses.

"Here's to the next chapter of a richer life," replied Uncle J with a broad smile on his face.

"So, how are we going to kill time today?" asked Umar. "We don't get picked up by Jez and company until eight-fifteen this evening. Has Jez laid anything on?"

"Jez has told me to be ready for collection at eight-fifteen this evening, nothing more," responded Uncle J. "Do you fancy doing anything for a few hours?"

"I know I said I'd like to go after all the business is done," replied an optimistic Umar. "But I'd really like to go and take a look at Coit Tower."

"Fine with me," replied Uncle J. "Let's finish breakfast and take a cab up there."

The pair finished their breakfast and then made their way by cab up to Coit Tower. The whole area had a peaceful tranquillity about it, which was much needed considering the stress that would be facing them later in the evening. The tower was at the top of a hill surrounded by soaring, broad trees. Uncle J and Umar paid scant attention to the ground floor historic displays. They were just itching to get in the lift to the top of the tower to take in the expectant fabulous views.

Once at the top of the tower, their hopes were not dashed in the slightest. The panoramic views of the bay were breathtaking. To their left, the impressive Golden Gate traversed majestically across the sea. To their right, the Oakland Bridge extended over the sea in an equally impressive manner. In front of them, they could make out the piers that made up Fisherman's Wharf, with the imposing outline of Alcatraz Island rising from the water in front of them.

"Wow!" exclaimed Umar. "Have you ever seen a view like this?"

"I haven't," replied an impressed Uncle J. "But some of the views from the Northern mountains back home take some beating."

"Yeah, but in a different way," argued Umar. "This has it all. There is no seascape in the mountains back home."

"You idiot," laughed Uncle J. "But I agree, this is a one-in-a-million view fit for a millionaire."

"And that will be us later," added a jubilant Umar.

Uncle J looked back at Umar with a wry smile.

"Let's just wait and see," said a sceptical Uncle J.

Uncle J and Umar spent the best part of an hour wandering the outer circumference of the viewing area, occasionally taking photos on their mobile phones as they roamed around. The tower along with its idyllic vistas seemed to have a magnetic hold on them.

Eventually, the pair returned to terra firma where they asked one of the tower patrons to call them a cab. Once in the cab, almost immediately, the cab driver quickly deduced that Uncle J and Umar were in the tourist mould. To stretch the fare, the cab driver talked them into a quick spin down Lombard Street on the way back to the hotel.

Uncle J and Umar's scepticism was soon overridden by surprise, as they proceeded down the tight, criss-cross novelty street on the hillside. Neither had ever driven down such a bizarre street.

Back at the hotel and sipping IPA at the hotel bar, the morning excursion was clearly a tonic for Uncle J and Umar. Spirits were high, the mood was positive and the non-stop conversation engaging, with not a single hint of nerves.

Uncle J and Umar drank three pints of IPA, devoured a giant burger and French fries and then returned to their respective rooms to ready themselves for the evening's affairs.

At seven forty-five p.m. as agreed, Uncle J and Umar met in the hotel bar for some last minute Dutch courage. Both selected a large scotch on the rocks for their tipple. As their glasses gently collided, toasting for a successful outcome, there were definitely signs of nerves etched across both of their faces. This was it. From the humble seed planted in a prison cafeteria, Uncle J and Umar found themselves on the threshold of fulfilling their criminal visions.

At ten past eight p.m., a sinister Jez appeared in the bar dressed in dark clothing.

"Ready?" asked Jez. "The cars are waiting in the car park, let's do this."

Uncle J and Umar gulped back the remaining scotch and leapt off their bar stools. The three comrades then strode confidently through the hotel reception area and into the car park, where two black pick-up trucks awaited them.

Uncle J followed Jez to his truck, while Umar, after a small embrace with Uncle J was led to the second waiting truck.

Bahir sat in the front seat of Jez's truck.

"You can move," demanded Uncle J aggressively.

Jez nodded his head at Bahir, gesturing towards the back seat of the truck. Bahir instantly jumped out of the truck and into the rear seat.

"How do you feel?" asked Jez.

"Nervous," replied a jittery Uncle J. "My heart is beating in my throat right now."

"No need for all of that," said a reassuring Jez. "We are all ready to go. Nerves are for the unprepared."

Uncle J nodded, then immediately averted his gaze out of the side window of the vehicle. They remained in total silence for the journey to Golden Gate Park. Once at the park, Jez pulled up in the same parking spot as the previous night, it was eight-fifty-three p.m..

"We will wait here until eight-fifty-five p.m.," commanded Jez.

"What if he's early?" asked a nervous Uncle J.

"He won't be," replied Jez with full confidence.

"How do you know?" quizzed Uncle J.

"We've been watching Rayan for weeks; he's never here before nine p.m.."

"That's just weird," replied Uncle J. "Not even once?"

"Never," snapped Jez.

"I find that hard to believe," added Uncle J. "What if he's on his game and gunning for a record time? What if he left the house early? What if he misread the time?"

"Don't ask me," responded an irritated Jez. "He's just always here at nine p.m., end of, and I've no idea how he just is. That's what the surveillance data tells us as well."

"Surveillance data, my backside," snorted Uncle J. "It just doesn't sound like the real world to me."

Still not satisfied, Uncle J reluctantly backed away from his verbal challenge and began to look around for parked cars, dog walkers or tourists that may prevent the extraction from going ahead. However, the coast was completely clear. Not a single car was parked and not a single person was in the proximity of the extraction site. This amazed Uncle J as during the two previous visits, at least there were other cars randomly parked up.

Eight-fifty-five p.m. arrived.

"Right, let's go," said a confident Jez. "Have you got the syringe, Bahir?"

"Yep," answered Bahir flashing a plastic-capped syringe back at Jez.

The three bandits jumped out of the truck and made their way to the shrubbery that was to act as their cover. They then ducked down into the bushes and waited for their target to enter the arena.

Uncle J's heart was beating like a big bass drum. A nervous sweat had formed on his brow, which he quickly wiped away using his sleeve.

Jez maintained a watch on his mobile phone screen, whispering to notify his companions as the minutes progressed.

At one minute past nine o'clock, Rayan jogged into the park. He could be seen on the dimly lit tarmacked pathway, running towards their position, getting ever closer.

As Rayan was within twenty yards of the shrubbery, Jez shouted,

"Now!"

Hearing the command, Bahir jumped over to Uncle J and sunk the syringe needle accurately into Uncle J's neck. Momentarily, Uncle J looked at Bahir with an angry look of disbelief in his eye, before falling in a heap to the ground.

"Excellent," said a joyous Jez. "Very well executed I must say."

"Thank you, sir," replied a proud Bahir.

Just as Uncle J's ample torso was hitting the ground, Rayan had trotted over to their position.

"Is it done?" asked Rayan.

"Like clockwork," replied Jez. "No resistance, he didn't suspect a thing. Like I said before, he's a few sandwiches short of a picnic. Come on then, help me to get him into the truck, we've got a long drive ahead of us."

Jez, Bahir, and Rayan then struggled to pick Uncle J up from the floor, but eventually, after a humungous struggle, they managed to bundle him into the load space of the parked truck. The load space cover was then slid back into place to conceal Uncle J's presence.

Once Jez was sitting in the front seat of his truck, he reached over to the glove compartment, he opened it and grabbed a radio that was stashed inside. Jez then switched on the radio.

"Park one to base, over," said Jez into the radio.

"Base receiving, over," came the response.

"Phase One complete," continued Jez. "Target down, in the truck and neutralised, over."

"Well done Park one," came the response. "We will notify the police to open up that area of the park and allow free movement. Proceed to the cabin without delay, reception party will be notified. Maintain contact and report progress regularly, over."

"Will do, over and out," added Jez.

Jez handed the radio over to Rayan who was now sitting in the passenger seat of the truck.

"Thanks," said Rayan. "I'm glad that's over, he could have been a handful if things had gone wrong. He's a big unit."

"Thanks to Bahir everything went to plan," replied Jez. "Never in doubt."

Jez looked over to the back seat, smiled at Bahir and offered his hand for a high five.

Bahir slapped the offered hand in elation.

"Just doing my job," said a smug Bahir.

"Let's get going," said Jez starting the truck engine. "The sooner we get to the cabin and get rid of our cargo, the better. But first I am going to cuff Uncle J, just in case. Come and help me, Bahir, I want to cuff Uncle J's wrists and ankles."

"No problem," said Rayan.

Jez and Rayan walked to the rear of the truck, slid open the load space cover and fitted handcuffs to Uncle J's wrists and ankles.

Once their load was secure, the truck pulled away gently, heading for the park exit and the highway.

Umar and Ramiz were parked at the marina car park a few miles away from Golden Gate Park. As their extraction was to be at ten o'clock, they had stopped off on the way and picked up a couple of take away coffees. There were several other cars parked up, plus every once in a while a dog walker would pass by.

"Are we still going ahead with all these people about?" asked a concerned Umar.

"Sure," replied Ramiz. "It's only nine-thirty p.m. The area will clear soon, you will see."

"How can you say that with any confidence?" quizzed a persistent Umar, who was now starting to follow Uncle J's thought train of suspicion.

"Like Jez has said before," replied Ramiz. "The Cell has selected this site based on data accrued over some time. Don't ask me why, but this area becomes quiet after nine-thirty p.m."

"Based on data," added Umar. "Data is cold, factual numbers, we are talking about people going about their business, real life. You can't guarantee that no random tourist or local will turn up tonight, maybe because they have a party to go to, or they feel like going for a jog, or anything else random."

"The thing with cold numbers is that they don't lie," replied an irritated Ramiz. "The Cell has looked at many sites and this one fills the criteria. That's all I can tell you."

"Did you ever come here on a surveillance exercise?" asked Umar.

"I didn't," responded Ramiz. "I was never asked."

"So, you can't confirm if you would see anyone here at ten o'clock?" added Umar.

"No, I can't confirm that," snapped Ramiz. "As I said, this site has been chosen for good reason by the powers that be."

Umar sat back in his seat. Seeing dog walkers and parked cars, he was not convinced that the extraction should go ahead. Uncle J had nagged Umar time and time again about the frailties in the plan, and this appeared to be a frailty.

"It's ten-to-ten now," said Ramiz breaking the tension. "I will drive the truck up to the holding position, ready for the extraction."

"If you are completely sure," replied Umar with a hint of scepticism in his voice.

Ramiz drove around the corner to a gate locked with a combination padlock. Ramiz got out of the truck, fumbled around with the lock for a short time and then opened the gate. Ramiz then drove the truck off the tarmac path and onto the grass to the top of the small hill. Ramiz parked the truck in the same position as the previous night's visit.

"We can get out now," commanded Ramiz as he removed a syringe from his coat pocket. "Make sure you stay low in the bushes."

"OK," replied Umar.

As the pair were lying in wait, Umar started to look around for potential witnesses. To his surprise, there was nobody at all, the place was void of people.

At almost exactly ten o'clock, Ramiz nudged Umar and pointed to his left. Coming out of the darkness was the figure of a jogger coming up the hill. With the target around thirty yards away, Ramiz turned towards Umar.

"Sorry, old boy," said Ramiz as he raised his hand to administer the needle into Umar's neck.

Umar was prepared. He had smelt a rat, so he blocked Ramiz's arm preventing the needle from reaching its target. As Ramiz fell towards Umar, Umar landed a headbutt on Ramiz's head. Unfortunately, it was more of a glancing blow, not a full and effective contact. The pair then wrapped themselves up in a violent struggle, each trying to land punches as they rolled around in the bushes.

By now, Talib had arrived on the scene. Greeted with an unexpected fight, Talib looked around for a weapon to help Ramiz with his struggle.

"Take this," said Ramiz throwing the syringe on the floor close to Talib, with a sense of desperation in his voice.

Talib took the syringe in his hand. He was unable to do much as the pair in front of him were rolling around, entangled in a violent struggle. Then, by chance, Ramiz managed to position himself on top of Umar, holding both of his arms firmly on the soil.

"Now," shouted Ramiz.

Talib seized the moment and plunged the needle awkwardly into Umar's neck and pressed the plunger. As the syringe fell away, a stream of blood flowed from the wound.

Umar continued to kick and struggle for five or so seconds, but gradually the resistance subsided as Umar passed out.

Ramiz and Talib waited for a few moments before they moved, just to make sure that Umar was out cold. Both were panting desperately for breath.

"What happened?" asked Talib.

"He rumbled me at the last minute," responded Ramiz. "He blocked me off, then started fighting back."

"At least we managed to get the job done between us," panted Talib.

"Thank goodness you were here," exclaimed Ramiz. "Let's get him in the truck and out of sight. Boy, do I need a drink right now."

Ramiz and Talib picked up Umar, bundled him into the truck loadspace, and fitted the load space cover. Once happy with the security of their consignment, they jumped inside the truck.

Once inside, Ramiz opened the glove compartment, grabbed the stowed radio, and switched it on.

"Park two to base, over," said Ramiz into the radio.

After a short period, the radio crackled into life.

"Base receiving, over," came the response.

"Mission complete, package on board safely, over," said Ramiz confidently.

"Well done, Park two," came the response. "We will notify the police to open up that area of the park and allow free movement. Proceed to the cabin without delay, reception party has been notified. Maintain contact and report progress regularly, over."

"Will do, over and out," added Ramiz.

Ramiz sank back into the driver's seat and looked across at Talib.

"I didn't need that," gasped Ramiz. "He sure put up a fight, I'm so glad that his headbutt didn't hit the spot."

"He headbutted you?" asked an astonished Talib.

"Yep," replied Ramiz pointing out a rising bump on his upper forehead. "I would have bet a lot of money that Uncle J would be the difficult customer. Just goes to show. I hope Jez and Bahir managed to capture Uncle J without a problem like this.

"Why don't you give him a ring and find out?" asked Talib.

"I think I will," replied Ramiz. "But let's get out of this park first."

Ramiz cranked over the truck engine and drove the truck down the hill and through the open gate. There were still police officers tidying up the tape and barriers that had closed off the area for the hillside antics. One police officer waved at Ramiz as he guided the truck back to the marina car park.

Once parked up, Ramiz used the truck's in-car system to dial up Jez on loudspeaker.

After three rings Jez picked up the call.

"Ramiz," exclaimed Jez. "All safe and sound, I trust?"

"Just about," replied Ramiz. "Umar didn't go quietly, put up a proper fight."

"Really," reacted a surprised Jez. "What went down then?"

Ramiz went on to explain in detail the events of the struggle with Talib adding to the story where he saw fit.

"Uncle J went down like a sloppy pussy cat," added Jez once Ramiz and Talib had finished their reporting. "He didn't suspect a thing. Like taking candy from a child."

"So, where are you now?" asked Ramiz.

We are on the freeway, about ten minutes outside the city limits," responded Jez. "Are you en route yet?"

"Not yet," replied Ramiz. "We are still in the marina car park. I just need to get myself together first before we set off."

"I get that," responded Jez. "Don't take too long though. The drugs will keep Umar out for about six hours. Do you have him restrained?"

"No," said Ramiz with a slight panic in his tone. "Shall I cuff him?"

"We have Uncle J cuffed, wrists and ankles," added Jez. "You never know how long these drugs really last."

"OK," replied Ramiz. "I'll go and cuff him now with Talib."

Ramiz ended the call and with Talib promptly secured handcuffs to Umar as instructed by Jez. This seemed to calm the pair down, knowing that their companion was suitably contained should he awake from his slumber.

A few minutes later, with adrenalin still running, Ramiz steered the truck out of the marina car park and set off for the cabin.

City traffic wasn't too heavy, so in no time they were out of the city limits and freely speeding down the freeway. They had pretty much a three-hour drive in front of them if they didn't stop on the way. Ramiz felt nervous at the wheel. Knowing that he had an actual person in the load space, he was concerned that any wrong moves could have consequences for his unwilling passenger. This put unwanted and additional pressure on Ramiz.

An hour into the journey, the centre console lit up. It was Jez on the phone, checking on Ramiz's progress, and making sure they were problem free. Ramiz reported their approximate position to Jez, also assuring that the journey was going well. This check was repeated an hour later by Jez.

"Does he not trust you?" asked Talib following Jez's second phone call.

"Yes, he does," replied Ramiz confidently. "He's just doing a professional job, making sure we are OK. It's not a question of trust, it's just teamwork."

"Oh, I see," replied Talib. "So, what happens when we get to the cabin?"

"I'm not one hundred percent sure," responded Ramiz. "I think some people are going to be there from the authorities. I've not been told officially, but that's what Bahir overheard."

"This whole business is all very weird for me," continued Talib. "Being told to go on a jog through the park three nights running, as close to ten o'clock as I could is a very strange request."

"Is that all they told you to do?" asked Ramiz.

"They?" replied Talib. "I was told that I needed to play my part in some kind of sting operation. That someone would be set up, and I was to help the person on the scene load the victim into the truck. Then accompany you to a cabin in Yosemite National Park where all would be revealed and make sense."

"When I say 'they'," added Ramiz, "I am referring to The Cell."

"The Cell?" quizzed a slightly confused Talib.

"You know, The Cell," continued Ramiz. "The operation that you are a high-ranking member of. A terror organisation that kidnaps people and fights the cause in the disputed lands back home."

"I haven't got a clue what you are on about," replied a totally confused Talib.

"So, who was it that gave you the instructions to go jogging at specific times then?" asked Ramiz.

My father, Mansoor," replied Talib. "I spoke with my brother, Rayan. He was also asked to go running, but in Golden Gate Park and at an earlier time."

"So, you don't really know what you are involved in?" quizzed Ramiz.

"Not completely," said Talib. "Maybe it's something to do with my father's kidnapping a few years ago. He was taken up north back home by some bandits and held as a hostage for eight months or so I think. They released him, but that's about all I know. He doesn't like to talk about his experience."

"Wow!" exclaimed Ramiz. "Is this getting weird or what!"

"What do you mean, weird?" asked Talib.

"Can I trust you?" asked Ramiz. "This is a really big deal to me."

"Implicitly," responded Talib immediately.

"Where do I start?" continued Ramiz. "So, you are not going to believe me, plus you might be angry with me, to begin with."

"Why would I be angry?" questioned Talib. "We've only just met."

"Let me explain," added Ramiz. "In my past, a past that I am not proud of, I was a small time street bandit back home. I used to pick pockets and commit petty robberies. Then I was introduced to this wanna-be big-time crook called Zaheer. He got me on board with this kidnap plan that had a big payout attached to it. Some guy who worked in Port Qasim, he might have even run the show."

"That's my father!" exclaimed Talib.

"It looks that way," continued Ramiz. "Anyhow, I was part of the gang. To cut a long story short, after the hostage release, our gang was hunted down by the authorities. I was captured and taken to the main police station, where I had to take part in an identity parade. I didn't know who was watching, as they were behind a two-way mirror. Bahir was also in that line up. After we were led out of the room, some guy dressed in a fancy uniform told Bahir and me to remain behind. We were led out into the yard where another police dude was waiting with a gun. I thought I was going to be executed, along with Bahir. But instead, the police dude shot off two rounds into the air, not even aiming at us."

"Strange?" interrupted Talib.

"Strange indeed," added Ramiz. "Then we were taken inside to a big posh office. We were given cigarettes and chai. I was confused. Here we were, guilty bandits, but these police guys were treating us so kindly. Almost too kindly. After a short time, some more people came into the office with papers. We were then given an ultimatum. Apparently, we had been selected to take part in a rehabilitation trial. The authorities were sick and tired of arresting the same petty criminals, which was filling the prison system to bursting point. They selected Bahir and me to take part in an experiment. We were kind of adopted by a well-to-do family, given jobs, new clothes, and all that. We even had our own bedrooms in a posh house. It was great at first. But Bahir and I aren't cut out for that style of life. We are streetwise and rise to a challenge. We don't want the responsibility of turning up to work every day. Then one day, a dude at work offered Bahir and me the chance to come over to the States and work for The Cell. We both jumped at the chance of fancy travel, but in particular, working with The Cell again. So, we took up the offer and here I am."

"That is incredible," said an astonished Talib. "It's a small world. What are the chances of this random meeting?"

"Well, is it a random meeting?" continued Ramiz. "I just don't think it's random. I think the whole thing is a set up, maybe to entrap Uncle J?"

"Who's Uncle J?" asked Talib.

"He's the person that your brother jogged past earlier," replied Ramiz. "I suspect Uncle J is the main reason for this charade."

"Charade?" quizzed Talib.

Yes, charade," responded Ramiz. "I think it's a sting operation to capture Uncle J and any of his associates. He's a wanted man. He's got brutal form that goes back a long way. Now I know you are not a member of The Cell, it's starting to make sense."

"This is just so confusing," said Talib. "Why would my father want me to get involved in this? I have a family. Why would he place me in such danger?"

"To be fair," replied Ramiz. "You weren't in much danger. Uncle J and Umar were unarmed, plus backup crews were watching on, just in case. You were pretty safe."

"I just wonder why he didn't tell me what was going on," said a dejected Talib.

"If you'd have known, would you have agreed to participate?" asked Ramiz.

"Absolutely not," responded Talib assertively.

Chapter Twelve

Jez and Bahir had reached their destination. Pulling up to the cabin, Bahir was surprised to see at least four other vehicles parked up in a line in front of them.

"Who are they?" asked Bahir gesturing at the line of parked vehicles.

"All will be revealed," replied a smiling Jez.

Jez walked to the back of his truck and pulled on the load space cover to check his load was still present and correct. Uncle J was lying in an awkward position, still out cold, but alive. To double-check, Jez placed his finger on Uncle J's neck where he detected a pulse.

"I'll go and get some help to move him," stated Jez walking towards the cabin. "You wait here."

A few minutes later, Jez returned with three more muscular-looking men all dressed in sharp suits. The posse then removed the load space cover, grasped the ample torso of Uncle J and carried him unceremoniously into the cabin. Once inside, the captive was quickly bundled into the secure bedroom. Uncle J was placed callously on one of the mattresses, still wearing the two pairs of handcuffs. The room emptied, and the sharp snap of the shoot bolts rang out as the door was firmly locked.

"What's all this then?" asked an extremely inquisitive Bahir. "Who are all of these people?"

Bahir scanned the room. There were about fifteen muscular-looking gentlemen dotted around the room. They all glared back at Bahir from expressionless faces.

"You had better sit down," replied Jez.

Bahir took a seat at the dining table.

"These are my colleagues from the FBI," explained Jez confidently.

"Why is the FBI here?" quizzed Bahir. "Am I in trouble?"

"Not as such," responded Jez. "You've actually worked alongside the FBI as part of the operation to bring Uncle J into our Federal Justice system. Uncle J has outstanding business with the FBI concerning war crimes committed in his more active and violent days up country, back home. When our troops were out there, Uncle J was not exactly an exemplary host. We have intelligence that he was behind executions and the torture of our soldiers. All in cold blood."

"What?" screamed a startled Bahir. "You are kidding me?"

"Nope," replied Jez. "The extradition process for Uncle J has broken down many times in the past. The only way that Uncle J could answer to his war crimes was to be arrested in America, in person."

"I thought we were working for The Cell?" stated Bahir, now in a state of utter confusion.

"The Cell!" laughed Jez. "They don't exist. They are a historic fabled bunch of no-hopers. There may be remnants of the old warlord way up country, but I can assure you, The Cell has no representation over here."

"So, you don't work for the Cell?" asked Bahir.

"Don't be ridiculous," snorted Jez. "I work for the American Government. I hatched a plan to bring Uncle J down two years ago. It's been a long time coming. I'm not going to go into any great details, as I want to see Uncle J's face when I tell you all about the sting operation."

"Uncle J will go berserk when he finds out," added Bahir. "Plus, I'm not too happy myself."

"Why are you unhappy, Bahir?" said Jez leaning over Bahir. "You were a simple, ineffective, small time street criminal, with no future. You even failed to get the ransom money after kidnapping Mansoor. On top of that, we gave you a second chance, which you blew. I guess you still remember Labid, don't you?"

"Yeah," responded Bahir. "He gave me and Ramiz the chance to come over here to work for The Cell."

"Really?" said Jez with a broad smile across his face.

"Labid is a high-ranking Cell officer I'll have you know," added Bahir.

"Labid works for us, you fool," replied Jez. "You were introduced to Labid by us, it was all part of the sting to get you over here. We thought Uncle J would recognise you. That would then add authenticity to the sting. Uncle J would then be convinced that some of his old boys had reformed in the States to continue the fight."

As Jez delivered his news to Bahir, a suited gentleman stepped forward and secured a pair of handcuffs to Bahir's wrists.

"You are kidding me!" scowled Bahir. "You set me up, use and abuse me, then arrest me. What sort of people are you?"

"We are not arresting you yet," responded Jez unsympathetically. "The jury is still out on that. You have been useful to us in your ignorance. You have delivered Uncle J and Umar into our hands. So, considering your achievements, I am sure you might be shown some leniency. This is just a precaution."

"Does Ramiz know about all of this?" asked Bahir.

"No," replied Jez, firmly. "He's as much in the dark as you."

Bahir angrily placed his face on the table and covered his head with his restrained arms in disbelief. Bahir had been played and he well knew it now.

"We'll get you some chai," said Jez in a more sympathetic tone. "You've suffered a shock, plus you've had a long journey here."

Bahir remained motionless.

An hour away from the cabin, Talib was still coming to terms with the predicament that he found himself in. Ramiz and Talib had travelled in silence for the past forty-five minutes. Mainly due to Talib attempting to comprehend Ramiz's involvement in his father's kidnapping. But his feelings were contradicted by the shared actions in bringing down Umar.

"I can't forgive you right now for your part in the kidnapping of my father," said Talib breaking the quietness. "Just give me some time to compute that, along with tonight's events. I'm feeling totally perplexed right now. My whole world seems to have been turned upside down."

"I understand," replied Ramiz. "If it's of any use, I totally apologise for the part I played in your father's abduction. I was stone broke at the time, and it looked like a golden chance to get back on my feet. Life is hard back home."

"As I said, give me time," responded a subdued Talib.

The pair completed the remainder of the journey in total silence.

As Ramiz drew up outside the cabin, both he and Talib looked in perplexity at the plethora of vehicles parked up outside the cabin. Ramiz and Talib looked at each other in total surprise.

"What the hell is going on here?" exclaimed Ramiz.

Forgetting their precious cargo, Ramiz and Talib rushed into the cabin. Once inside, they were both as shocked as Bahir was by the picture that greeted them. Bahir was not visible at this time as he had been moved into the secure room next to Uncle J, who was still out for the count.

"Greetings!" exclaimed Jez. "Good journey?"

Ramiz was too preoccupied with the roomful of welcome party members to answer. Ramiz studied the room to see if his buddy had arrived yet.

"There is chai if you require," continued Jez. "It's freshly made, nice and hot."

Talib was equally as confused as Ramiz. Also scanning the room, Talib immediately spotted his brother amongst the crowd. Talib walked over and hugged his brother.

"What a situation we find ourselves in," whispered Rayan in Talib's ear.

"I'm so confused, I don't think I know what planet I'm on, or what day of the week it is," responded Talib.

As Ramiz walked forward to claim his chai he was approached from the rear by two of the muscular gentlemen, who held his arms firmly. Another cohort snapped a pair of handcuffs firmly on Ramiz's wrists.

"What are you doing?" shouted Ramiz. "Release me!"

"Calm down," said Jez walking towards Ramiz. "The cuffs are just a precaution."

"A precaution for what?" begged Ramiz.

"All in good time, young man," replied Jez. "Take him to the secure room."

Three of the attending officers stepped forward and ushered Ramiz into the now unlocked secure room.

"Go and fetch Umar," ordered Jez. "We don't want him waking up in the back of the truck. Let's get him locked up before he is capable of making things difficult."

Four more attending officers rushed out of the cabin to fetch Umar. A few minutes later, the officers reappeared carrying the limp body of Umar.

Jez strode across the wooden floor and placed his middle finger on Umar's neck.

"Yep," said Jez. "He's still with us. Go and put him in the secure room with Uncle J."

Umar was carefully taken to the secure room and deposited on the floor with the other captives."

"This is nice," said Jez rubbing his hands together.

"What happens now?" asked Rayan.

"We wait," replied Jez, "until Uncle J and Umar come round. Then I will deliver some unwelcome news to Uncle J and Umar. It will be like a dagger blow through their hearts."

"What about Talib and I?" begged Rayan.

"Just be patient," responded Jez. "I want you here when I talk to Uncle J. It might give you some more closure concerning your father's kidnapping."

"We don't need closure," replied Rayan. "The fact that my father is free, safe and well. That's enough closure for us."

"What about your feelings for Uncle J?" quizzed Jez.

"You don't understand our family way," responded Rayan. "Why hold all that negative feeling inside your body? It will just eat you up from the inside. We have put my father's experience behind us as a family and moved forwards in a positive manner. We don't hold grudges."

"More fool you," snorted Jez.

"It's just the way we are," added Rayan. "And I prefer it that way."

An hour later, Uncle J and Umar began to awake from their induced slumber. Uncle J attempted to look at his surroundings trying to make out where he was, but his sight was blurred. Gradually, Uncle J's vision cleared.

"Where the hell am I?" exclaimed Uncle J. "And what the hell has been going on?"

"We've all been duped," replied Ramiz who sat in the corner of the secure room.

"Duped?" replied Uncle J now aware of the presence of handcuffs on his wrists and ankles. "By whom?"

"That slippery Jez, that's who," responded a downbeat Ramiz.

"I told you!" added Uncle J vociferously. "What did I say, I never trusted that low life from the start."

"For once you were right," interrupted Umar.

Uncle J swung his head around to his right. He was unaware that Umar was also being held captive. Umar had also come round.

"Ha ha," chortled Uncle J. "They've got you as well."

Umar did not respond. He just bowed his head and stared at his feet.

"What a complete mess," continued Uncle J. "I guess we're not going to be millionaires after all. I guess it's back behind bars for me."

In the dining area, Jez cocked his head after hearing what sounded like conversation coming from the secure room.

"Let's get them out here now," ordered Jez. "I don't want too much debate in there. Arrange four chairs in the centre of the room. Whatever we do, it's extreme caution from here on in. These people will do anything to evade captivity."

Two attending officers started to pull chairs from the dining table, arranging them in a neat line in the centre of the room. At the same time, two more officers walked to the secure room door and released the shoot bolts. As they did so, two other officers brandished and cocked their rifles in readiness.

Uncle J, Umar, Ramiz, and Bahir were escorted to the awaiting chairs; Uncle J and Umar shuffling across the room because of their ankle restraints. All four took their seats in anticipation.

"How are you feeling, Uncle J?" asked Jez. "What do you make of good old Californian hospitality?"

"I'd rather go to Miami," retorted Uncle J.

"Not for a while, I fear," snapped Jez. "Let's get all the official stuff out of the way. Let me tell you what's happening here as I'm sure you are dying to know, gentlemen."

"Can't wait," replied a sarcastic Uncle J.

"As you know, Uncle J," continued Jez, "we have been after you for some time now without success. Extradition negotiation breakdowns, the terrain, along with the remote locations of your Northern bases back home. Then there is the incompetence of your own authorities, and so on. So, I hatched a sting plan to get you in our backyard, so I could control how we got you in our custody. Fortunately, we've had some people help us along the way by people who want to see you permanently behind bars. From the outset, we've been playing you, Uncle J, and Umar."

"Me?" scowled Umar. "Nobody's been playing me."

"Let me explain," continued Jez. "Let's take Umar. You were in prison for fifteen years, right?"

"Yes, I was," replied Umar.

"So, how come you are sat here in front of me and not still in prison then?" asked Jez.

Umar remained silent.

"We had many meetings," added Jez, "with your government, discussing the possibility of a joint operation with your authorities and your prison system. They were on board with my plan from the start. The governor's role was pivotal. He had to ensure you both remained safe and out of harm's way. We didn't want a gang of prisoners doing away with you on the inside as you were more useful to us on the outside. Then there is the parole hearing panel. They were all completely fake. They were working on behalf of our government, so the success of your release hearing was always predetermined. Didn't you and Uncle J. ever wonder how you remained relatively untouched, while all around you inmates were getting in fights, receiving prison guard beatings, and constantly being placed in solitary confinement? That was no accident. We were controlling prison affairs remotely. We have that power and influence."

"What about the visits from The Cell to develop plans?" asked Umar.

"Our people again," smirked Jez, "feeding you lies, filling your mind full of a plan, but it was my plan. Let's be fair. A man like you, of little or no status, how on earth do you think you were allowed to receive a constant flow of visits? It just doesn't happen for people like you."

"I guess the meetings with The Cell after my release were also staged?" quizzed Umar.

"Exactly that," replied Jez. "Every meeting was recorded and filmed using covert equipment. Every step of the way was controlled by me and my team. We even have a full report of Uncle J's internet activity in the prison library. Minute by minute, page by page, website by website. You looked all around this area for cabins, Uncle J. Am I right?"

"Maybe," replied a subdued Uncle J.

"So, what about that story about your father you told me?" asked Umar. "You told me about him working with The Cell, up north. And how he was shot?"

"Fabricated," replied an arrogant Jez. "My father is a delivery driver, he's never been in a fight in his life, let alone shot a weapon."

"You really are a low life," responded Umar angrily.

"Let's move on," resumed Jez. "Uncle J, for starters, your hill-walking charade, pretending to live a healthier life is also well documented, Uncle J. We have a dossier full of photographs, along with a full timeline. We have your every move on record. Your manservant, Faisal. We have a dossier full of his movements as well. We were well aware of the change of shopping outlet. We assumed it was a poor attempt to distract us from an impending trip to the airport. We even had both trips to the airport under surveillance, partly completed in the load space of your truck, if I am correct. Why on earth you wanted to travel in such discomfort is beyond me."

"I like to inspect my load space for paint damage sometimes," quipped Uncle J.

"Sure," replied Jez. "Then there are the airport experiences themselves. Let's start with the papers. They were perfect in every way, wouldn't you agree? And the assumed names you took for your transit. Don't you think if these named people went on trips but didn't return, this might cause a reaction from relatives, friends, or associates? When people go missing it leaves a void. You didn't give that too much thought, did you, Uncle J? You were absolutely guaranteed passage, as the immigration guards were again our agents, at both airports. We made sure you went to their counter to be processed. If you recall, an officer came on shift when you were in the queue. His start of shift timing was driven by your position in the queue. His strict instructions were to ensure you got on the plane without a hitch. You too, Umar. You were checked by the same agent at your home airport and our agent at the San Francisco airport."

"Unbelievable," said Umar rolling his eyes and looking to the heavens.

"Now let's move on to the cabin," added Jez. "I chose the location, I funded the modifications, my department has provided the manpower, and here we are. To be honest, Uncle J., your internet activity in prison, trying to find a suitable place to hold your targets was completely in vain. But at least it kept you away from trouble in the prison."

"What I don't fully understand," responded Uncle J, "is why would you go to all of this trouble? Why not just arrest me at the airport and send me to trial?"

"Good question," responded Jez as he paced up and down the room, with his hands behind his back. "For several reasons. Firstly, we are going to incarcerate you here for eight months and feed you porridge and stale water. This will give you some idea of what you put

Mansoor through. We are going to modify the secure room now our little secret is out. That is why there is a truck outside laden with timber. We are going to construct two boxes in the secure room, the same dimensions as the box in which you made Mansoor suffer so brutally. We want you to really get the full experience."

"Surely that's not legal?" growled Uncle J. "That is barbaric. I want to see an attorney, straight away, it's my right."

"Barbaric!" shouted an angry Jez. "So how come it was not considered barbaric when you stuffed Mansoor into a similar tiny box?"

"I don't have access to fancy cabins like you." quipped Uncle J.

"I'm not interested," responded Jez aggressively. "It's been signed off by my people and that's that. You fully deserve what's coming to you."

"We'll see," replied Uncle J.

"Reasons for an elaborate plan," resumed Jez. "Secondly, we now have you involved in criminal activity on our soil. Your leadership and participation in the attempted kidnapping of Rayan and Talib are good enough alone to get you locked up for a long time. Added to your known war crimes, you aren't going to see the light of day in the outside world again."

"So where do Ramiz and Bahir fit in?" asked Umar.

"Another good question," responded Jez. "They were part of an experimental rehabilitation plan. But your authorities could see that it was not working as Ramiz and Bahir gradually returned to their old ways. During our planning meetings for this sting, their names were mentioned as possible candidates to support the plan. They could be of use to us in the plot to snare Uncle J. So, I sent an agent to tempt them over here to work for 'The Cell'. They took the bait and I've been controlling their puppet strings ever since."

"Outrageous," snarled Ramiz. "It's all a lie. I've been working for The Cell."

"Ramiz," said Jez angrily. "Were you in a position to afford the expensive flights to San Francisco? Were you in a position to pay your way with the board and lodgings? Were you in a position to secure a job in the States? I don't think so. Now stop whinging on about being a victim. You went into this with your eyes wide open."

Ramiz looked away in contempt.

"Then we have fooled you all with a watertight plan then," replied an arrogant Jez. "All in all, I'm really pleased with how this has worked out. We have Uncle J in custody, we have his accomplice, Umar, in custody, and we can now deport two street urchins so that their own authorities can deal with them."

"What have we done wrong over here?" begged Bahir. "After all, we've done what you have asked, albeit in ignorance. How can we be deemed as criminals when we have, in reality, been following your orders?"

"Agreed," replied Jez. "But under the premise that you were working for The Cell. Am I right?"

"I guess so, but it's still totally unjust," responded Bahir after a moment's deliberation.

"Criminals," continued Jez. "The lot of you, and I've managed to get you off the streets. Boy am I in for a promotion and a pay rise now."

"So, what about my brother and I?" said Rayan from the back of the room. "Have you considered that?"

"What do you mean?" asked Jez turning to face Rayan.

"Remember, I was contacted by you Jez, saying you had instructions from my father," added Rayan. "You asked me to jog three times in Golden Gate Park at a specific time, not get involved in a bizarre scheme to entrap international criminals."

"And I was asked to do the same in Black Point Gardens," interrupted Talib. "I didn't realise when I agreed to this request that I would be involved in a warped entrapment scheme."

"Here, here!" bellowed Uncle J.

"So, your father didn't fully explain what was going on?" asked Jez.

"No," replied Rayan and Talib in unison. "We didn't even talk to him, it was you who said my father had requested this."

"Then your beef is with your father," replied Jez in an attempt to absolve himself. "I can assure you, your father was fully aware of all phases and actions within the operation and he was fully on board."

"I need to speak with him, now," stated Rayan.

"Look," said Jez trying to distract and delay Rayan. "That can wait, we need to sort this situation out first."

"I insist," replied Rayan adamantly. "Come with me, brother."

Rayan and Talib left the cabin, Rayan clutching his mobile phone in his right hand in readiness. One of Jez's officers started to follow them, but Jez gestured his hand to stop the officer from moving in. The officer stopped in his tracks.

"You didn't think this completely through, did you, Jez?" said Uncle J attempting to agitate Jez. "Involving innocent civilians for your selfish benefit."

"They were in no danger," snapped Jez. "Their father is at fault for even involving them at all. I wanted to plant agents to act as Rayan and Talib, but Mansoor would have none of it."

Five minutes later, Rayan and Talib returned to the cabin, both with expressions of anger on their faces.

"We've spoken with our father," announced Rayan. "He told us that you would contact both of us, give us a full brief, plus some self-defence training. Just in case things went wrong. But the reality is that he was against our involvement."

"That's rubbish," said an embarrassed Jez.

"Let me get him back on the phone right now," said Rayan. "I'll put him on loudspeaker, so we can all hear what he has to say. My father also told us that he didn't want us to take part at all because of the exposure to known and dangerous criminals. But my father told me that you talked him out of it, wanting your plan to be authentic in every way."

Jez turned away from Rayan and Talib to collect his thoughts.

"Look," Said Jez after a moment's pause. "You have to look at it from my perspective. What if Uncle J and Umar actually knew what you two looked like? If I used substitutes, and Uncle J and Umar twigged that all was not right, it would have blown the plan out of the water. I just couldn't risk it."

"I haven't a clue what they looked like before today," sniped Uncle J.

"Me neither," added Umar.

Jez was backed into a corner. His need to have a totally authentic plan, right down to the last tiny details, may have come back to bite him. Jez needed to remedy the situation as quickly as possible.

"OK," said Jez. "I admit it. I did say those things to your father. But if I had explained the operation to you two, I pretty much guarantee that you would have refused to take part. Am I right?"

"Absolutely," replied an angry Rayan. "Your plan is dishonest from the core. All of these people you have tricked and manipulated. You need to take a good look in the mirror. And as far as your plan to hold Uncle J here, as you said you would, that is totally unacceptable."

"Here, here," chanted Uncle J, again trying to stir the pot.

"I totally agree with my brother," added Talib. "I want nothing to do with this twisted plot. What happened to good old-fashioned police work?"

"You don't understand the big picture," begged Jez, trying to win back the room. "Uncle J is not only a war criminal, but he has also been heavily involved in two failed kidnapping attempts, amongst a mass of other crimes. He needs to be brought to justice. I have played by the book in the past and failed. This way I get my man and nobody gets hurt."

"Speak for yourself," added Umar rubbing the injection wound on the side of his neck.

"You failed before on a level playing field," stated Talib. "This time you say you have won, but the odds were stacked dishonestly in your favour. How can you take comfort from that? You have won by cheating and manipulation. And what if my brother and I had come to harm? What then?"

"This is the real world," snapped an angry Jez. "My job is to bring criminals to justice whatever it takes. End of. And, as luck would have it, you came to no harm."

"Whatever," responded a disinterested Rayan. "But Talib had to come to the rescue when you tried to take Umar. What if the fight was won by Umar, and he beat Talib?"

"People," said Jez raising both his hands above his head in frustration. "Don't forget who the good guys and the bad guys are in here. You are starting to make me feel like the criminal. All I have done is my duty. Maybe I have stretched the rules a bit along the way, but I got the job done. At the end of the day, right here, right now, nobody came to harm."

"But look at the fallout," said Rayan. "My brother and I are in turmoil. We've unwittingly been used like pawns in a sordid game of chess, for your convenience, Jez, so that you can get a pay rise and promotion. My brother and I have got to live with the deception you have led us to."

"And what about me and Ramiz," growled a disgruntled Bahir. "We have equally been used and abused for your gain. I was heading for the straight and narrow before you and your team tempted me into this trap."

"That's utter rot," replied Jez angrily. "You were back on the downward slippery slope, and well you know it."

"I wasn't," argued Bahir. "I liked my new life, with a job to go to and hard-earned money in my pocket. How do you know what I was feeling, Jez?"

"Once a criminal, always a criminal," stated Jez. "In any case, you are just saying that now you are aware of the facts."

"So why have the rehabilitation programme in the first place?" said a vexed Ramiz.

"We are getting off track," bellowed Jez. "I am not in the courtroom being accused of my misdeeds. Let's get back to the reasons why we are here in the first place. I will answer for the rights and wrongs of the operation when I've tidied up this situation. Until then, let's get on with matters in hand."

"Don't I get a say in all of this?" demanded Uncle J with a raised voice.

The room fell silent as attention focussed on Uncle J, who had been sitting quietly taking in events as they unfolded.

"Actually, no," replied Jez firmly. "You of all people have no say whatsoever."

"Actually, I disagree entirely," responded a smug-looking Uncle J. "Jez, I'm afraid we haven't discussed all of the options yet. I have some of my own if you'd care to permit me to share?"

"Look around you," growled Jez. "You are out of options. We have you surrounded, in handcuffs. We have your accomplices in custody. I'm not interested in what you have to say. It will probably be all lies in any case."

"I can assure you that I will tell you no lies," responded Uncle J confidently. "In fact, it could save your life if you listen to what I have to say. Plus, the lives of everyone in this cabin right now. It's your call, Jez. For the record, be it on your head if anything should happen."

"Nice try, Uncle J," replied Jez. "You don't intimidate me. Your name might carry weight back home, but on my turf, you are just a low life criminal, and I'm going to give you what's been coming to you for years."

"Don't say I haven't tried to reason with you," added Uncle J. "Be it on your head. My suspicions were aroused early on. When the appointments we should have fulfilled in Monterrey, Los Angeles, and San Diego didn't even get a mention, not to mention the fun runs. I was curious at first which encouraged me to take my initial steps towards self-preservation."

"What! If he's for real?" interrupted Rayan. "He is a man of resources and a born survivor. What if he's actually got something to say?"

"He's a blag artist," said Jez. "Always has been, always will be."

"Well," responded Uncle J confidently, "on this occasion I am not trying a last minute blag. I can assure you. It's very much in your interest to hear me out."

"Jez, it's not just your life at stake here," begged a frightened Talib. "It will cost nothing to hear him out."

"Let's hear it, for what it's worth," said a resigned Jez.

Chapter Thirteen

"The way I see it," began Uncle J, "there are two options. Option one, you let, Umar, Ramiz, Bahir and I go, let us walk away and don't track us. Option two, we all die here together in a great big fireball of hell."

"That's pretty desperate, Uncle J," responded Jez arrogantly, "even for you. Firstly, even considering letting you go is preposterous. Secondly, die in a fireball from hell? What are you? Covered in explosives?"

"Not exactly," responded Uncle J coyly. "I do, however, have one of these."

Uncle J lowered his shirt to reveal a hidden wire.

Jez looked at Uncle J in amazement.

"With all of your fancy planning to the 'enth degree," added Uncle J. "You didn't stop for one minute and try and pat me down for weapons or wires, did you? You see, I'm not the dumb old anti-technology dinosaur that you think I am. Your so-called guardian angels also didn't know that I purchased a burner phone when I was in San Francisco. I never trusted you from the start, Jez, so I made sure that I had my own back covered. I've been in regular contact with the only person I truly trust on this earth, my long-standing manservant and real friend, Faisal. I know that Faisal will come through for me, and he has. Jez, you aren't the only person here who has guardian angels, I have them as well. And they are outside right now, waiting for my commands."

"Bullshit," snarled Jez who was now reeling.

"Bullshit?" responded Uncle J confidently. "Let's see, shall we?"

"You are just grasping at straws, Uncle J," replied Jez nervously. "You just never know when you've been beaten."

Uncle J lowered his chin.

"This is Eagle One," continued Uncle J speaking into his wire. "Take out a tyre."

Almost immediately, the shrill crack of a gunshot filled the air. In the parking area, a bullet struck the tyre of one of the agent's vehicles with complete accuracy, causing the tyre to explode, instantly dropping the vehicle onto its wheel rim.

Everyone in the room that could dropped to the ground in self-preservation. The attending agents who were armed crept their way towards the windows, with their rifles cocked.

"What the hell was that?" yelled Jez.

A sense of fear enveloped the cabin.

"That, my friend, was one of my guardian angels," replied Uncle J confidently. "And there's more where that came from. So, do I have your attention now, Mr Jez?"

"I don't believe it," said Jez, angrily smacking his hands on the wooden floor.

"So, can we discuss my terms now?" asked a super confident Uncle J.

"Ah," screeched Jez. "Maybe I have another card to play. You are unarmed, but I have armed agents."

As Jez delivered his counter move, the two armed agents trained their rifles on Uncle J.

"You can shoot me now if you like," added Uncle J. "But I must warn you, my guardian angels have brought with them many weapons. Some of them are particularly nasty. They have a bunch of R.P.G.'s with orders to open fire with them should anything happen to me in here. So, I guess it's your move, Jez. Do you want to take that gamble? But think hard, young man, it's not just your life at stake now, is it?"

"You are lying," snapped a frightened Jez. "You don't have that firepower."

"It's a demonstration you are after?" responded Uncle J.

"No," shouted Jez. "Just hang on a minute."

"I think it's you that is now out of options, Mr Jez," said Uncle J. "Maybe your people need to stop intimidating me and cease pointing the business end of their rifles at me as my angels can hear what's going on, you know."

Jez gestured at his men to back off and lower their weapons, in an attempt to show a willingness to concede.

"For starters," said Uncle J. "You can remove these cuffs from us all."

Jez stared back fearfully into Uncle J's cold eyes. Jez had never been in a violent or threatening situation since joining the force.

"Remove the cuffs," barked Jez after a short time of deliberation.

Three agents stepped forward and removed the handcuffs from the four interns.

Uncle J stood up, casting an impressive, bulky shadow on the floor. Looking around the cabin, Uncle J spotted a dustbin in the kitchen that was lined with a plastic bin liner.

"Umar," commanded Uncle J. "Go in the kitchen and find me a few of those bin liners, pronto."

Umar scampered into the kitchen to search the cupboards. In no time, Umar returned to the room holding several black plastic bin liners.

"Phones, radios, weapons, truck keys," boomed a now confident Uncle J, "in the bag, now!"

"You are kidding me," japed Jez. "You really think we are going to play along with your game?"

Uncle J again lowered his chin.

"This is Eagle One," continued Uncle J speaking again into his wire. "Take out another tyre."

Again, almost immediately, the distinct crack of a gunshot once more filled the air. The bullet crashed into the rear tyre of the same vehicle, causing a repeat explosion of the tyre and a repeat collapse of the car to its wheel rim.

For a second time, hearing the gunshot, everyone dropped to the floor except Uncle J and Umar.

"We are going to do this," repeated Uncle J assertively. "Now, phones, radios, weapons, truck keys in the bag. Ramiz, Bahir, get busy."

Ramiz and Bahir split the bin liners between them, offering them to Jez and his agents. In total silence, Jez and his team conformed to Uncle J's demands.

"Not the rifles," demanded Uncle J. "Give them to me."

Bahir handed the two rifles to Uncle J, who slipped them over his head and onto his shoulders.

Once the demands had been fulfilled, Uncle J walked over to the window and peeled back the net curtain. Uncle J then turned and faced Jez.

"Now search them," growled Uncle J. "Thoroughly."

Seeing his moment, Jez leapt forward and grabbed Uncle J by the throat. Umar moved forward to help Uncle J but was struck from behind by one of the agents. Umar fell to the floor holding his head.

As Uncle J grappled with Jez, three more agents stepped forward to help Jez restrain Uncle J. In the heat of battle, Uncle J forcefully lowered his head to his chest.

"This is Eagle One," chanted Uncle J in desperation into his wire. "Smoke the truck."

A few seconds later there was an explosion outside. Uncle J's support team had set off an I.E.D., trying to simulate the effects of an R.P.G. Uncle J didn't want to be responsible for starting a huge wildfire, so had instructed his team to carry out a simulated explosion using a small I.E.D. placed under the truck. Uncle J deemed this sufficient to trick Jez into thinking Uncle J had ordered the firing of R.P.G.'s. The I.E.D. had been placed under the truck with deflated tyres. The device had only marginally damaged the truck but was designed to expel a significant sound to mimic a large explosion. A minor fireball was also discharged, but this only had a minimum effect on the surroundings. Debris from the explosion flew in all directions, some landing on the cabin roof and rattling against the windows. It was almost like a group of delinquent schoolchildren throwing stones at the windows. But it had Jez and his agents convinced.

Uncle J broke free from the grip of Jez and his agents, who were paralysed in shock by the explosion. The sound of the explosion could still be heard reverberating down the valley, like a violent crack of thunder.

"Now do you see the predicament you are actually in?" said a flustered Uncle J, getting to his feet. "I told you, they have brought some serious hardware with them. Enough to make kindlling of this cabin in an instant. So, you had better start taking me seriously, Jez.

As I said, two options. Now, get back to the searching duties, you pair."

Ramiz and Bahir resumed their search of Jez and his agents. The pair were as staggered as Jez and his team when the explosion erupted. They were also convinced that Uncle J's warriors were heavily armed and not afraid to use them. During the searches, Bahir uncovered three small revolvers tucked inside the trouser legs of the agents. It was a good move by Uncle J to frisk the agents.

"You know you won't get away with this, Uncle J," said Jez. "You can't wantonly fire off missiles in a public park. What if there are tourists or locals in the vicinity? I will hunt you down until I take my last breath."

"If you carry on talking like that," growled Uncle J, "your last breath might be sooner than you think. You chose this location, so I am guessing it is relatively tourist-free. So, the public is in as much danger as you placed Rayan and Talib in?"

Once Ramiz and Bahir had completed their searches, Uncle J summoned the first agent to him. Uncle J patted him down thoroughly, leaving nothing unchecked. Uncle J wanted to be doubly sure that his prisoners had no means with which to affect an escape. Once Uncle J was happy that he was clean, he gestured to Ramiz.

"Put him in there," demanded Uncle J pointing at the secure room.

The agent cooperated, walked unwillingly into the secure room and sat down on the floor.

"Next," boomed Uncle J.

Uncle J then proceeded to check all of the remaining agents, even Rayan and Talib, leaving Jez until last.

"I am genuinely sorry about having to do this," said Uncle J to Rayan and Talib. "But I can't have you two running around telling tales, can I?"

"But we are nothing to do with this," appealed Rayan.

"I know, I know," replied Uncle J. "But as I said, I can't have you two loose cannons out there, before I've made good with my escape."

"Of course," said Ramiz randomly. "I get it now."

"What are you on about now?" asked Uncle J.

"When we were here before," continued Ramiz. "You went out for a walk to clear your head. Now I know, you were just working on vantage points for your guardian angels, weren't you?"

"I was indeed," replied a cocky Uncle J.

"I knew I shouldn't have let you out of the cabin," admitted Jez. "What was I thinking?"

"You know," said a calm Uncle J, "you think you are a big shot, Jez. You pride yourself in professional planning, leaving no stone unturned. In fact, from the outset, Umar was using your phrasebook, I think. All this garbage about how the new Cell leaves nothing to chance. I know now that it's you and your organisation that was actually preaching that sermon through Umar. Then along comes a stupid, old, vulnerable antique like me, who blows holes in your plan for fun. You need to go back to school, Jez, or better still, get a load more front line experience. It works wonders, you know."

"Fair play, Uncle J," replied Jez. "But you know we will have you back in custody pretty much as soon as I get out of here."

"Depends how long you stay in here," snapped Uncle J in reply.

"The whole department knows what's going on," responded Jez. "As soon as they stop getting updates, they will send in the backup teams."

"Don't you think I've thought about that?" replied Uncle J. "And who do you think has got the radios? And who knows the call signs and jargon?"

Jez rolled his eyes in frustration. It appeared that Uncle J was holding all the trump cards.

"OK then," added Jez. "What about cutting a deal with me?"

"And why would I want to cut a deal with you?" barked Uncle J, "after all, you are not exactly in a position to cut a deal, are you?"

"Think about it," continued Jez. "I can make up some story. I can help you get a reduced sentence. I can make some of the evidence we have collected 'disappear'. We can also sign like a prenuptial agreement."

"Prenuptial?" boomed Uncle J laughing. "I'm not going to marry a two-faced worm like you."

"You know what I mean," responded Jez. "We can sign a contract or agreement before you go into custody. As long as my people get you behind bars, the time you spend behind bars can be negotiated down to an agreeable level."

"You really do think I am soft in the head," chuckled Uncle J. "Make a contract with a lying, devious, manipulative, self-centred creep like you. I've seen how you work and I don't like it. Not even Rayan and Talib like the way you work."

"I won't offer again," begged Jez.

"Enough!" snarled Uncle J. "Get them all in the secure room and lock the door. Umar, what are your mechanical skills like?"

"Pretty good," replied Umar.

"OK," continued Uncle J. "Get yourself outside. Make sure there is no threatening fire from the R.P.G. Take Ramiz and Bahir with you just in case you need some help. Maybe look around for some buckets. We don't want to send smoke signals to the neighbourhood. Then do what you can to disable all of the trucks, including the ones that we were transported here in. I have the escape plan covered."

"Right you are, boss," replied an upbeat Umar.

"You want us to help you?" asked Ramiz.

"Absolutely," replied Uncle J. "You don't want to stay on the same side as that lying, cheating team, do you?"

"No way," smiled Ramiz.

With everyone who should be in the secure room, Uncle J wandered over to the door slammed it, and engaged all of the shoot bolts. Uncle J picked up his mobile phones, along with Umar's, Ramiz's and Bahir's mobile phones and possessions off one of the dusty kitchen worktops. He placed them in a black bin liner before taking a final look around the cabin.

"You won't get far," came a voice from within the secure room.

Uncle J refused to get engaged in any more games with Jez and remained silent.

Umar, Ramiz, and Bahir rushed out of the cabin to inspect the damage caused by the so-called R.P.G. Fortunately, the ground appeared to be slightly damp, so the fires were small and sporadic and hadn't taken hold on any of the surrounding combustibles. Bahir searched the grounds around the cabin, unearthing a hose pipe on the side of the building. To his joy, water flowed from the nozzle when he turned on the tap.

"You little superstar," said Ramiz, congratulating Bahir on his most useful find.

Bahir unravelled the hose down to where the trucks were parked, directing the water to the fires in front of him. Seeing that firefighter duty appeared to be covered, Umar set his attention on disarming the vehicles. Due to the remote and sparsely populated location, the agents hadn't bothered locking their vehicles, so Umar was able to pop the bonnets of all of the trucks to get his hands on their engines.

Inside the cabin, Uncle J was scouting around for evidence that may incriminate him. He wanted to leave as clean a crime scene as he could. Finding nothing, Uncle J joined his team outside.

"How's it looking?" asked Uncle J, fishing for updates.

"Fires are pretty much out," responded Bahir.

"Great," replied Uncle J. "Just make sure there is no smoke. We don't want to send smoke signals down the valley, giving away our position"

"Right you are," replied Bahir.

Uncle J walked over to Umar, who had his head buried inside the bonnet of a truck.

"Sorted?" asked Uncle J.

"Give me a minute or two," responded Umar. "I've cut the H.T. leads. These trucks are going nowhere fast."

"Excellent," replied Uncle J. "Top speed please, we don't have much time."

Uncle J rushed back to the cabin. He walked over to the secure room door, double-checking that it was secure.

Uncle J then rushed out of the cabin, locking the door as he left, then threw the key deep in the undergrowth to the side of the cabin. Uncle J walked over to Umar.

"Are you done yet?" asked Uncle J.

"Last one," responded Umar. "There we are."

"Right," said Uncle J assertively. "Let's get to the rendezvous point. Here are your phones and belongings. They are all I could find that were visible in the cabin."

"Why don't we push the trucks down that hill over there?" asked Bahir. "That will really screw them up and mess with their heads."

"Pointless exercise," responded Umar. "The trucks are going nowhere as they stand. What's the point of wasting time and energy?"

"Agreed," added Uncle J. "We need to get out of here now. Time is not our friend at the moment. If Umar says the trucks are disabled, then I trust him. Now, follow me."

Uncle J led his band of fugitives into the tree line. Uncle J glanced back at the cabin for a last look before he proceeded to duck under the first low-lying branch. During his 'head clearing walks' when previously visiting the cabin, Uncle J had scouted around, and along with some help from the internet, plotted a path out of the area. Once under the thick canopy of pines, Uncle J headed down a pine needle-laden slope. His accomplices struggled with the tricky terrain, not really prepared for this hardcore hiking, they were quiet life appreciators, preferring a cold beer and a warm fireplace to the rugged terrain of Yosemite Park. It took the assemblage quite a time to negotiate the slope. Uncle J selected a more difficult route, thinking that if he was pursued, then maybe his chasers would consider the route too hardcore for Uncle J. As they were reaching the lower section of the initial slope, the terrain began to change. The needle-clad landscape became a rockier affair, as huge boulders faced the team.

"We must be closing in on the river," panted an out of breath Uncle J. "There should be a guide at the river waiting for us."

"How much further?" begged an equally breathless Umar. "I need a rest."

"Soon," snapped Uncle J. "Just keep going."

The four comrades battled against the difficult conditions. Some of the boulders that they had to encounter were reminiscent of small buildings. But they simply had to keep going, just in case, the news of their breakout had reached a wider audience.

After clambering over another huge, grey boulder, Uncle J started to make out the familiar sound of a babbling river.

"Listen," declared Uncle J. "Over there, can you hear it?"

The posse stopped in their tracks and listened. Each could make out the sound of running water.

"Got it," said a smiling Umar. "Over that way."

Umar pointed slightly to his right, in the direction where he could hear what he thought to be moving water.

Uncle J guided himself down another immense boulder on his backside, landing on the edge of a beautiful-looking mountain river. The water was perishingly cold, but that did not deter Uncle J from completing a small celebration jig.

One by one, Umar, Ramiz and Bahir slid down the final boulder into the ice-cold water below.

Uncle J crossed the shallow water, finding a vantage point on top of another large boulder located on the far bank. Uncle J scrambled to the top of the boulder and started to look up and downriver for his awaiting guide. Taking out his burner phone, Uncle J used his speed dial. After a short time, his call was answered.

"Where are you?" demanded Uncle J assertively.

There was a pause as Uncle J listened to the response.

"OK, got you," replied Uncle J as he hung up. "We need to follow the river downstream for about half a kilometre. He is waiting for us."

"Are you sure it's downstream?" asked Bahir playfully. "You don't want to get lost now."

Uncle J pulled back his right arm as if in readiness to deliver a slap to Bahir.

"Get off with you," smiled Uncle J. "I know exactly where we are."

"What about the radios?" asked Umar.

"Radios?" replied Uncle J. "What about the radios?"

"Don't we need to check-in?" added a concerned Umar. "Jez will be in constant contact via radio with his base. Don't you think we should make a call, telling them that everything is OK? To make them think that we are still being held captive in the cabin?"

"First of all," responded Uncle J. "I haven't got a clue how to unlock the radios. I don't know if you noticed, but they all keyed in a code before they used their radios. Secondly, I was blagging when I said I knew the call signs and jargon. Thirdly, who here even remotely sounds like Jez? I couldn't mimic his broad Californian twang if I tried. Neither could any of you."

"Well, you had me fooled," said Ramiz. "I was totally hooked when you said you knew the call signs."

"Years of practice," quipped Uncle J. "If I had you lot fooled, then I must have fooled Jez and his cronies."

Enjoying the warm sun on their backs and after a short rest, the four comrades started to follow the river downstream.

Back at the cabin, Jez was still pacing around the secure room. His mood was dark and his temper short.

"Has anybody got a phone, radio, anything that can transmit a message?" said Jez to his team.

Jez looked around the room. All of his loyal agents were silent, staring down at their feet in embarrassment.

"Uncle J's search was a good one," replied Rayan. "He searched everywhere, and I mean everywhere. Pity you didn't search Uncle J, then maybe you would have found his wire."

"Yes, I get it," snapped an angry Jez. "I still can't believe how that dinosaur turned the tables on me. How could I be so naïve?"

Jez proceeded over to the window and he grabbed and shook the metal bars guarding the window in rage.

"When you want someone to do a proper job, you get this," said Jez in frustration. "It's because of my thoroughness I'm in this pickle."

Jez then wandered to the locked door. He charged at the door with his shoulder, but he bounced back into the centre of the room holding his shoulder in pain. He then gave the door a few good hearty kicks. The door didn't budge an inch.

"Ah!" screamed Jez. "It's pointless shouting for help. The backup team are by the entry gate, they will never hear us from here. Any ideas anyone?"

"What about the ceiling?" asked Talib. "I have handcuffs here, they are metal. Maybe we could loosen that wood around the light fitting?"

"At last," replied a jubilant Jez. "Someone with common sense."

Jez snatched the handcuffs from Talib and ordered two agents to lift him to the ceiling. Once next to the light fitting area, Jez started to try and pry at the wood to loosen it. Bit by bit, small pieces of wood started to fall away, but Jez's arms were starting to tire.

"Lower me," ordered Jez. "Someone else take over."

Another agent stepped forward and was raised to ceiling height. Bit by bit they started to make progress, but it was slow.

"Every minute we spend on this gives Uncle J more time to evade us," snorted Jez in temper. "Come on, let's get this done."

The agents swapped and changed, chiselling away at the wood as if their lives depended on it.

Back alongside the river, Uncle J and his team had reached the rendezvous point. A slim figure was waiting for them, dressed in professional hiking garb, and wearing top-of-the-range hiking boots.

"Hi, I'm Wasim," greeted Uncle J's guide. "Great to see you, are you having a great day in the California sunshine?"

"Enough of all that small talk," grunted Uncle J. "Where are we going now? We will have half of the U.S. police force on our tails soon, we need to get moving, and fast.

"OK, OK," replied Wasim. "Cool those beans. I'll get you out of here. We don't need to go far. We have a tanker waiting about two miles away. The terrain isn't easy, so we need to be careful in our haste."

"Tanker?" asked a totally perplexed Uncle J. "That wasn't the plan."

"I know," replied Wasim. "You asked for off-road motorcycles to get us far away from here. But once the authorities know you are on the run, they will get helicopters up there, armed with heat-sensitive cameras.

The heat from the engines will give you away in no time. Even if you are under the forest canopy. Our plan has a better chance of getting you out of here undetected."

"But a tanker?" added Uncle J. "That will be slow. How do you intend transporting us? Inside the tanker in a load full of beer?"

"Time is not on our side," responded a frustrated Wasim. "Let's get going. I'll fill you in with the details on the way. Now, watch out for bears and mountain lions, and I am not joking."

Umar and Uncle J looked at each other with total surprise on their faces. The thought of a real threat from actual wildlife was a novel experience for them both.

With Wasim's words ringing in their ears, the five fugitives disappeared again into the forest, using the blanket of pine trees as cover.

Over an hour had passed in the cabin. Between them, the captives had all but managed to chip away the wooden cover over the light fitting. A final few strong pulls at the wood saw the final piece fall away. The ceiling boards were now exposed, giving Jez and his team something to put pressure on to make a large enough hole to get someone into the loft space.

The agents took turns in pulling on the exposed boards. The wood started to crack and split under the strain. Suddenly, the pyramid of support fell to the floor as a main board gave way. Once the dust had settled, Jez took a look at the hole. Eyeing up Rayan and Talib, Jez was trying to determine who was the smallest of the pair.

"Talib," shouted Jez. "Over here."

Talib shuffled to Jez's side.

Jez measured Talib with his hands, then offered his hands to the hole in the ceiling.

"Just a little more and we can get Talib through the hole," commanded Jez.

"Get Talib through?" stated a nervous Talib. "You want me to go up there? There may be rats or anything."

"Don't be a princess," replied Jez. "We need you up there to get us out of here. When you are up there, look for the loft hatch. Deploy the ladder and climb down. Then unlock the secure room door and we will be free."

"I'm not sure about this," responded Talib nervously, looking at his brother."

"You will be OK," said a reassuring Rayan. "Do it for us."

Talib smiled back at his brother, then averted his attention to the hole in the ceiling.

Fifteen minutes later, the agents had widened the hole and removed some of the sharper pieces of wood around the hole.

"Let's get you up there, laddie," said Jez with vigour, sensing his imminent freedom.

The agents carefully lifted Talib, guiding him into the hole. It was going to be a tight squeeze. Bit by bit, Talib disappeared into the hole. His clothes were catching on the rough, sharp surrounds of the hole, but as they got caught, agents carefully freed the clothing. As Talib's feet disappeared, a small cheer rang around the room.

"I can see the hatch," said Talib from the loft space.

Jez ordered the agents to lift him so he could see what was going on and issue orders when required.

Talib reached the loft hatch which was covered in a three-section access ladder. After a short time messing about, trying to unlatch the roof hatch, Talib appeared beaten.

"It's locked from the outside," announced Talib. "I can't open it from this side."

"Keep trying," snarled Jez. "We need you to get this job done."

Talib continued to poke and rattle the construction.

"It's no good," replied Talib. "It won't budge."

"Jump on it then," shouted Jez. "Try and break through using your body weight."

"I'm not doing that," responded a belligerent Talib. "That's far too dangerous, I might break my neck."

"Screw this," growled Jez hacking at the hole in the ceiling. "Come on, help me widen this hole. I need to do this myself, as always."

Jez and his agents started to brutally hack at the hole, widening it as quickly as they could. But without tools it took time and its toll. Two agents had given up already, sporting nasty cuts to their hands caused by the sharp and distorted wood.

Another half an hour passed before the hole had been widened enough for Jez to squeeze through.

Once in the loft space, Jez went over to the loft hatch and glared angrily at Talib. Jez then wrapped his arms on the roof beam, positioned himself above the hatch and kicked down violently with his feet.

The latch assembly shuddered and dropped slightly but remained in place.

Jez again took another kick at the hatch. The whole hatch assembly gave way. The hatch lid dropped to the floor, while the ladder assembly dangled in mid-air. A third firm kick sent the ladder assembly to the floor. The hatch was open.

Jez scrambled through the hatch, holding onto the hatch frame as he lowered himself, then dropped to the floor, covered in dust.

"Come on, I'll catch you," said Jez looking up into the loft, beckoning at Talib.

Talib dropped to his knees and lowered himself through the loft hatch, where Jez was waiting to catch him.

Once Talib had both feet on the floor, Jez ran to the secure room and removed the shoot bolts. The captives collectively clapped and started to filter out of the secure room.

"Right," said a confident Jez. "Let's go and capture those dinosaurs."

Chapter Fourteen

Jez ran to the front door of the cabin. After trying the handle, he discovered that the door was locked. Unperturbed, he rushed through to the kitchen and tried the back door. That was also locked.

"Damn it!" yelled Jez. "We are going to have to break through one of these doors."

Agents, reacting to Jez's frustrated yells, had turned up in the kitchen. One of them stepped forward and delivered an energetic kick to the back door, just under the handle.

Instantly, the door gave way and flew open. They were now completely free of their temporary prison.

Jez confidently walked outside, looked up at the clear azure blue sky and took in a lungful of fresh air. He then walked round to the front of the cabin.

Some of the agents had already beaten Jez to the front of the cabin and a number of them had been checking the trucks for ignition keys. They also checked the glove compartments and cab areas, even the sun visors.

"Anything?" asked Jez, more in desperation than hope.

"Nope," responded one of the agents. "It looks like the H.T. leads have been severed on every vehicle. These trucks are of no use to us right now. I'll contact base when I can and sort out the recovery."

"Damn!" snarled Jez. "And the radios? Any sign of the radios?"

"No sign of radios in the trucks, we'll take a look around," answered another agent.

Rayan and Talib joined Jez.

"What's going on?" asked Rayan. "Are we getting out of here?"

"Not for a while it seems," answered Jez. "Our friends have disabled the trucks and either taken or concealed the ignition keys."

"Can't we use the radios?" quizzed Talib.

"Maybe," replied Jez sharply. "Once we find one."

Jez then joined the agents, searching undergrowth, bushes, and grassy areas adjacent to the cabin. It was like looking for a needle in a haystack, as the fauna around the cabin was dense.

Meanwhile, deep in the forest, Wasim held his arm aloft in the air. Uncle J and his followers stopped in their tracks.

Wasim took a folded-up map from the back pocket of his shorts and unwrapped it. After a short time examining the map, Wasim folded the map and returned it to his pocket.

"See that ridge up there," said Wasim. "By my reckoning, once we get to the other side, we will be able to see the forest track we have to follow."

"How far then until we reach the tanker?" asked Uncle J.

"Less than a mile," responded Wasim.

"Let's take a break?" asked Umar. "I am weary, I need to sit down."

"We'll rest when we are in the tanker," snapped Uncle J. "For all we know, there may be people close by looking for us. While we are outside in the park, we are vulnerable. We need to keep going."

"Agreed," said Wasim. "The sooner we get to the tanker the better."

The group commenced the ascent up the rock-strewn hillside towards the ridge. Progress was difficult. The way was not only strewn with rocks, but with fallen branches, a build up of pine needles and general natural rubble, which made for a very difficult and unstable terrain. However, the strong desire for safety and freedom drove the group up the tricky hillside.

An hour later, after a frantic and difficult ascent, the gang had reached the top of the ridge. The view that greeted them was as magnificent as it gets in Yosemite Park. The distant turquoise mountains punctured the cloudless deep blue sky, giving way to what seemed to be a never-ending canopy of glorious pine trees. The occasional caw from a bird of prey filled the air, giving the whole area a sense of atmosphere and adventure. It was hot, sunny and the most beautiful place to be. But Uncle J and his cohorts needed to be out of sight, and fast.

Jez and his team had been searching the areas around the cabin for nearly an hour. In addition, Jez had sent one of the agents to run down the forest track to the access gate, to find the backup team. That is where they should have been waiting for orders according to the plan. Jez needed to alert his people that the operation to capture and humiliate Uncle J had gone wrong, and to request immediate assistance to track and find Uncle J and his accomplices.

Rayan and Talib had joined the search in the undergrowth.

"Is this any good?" said Rayan holding up an ignition key in his hand.

One of the agents rushed to Rayan, snatching the key vigorously from his grasp. The agent then ran to the line of trucks parked up outside the cabin, trying the ignitions one by one until he had a match. The key snuggly fitted in the ignition barrel of the penultimate vehicle. The agent cranked the engine, but that's all it did. The engine failed to fire up as Umar's stealthy work was biting Jez and his team in the backside, big-time.

"This is fruitless," said a demoralised Jez. "Just look for radios now, any keys will be of no use to us. The trucks are going nowhere, except on the back of recovery trucks."

Another hour passed and, as Jez and his associates were still trying to locate a radio, the agent sent to find the backup team seemed to have returned, as three pristine black pick-up trucks appeared in convoy along the forest track.

Not wanting to waste any more time, Jez ran towards the trucks.

"Give me a radio, now!" barked a frustrated and angry Jez.

In no time at all, a small black radio was thrown at Jez. Instantly, Jez alerted his base, updating them with his grim news of failure. Begging for immediate air support, Jez also demanded roadblocks and search squads in the forest, demanding that every available agent was rallied to get on the trail of Uncle J and his posse.

After spending ten minutes ranting into his radio, Jez returned to where Rayan, Talib, and his agents were standing.

"There's good news and bad news," said a resigned Jez.

"What's that?" asked Rayan.

"They are going to assign me two helicopters," replied Jez, "with heat-seeking capability. But the roadblocks are a no-no. Apparently, my case doesn't justify the manpower allocation. Despite them knowing all about the importance of recapturing Uncle J and his associates, my people have other 'more pressing' operations to cover. So, they are not letting me have any more manpower. In fact, these agents you see here are about to leave on another operation. That's a sign of the times."

"That's just a big joke," stated Talib. "Why go this far, then pull the plug?"

"They are not pulling the plug per se," responded Jez. "They are giving me two choppers. In fairness, they can cover more ground faster than a whole load of foot soldiers."

"But you can't do this alone with two helicopters." added Rayan. "Can you?"

"I've been told that I should have Uncle J in the bag," continued Jez. "I guess it's because of me and the failure of my plot that he broke free, and my people seem to want to make an example of me by withdrawing the manpower."

"Harsh," replied Rayan. "Borderline childish."

"It is what it is," responded Jez. "The choppers should be here in about half an hour. Once they are here, I need to decide where to send them to start to look for Uncle J."

Wasim had led Uncle J and his friends to the forest track that would lead them to the highway. The track was narrow, meandering under the welcome cover of the forest canopy.

"Ten minutes and we should reach the highway," said a sweaty Wasim. "The Mexicans usually come through. Nobody wants to cross them as they are brutal.

Life is cheap where they come from, and bullets are even cheaper. They are bad arse, that's for sure."

"Then I will start to relax a bit," replied Uncle J. "No sign of any search team in the sky yet, but I'm still not confident."

Just as Uncle J spoke, the faint but familiar pounding buzz of helicopter rotors could be heard in the distance. Fortunately, the noise was well to the right of the group.

"We need to speed up," announced Wasim. His voice was far more serious than normal. "Those could be surveillance helicopters. If they fly directly over us, we will be done for."

The group picked up the pace, almost breaking into a trot down the dusty forest track. Fortunately, the helicopters were well to the side of their position. If the aircraft were overhead, there was a high risk of not only Uncle J and his party being rumbled, but the awaiting tanker also being spotted.

As Wasim led his followers around the next sharp bend in the track, the beautiful sight of a gleaming silver tanker came into view. The tank itself had 'Fernandez Bulk Logistics' emblazoned on the side in bold red letters. Never had Uncle J been so delighted to see a lorry.

The group ran the last one hundred yards to the tanker. As they reached the tanker, the driver leapt from the driver's door and embraced Wasim.

"We have no time to lose," said a flustered Wasim. "Let's get you inside."

The driver climbed the rear access ladder, walked down the length of the tanker, and opened the forward service hatch.

"Come," beckoned the driver in a thick Mexican twang. "Quickly, in here."

Uncle J led the climb. He followed the driver's route up the rear access ladder to the service hatch. There was a wooden ladder inside the tank to assist Uncle J to enter the awaiting gloom. Uncle J carefully climbed down the unstable wooden ladder. He was greeted by an inhospitable cramped space. There appeared to be a false bulkhead, leaving just a few, cramped metres for Uncle J and his buddies to settle down in. There were also makeshift, crude handles welded to the inside of the tank. These were positioned so that Uncle J and his cohorts had something to grab hold of once they were on the move. In no time, Umar, Ramiz, and Bahir had scurried down the ladder to join Uncle J.

Wasim poked his head into the tank.

"We are going to lock you in now, Uncle J?" said Wasim. "We will padlock the lid. This will make inspection difficult at the border, plus there are many criminals where you are going, it's normal practice. Once you reach your destination, there will be someone to let you out. Fear not, you will be able to breathe as the lid is subtly vented."

Wasim lifted the rickety wooden ladder out from inside the tanker.

"Will they have a ladder at our destination?" asked Uncle J.

"Sure, don't worry," replied a smiling Wasim.

"Thanks for all of your help," said a genuine Uncle J. "We couldn't have got here without your help. I hope they are paying you well for your services."

"No problem," replied Wasim. "Good luck with the rest of your journey, you're gonna need it."

The hatch closed with a loud bang above their heads. The driver fitted a large padlock to the service hatch, double-checking it was secure by shaking the lock vigorously.

Uncle J followed the sound of the footsteps in his dark, sauna-like temporary slammer, as the driver proceeded to make his way to the back of the tanker. Once on the ground, Uncle J could hear a muffled short conversation between the driver and Wasim, before the driver climbed in his cab, slammed the door shut and fired up the tanker. They were on their way. Gripping the makeshift handles like his life depended on it, Uncle J started to feel a little easier with his plight, although not in the discomfort he was experiencing for his escape.

At the cabin, the two helicopters were now within direct sight of Jez. Using his radio, Jez discussed potential search sweeps to be made by the pilots, trying to cover as much ground as they could in as little time as possible. Jez was unsure of the direction Uncle J and his friends made off in, but Jez ruled out the access gate direction, assuming Uncle J would think it would be manned.

Once he was happy with the surveillance plan, Jez walked over to Rayan and Talib.

"Let's try and get you back to civilisation," said Jez. "I'm sorry about how this has turned out, and what you've been put through, but we are all safe and sound now."

"Maybe," responded Rayan. "But I can assure you that we will be taking legal advice when we get back."

Resisting a bad-tempered response, Jez just ushered Rayan and Talib to an awaiting black pick-up truck to get them out of his sight. He saw it as one less problem to worry about right now.

With Rayan and Talib out of the way, Jez turned his attention to his radio.

By now, the gleaming silver tanker had reached the main highway. It was tourist season, so traffic was not light. This played into the hands of Uncle J and his party. The tanker would look like part of the regular traffic, going about its normal routine from above, not standing out from the other tankers and trucks that littered the highway.

Inside the tanker, Uncle J, Umar, and Bahir were attacking the bottled water and snacks that had been provided for them. It seemed like Wasim knew what he was doing. Ramiz was just standing in silence, trying to come to terms with his black, bumpy, and incredibly hot residence.

"Are you OK?" asked Uncle J looking at Ramiz.

"I guess so," responded Ramiz. "Just trying to sort my head out."

"What's eating you then?" asked Bahir.

"I think it's obvious?" replied Ramiz. "Coming over here, working for The Cell, or so I thought, then ending up in this most unappealing tomb, not knowing if the people who open that hatch are going to be friend or foe, not knowing how long we are going to suffer in this darkness. It's certainly not the trip I had pictured in my head."

"I understand," said a reassuring Uncle J. "Just stay positive. It will all work out fine. You'll see."

"I hope you are right," replied Ramiz.

Bahir sidled up to Ramiz and did his best to give Ramiz a man hug.

"Let's hunker down," said Uncle J. "We have a long journey home ahead of us."

"How are we actually getting home?" asked a concerned Umar.

"First stop, Mexico," replied Uncle J. "The driver will drive south from here to the Mexican border. Once in Mexico, we will hook up with an old friend of mine, near the coast. We will be taken to a ship, lying offshore I hope, which will take us back home. I don't think it's wise for me to go back to my home city. I suspect Jez might go to extra lengths to get his revenge on me. So,

I have decided to head north, back to my old stomping grounds. I know that place like the back of my hand, plus I have many allies that I can call upon to take me in. After all, I am supposed to be a living legend."

Umar, Ramiz, and Bahir, all captivated by Uncle J, smiled in unison.

"Maybe I can come up north with you?" asked Umar. "I could be your right hand man?"

"That's not such a bad idea," responded Uncle J. "After all, we've been through a lot together. What about you two?"

"I'm going to stay down south," replied Bahir. "I have learnt a lot from this experience, so I want to use it and maybe start up my own operation in the ghettoes. There's many a dollar to be made out there."

"Me too," agreed Ramiz. "I want nothing to do with The Cell ever again. I will maybe team up with Bahir and become the new threat on the block."

The four comrades carried on the conversation for the remainder of their transit to the Mexican border, it passed the time, plus gave them all a real chance to get to know each other properly.

With the tanker long lost in daily traffic, Jez was still impatiently pacing up and down in front of the cabin. Jez had managed to commandeer some binoculars from an unwitting agent, so Jez could try and track the sweeps made by the helicopters.

However, the longer the search went on, the deeper the pain was for Jez. He knew that the choppers only had a limited time before they needed to refuel. Due to the distance they were from base, this gave Jez only around thirty minutes of airtime over the park.

Jez's radio cracked into life.

"This is Oscar Romeo Three," came a voice over the radio. "I'm getting low on fuel, returning to base, over."

"This is Cabin One," replied Jez. "Understood. Thanks for the heads up. Over."

Moments later, the second helicopter informed Jez that he was returning to base to refuel.

"Damn," shouted Jez as he launched his binoculars through one of the cabin windows. "That's about it, I bet you that they don't return."

Jez walked back into the cabin. He retrieved the binoculars that had ironically found their resting place in the secure room. Jez walked over to the pile of loft ladders and rubble that covered the floor in front of the kitchen door. Jez had a wry smile on his face as he walked out of the cabin door for what he deemed to be the last time. As he appeared in the open air his radio again crackled into life.

"This is Oscar Romeo Three," came the voice over the radio. "New orders received, we will not, repeat, not be returning to resume the search, over."

Jez bowed his head in total disappointment.

"Yeah," replied Jez into his radio. "Cabin One here, received and understood. Out."

Jez looked to the heavens, rolled his eyes, and switched off his radio. Jez then turned to the one remaining agent.

"Let's get out of this dump," uttered a dejected Jez.

Apart from regular toilet breaks, the tanker driver plundered on in a determined manner. Ensuring he observed the speed limits and rules of the road to the letter, the driver was determined to get his load safely to the Mexican border.

Night had passed and the tanker was still rolling. As the sun started to appear over the mountains to the left of the driver, the tanker passed a signpost indicating ten miles to the Mexican border.

Seeing the sign, the tanker driver took to his CB radio.

"UJ Cargo to X-ray One, over," said the driver confidently.

"X-ray One here," came the muffled response. "What's your twenty? Over."

"Ten miles out," continued the driver. "Time to get busy."

"Ten-Four, over and out," responded X-ray One.

The tanker driver replaced his CB microphone and let out a huge smile. His task was nearly at an end.

Around five miles from the border, the driver spotted a lay-by on his right hand side, big enough to fit his tanker. He then pulled in, parked up and jumped out of his cab. The driver proceeded to walk to the front of the tank and tapped the tank twice.

"Uncle J, can you hear me?" asked the driver.

"Yes," replied Uncle J from inside the tanker.

"We are almost at the border crossing," continued the driver. "Total silence from here. Take off your shoes if necessary. Absolutely no noise, we can't afford to be discovered at this late stage."

"Right you are," replied Uncle J.

The driver returned to his cab and fired up his rig.

As the driver joined the queue of trucks at the border crossing, his hands grew sweaty. This was his final hurdle, and if successful, a big payout awaited. The line of trucks seemed to be moving quicker than normal, but this didn't surprise the driver. One of the driver's associates had been detailed to mess with the X-ray machine used by the border patrol. The last thing that the driver wanted was to be pulled out of line and guided through the X-ray machine. That could be the end of Uncle J's quest.

The driver waited in the border crossing queue for about forty-five minutes. It was now his turn as a border guard waved his arm, gesturing for the tanker to pull up.

"Papers," demanded the border guard.

The driver provided his passport and a carnet for the empty tanker. The border guard closely examined the passport and papers.

"What's your business in Mexico?" asked the border guard.

"Work," replied the driver. "I'm on my way to collect a load of vegetable oil from Tijuana. My work permit is in with my passport."

"I can see that," snapped the border guard.

As they spoke, a second border guard joined his colleague. The second guard walked to the tanker and started to bang on the side of the tank with a metal baton. He then proceeded to the back of the tanker and climbed up the rear access ladder onto the top of the tank. Inside, Uncle J and his gang held their breath in anticipation of possibly being discovered.

The guard looked at the rear service hatch which was padlocked.

"Why's this padlock on here?" shouted down the guard to his colleague.

"That's normal," replied the first border guard. "This is bandit country."

The second guard looked at the remaining three service hatches. Spotting that they were all padlocked, thought that this looked like a task in the 'too hard to do' box, so climbed off the tanker via the rear access ladder. Banging the tanker again with his baton, the second guard joined his partner.

"Tank appears to be empty," stated the second guard. "Unless they are people smuggling."

The first guard laughed.

"In there?" said the first guard. "They must be desperate if they are. Who wants to be smuggled into Mexico?"

The first guard walked across to his booth, stamped the driver's passport and carnet, and returned them to the driver.

"You have a great day," said the second guard, as the driver hastily steered his rig into the Mexican customs area.

As the U.S. border guards had not questioned the driver with any great vigour, the Mexican border police were more relaxed. The controls on the American side were tougher. If the truck had gotten this far, then the likelihood was that it was clean. After quickly examining the driver's paperwork, the tanker was ordered to roll out of the customs area and into Mexico.

Thirty minutes later, the tanker came to a halt, but this time, the engine was turned off. An expectant Uncle J hoped that they had arrived at their destination. Uncle J again followed the sound of footsteps as they resonated up the rear access ladder. Within a minute, Uncle J could hear the rattle of keys as the service hatch padlock was released. As the hatch opened, a burst of blinding light filled the lair. All four shielded their eyes from the dazzling light.

"Uncle J, I presume?" came a voice through the service hatch.

"Am I glad to see you!" replied Uncle J with gusto.

As Uncle J replied, a sturdy wooden ladder was fed down through the hatch. In no time, Uncle J, Umar, Ramiz, and Bahir stiffly clambered up the ladder to freedom. They clambered along the tank and scrambled to terra firma down the rear access ladder.

No sooner had their feet touched the ground, than a mean, tattooed, fierce-looking man with scrawny black hair walked up to Uncle J.

"Boss wants to see you, right now," said the intimidating bandit. "Follow me."

As the four friends followed the hostile-looking host, Uncle J looked around, to try and get a feel for the place he now found himself in. It was a bedraggled-looking run down factory. The buildings he could see were all in a poor state of repair. The rusty corrugated iron roofs stained the crumbling beige-coloured brickwork, and all the windows were either filthy dirty, cracked, smashed, or missing.

They were led under an overhanging roof that covered a suite of well-used dock levellers, into a vast, empty warehouse. Umar spotted three or four rats scurrying around some discarded cardboard boxes. The air was full of tension and there were no words exchanged.

In the far corner of the warehouse was a single-story office. Umar, Ramiz, and Bahir were told to wait as Uncle J was led inside the office alone. As the door shut, two more bandits appeared brandishing automatic weapons and stood next to Umar, Ramiz, and Bahir.

"No sudden movements," said one of the guards to the three terrified associates.

"You must be Uncle J?" said a large, smartly dressed gentleman sitting in a comfy seat behind an out-of-place but impressive oak desk. "I'm Mr Sanchez, I run things around here. My people have been speaking with your people, about getting you out of the States and back home."

"Good to meet you," said Uncle J offering a handshake.

Mr Sanchez remained unmoved which made Uncle J's nerves jangle with fear.

"We did our part as you can see," added Mr Sanchez. "You are standing in front of me, safe and sound, away from the clutches of the incompetent FBI and alike. Spinning this sort of deal ain't easy and it don't come cheap, if you know what I mean."

"What did you agree with my people?" asked a nervous Uncle J.

"Ten thousand," snapped Mr Sanchez.

Uncle J reeled back on hearing the amount required for his liberation.

"Dollars?" asked Uncle J.

"Yes, dollars," ranted Mr Sanchez impatiently. "Is there any other currency to deal in?"

"OK, OK," mumbled Uncle J. "When do you need it?"

"Right now," growled Mr Sanchez. "Do you actually know who you are dealing with here? It sure as hell ain't the boy scouts."

As Mr Sanchez ranted, one of the attending bandits cocked his automatic weapon.

"I don't carry that sort of money," replied a now-shaking Uncle J. "But I have it, not right here. I was not prepared for this, Wasim didn't tell me anything about payment details."

"Then you should have asked him," snapped Mr Sanchez.

"So, what now?" asked Uncle J.

"Looks like we got ourselves a situation," replied Mr Sanchez arrogantly. "Maybe my men are in need of some live target practice. We sure have four great candidates right here."

"Come on," begged Uncle J. "There has to be a better way, surely? What happened to honour amongst thieves?"

Mr Sanchez looked at Uncle J and laughed.

"I've been told about you, Uncle J," said Mr Sanchez. "You're a slippery character, one of life's great survivors. Just think what terminating you would do to my already fearsome reputation."

"Come on," said a now desperate Uncle J. "There must be another way. I'm sure you are feared but are a reasonable man. There must be some way you can cut me some slack and give me time to get the money to you. It's not like I haven't got it, it's just back home right now."

"So, if you want to cut a deal," responded a determined Mr Sanchez, "then the price goes up and you do something for me in return."

"That sounds fair," said Uncle J clutching at straws. "What is the new price? And what do you want in return?"

"Thirty thousand," boomed Mr Sanchez. "Plus, you become my new and prime Asian agent."

"Asian agent?" asked Uncle J. "Agent for what?"

"Show him," barked Mr Sanchez gesturing at one of the bandits in attendance.

The nominated bandit walked over to a table in the corner of the office. On the table was a brown, scruffy holdall. The bandit reached in and picked out a package. The bandit gave the package to Mr Sanchez.

"White gold," replied Mr Sanchez. "I'm looking to expand my operations into Asia. You couldn't have come at a better time, Uncle J. I can organise operations from this end. I already have established routes into your country. The problem is that my previous Asian agent met with an unfortunate messy demise. Hence I'm in the market for a replacement"

Uncle J rocked back. He had never dealt with drugs any stronger than weed. This could be a big-time operation with plenty of muscle judging by the hardware on show. Then there were the already established drug runners in the city back home. Uncle J was extremely nervous even considering stepping on anyone's established toes, but the other choice looked equally as fatal.

"Can I talk with my people outside?" asked Uncle J.

"I thought you were the big man," growled Mr Sanchez. "If you call the shots, what's the point of talking to them? You are either in or out. If you're out, I'll deliver the four bullets myself."

"Four bullets?" responded Uncle J angrily. "Why bring my friends into this? It's me you need the money from, not them. I beg of you, please let them go free and I will answer your demands."

"Not possible," grunted Mr Sanchez as he slammed the palms of his hands firmly on the desk in front of him. "They have seen my place of work. They have seen my face. I can't consider letting them go. They are in this as much as you, Uncle J."

"Then you give me little choice," replied a despondent Uncle J.

"What's it to be then?" asked Mr Sanchez impatiently.

"Welcome from your new Asian partner," said Uncle J begrudgingly, offering his hand out for a handshake.

Mr Sanchez took Uncle J's hand and shook it firmly, almost causing Uncle J to wince in pain.

"Welcome on board, Uncle J," replied an ecstatic Mr Sanchez. "Now where's that whiskey, we need to seal our new partnership with hard liquor."

Uncle J turned and looked at Umar, Ramiz, and Bahir who were still standing outside the office looking frightened under armed guard.

"What have I let myself in for?" said Uncle J under his breath.